The Owner
My Part in His Breakfast

JACK LABRADOR

ISBN:-10:1480020036
ISBN-13:978-1480020030

DEDICATION

To my children, Linda, Cherry and Sky, in the hope that one day I can prove myself worthy of their patience and love, and to my Dad, Peter, living proof that heroes aren't just found in comic books. And to all who have encouraged me to put this down in print.

Jack Labrador
XX

About Me

Born and trained on Lord Bath's estate at Longleat, I didn't like the bangs the guns made (I don't like the noise The Owner's Dyson makes either.) So I was 'released' from my training (given my P45). I was picked up and deposited rather unceremoniously in the back of a Land Rover and taken back to The Owner's cottage, although I did get my own back by depositing a large amount of regurgitated breakfast in the back. There then followed a rather more challenging form of training, on matters such as 'How to behave indoors!' and 'Not pooing on the carpet!' I must have passed this training because I was allowed to stay and am still here today. The Owner can be a grumpy git but he puts up with me and he's my bestest mate! He also keeps me in Bonio's as well

The Food Bin

Knocked food bin over this morning but managed to clear most of it up before the owner got up and got visiting small boy blamed for whole thing!

Still had breakfast though, The Owner left a croissant unattended on his plate. I think I got the small boy blamed again. It's been a good morning!

The Nice Man's Big Car

The Owner took me for a ride in the car today, dogs do cars! Cars are my favourite!

When we got back he took me for a nice walkies across the fields, it was really muddy, such fun. On the way home we met a nice man with a big car who opened the boot lid for me, I like cars! I think he must have had a headache or something coz he kept holding his head with his hands and shouting the name of his car. The owner came up and they started shouting at each other but they must have known each other already coz the nice man in the car patted him by his ear.

Now the owner has a headache as well I think, coz he's holding his head now! The Owner put me in the car and we drove to the hospital, there were lots of people and they were ever so friendly and I made lots of friends. I think The Owner must be feeling the cold a bit today as he was wearing lots of bandages around his head when he came out of the hospital. I think he was a bit jealous when he saw me being friends with all these new people as he isn't talking to me much tonight and he's shut me in the boot room now. But I have found the remains of the food from yesterday that I didn't clear up and I've got his new jumper out of the washing basket to lie on, so all's well I guess.

The Walk to Work

There was lots to sniff at on the way to work this morning and even tried to get in the stream to see where that otter had gone to. The Owner called me away, I expect he's jealous! That badger on the side of the road is starting to get particularly interesting, I think if I give it a few more days it should be about ready to roll in. I think The Owner has got his eye on it as well coz he keeps calling me away from it. I may have to employ a little K9 subterfuge here and get far enough ahead on our walk to work that he can't get to me before I get my shoulder right down in it!

The Stick in the Pond

We had a nice walk in to work this morning, the sun was shining and warm and we stopped for a look at the pond. It's a peaceful spot, where they used to drive the horses and carts into it to wash the wheels and hooves at the end of the day before putting them to bed for the night. Then he threw a stick in! Hello... I'm a Labrador....... We retrieve things..........That's what we do.........! Now he's got a strop on with me coz I'm all wet and he reckons I smell. I've now been sent under the desk out of the way.

Problems

I think the owner had a problem today, there was water running everywhere and a big yellow thing was called. The driver dug a big hole outside the office door and water sprayed everywhere. They all stood round the hole and looked excited so I ran around looking excited and sprayed some of my own water. The Owner wasn't pleased with me! I've taken myself off to the boot room tonight! I'll lay on his jumper again!

Ooops!

Decided I may come back in and give The Owner a second chance. I crept in from the Boot room as much on my belly as I could manage after clearing up the bag of food I knocked over. Nobody told me that he had got the wire attached to the laptop across the door way. There was a big crash! ... I'm back in the boot room. Door closed this time!

The Village Pond

Me and The Owner are going to the pub tonight. Pubs are my favourite. I keep him on just the two drinks as a safety precaution. He had a few more one Sunday afternoon and we had to walk home. I like walks home from the pub, but on this occasion he decided that the walk should go through the village pond. I was on a lead and had to go with him. Now if I had done that he would have sent me to the boot room again!

The Guinea Pig

Well, I've got The Owner back from the pub. We had to walk, but I like walkies. The Owner let me off the lead so I found him a present. Well it seemed only fitting! Well it looked like a rabbit to me and that's what I do, bring rabbits back. Apparently it was a Guinea Pig, but it was dark so an easy mistake to make I felt. It was alright when I gave it to him, stunned, but alright. I'm in the boot room again!!!!!!

The Missing Car

The Owner is in a good mood this morning! Don't think he's realised yet we have to walk back for the car. We're off to The Owner's niece's wedding today, dogs do weddings they're my favourite. I've even done my little excited run out round the bush and back a couple of times. What IS a wedding? Should I be having one?

The Owner's good mood has evaporated! He's been outside and realised the car is not there and he's got to walk and get it. I think he has just remembered my little mistake with the guinea pig last night as well. I think I'll go and find a nice sunny spot up the garden somewhere.

The Postman

When the postman brings envelopes to The Owner he normally groans so I growl as well and then I get told off. Today Postman came up the pathway and I started to practice my best growl when he gave me a letter from an anonymous fan. There were treats in it.... for me! I like treats, they are my favourite. In fact I don't know why The Owner grumbles when Postman comes. I like Postman now, he is my favourite!

The Garden Centre

We've been to the garden centre today, garden centres are my favourite. The Owner always visits the pet's section and brings me back a treat. I like treats! He put all the seats down and put loads of plants all over the floor of the car and left me a little space in the corner to sit. That was ok until some yoof pulled up beside him at the traffic lights in a fast car and The Owner wanted to prove he was fastest...

He pulled away so fast that I stumbled onto the plants. He said "Oh no, Jack!" so I sat down where I was. Always best to sit if you're in trouble. It seems that where I sat perhaps wasn't the best place to sit. We've been back to the garden centre again to get more plants only this time I didn't get any treats. Dinner seems late tonight!

Thoughts on a Bath

The Owner took me for a bath today. Baths are my favourite! No, honestly, they are! But why does he always get warm water and bubbles?

The Owner has one like this but I'm not allowed in it, I suspect his one is warmer.

Destroying the Computer

After my bath in the trough up on the hill, The Owner went to the office for me to "dry out for half an hour". That was five hours ago but I nearly stopped all his computers permanently, which would at least have meant that I could have had a walkies again. The Owner had been listening to the music with them funny things on his ears when someone knocked at the door selling a funny paper, which didn't seem to please The Owner somehow.

It pleased him even less when I ran out from under the table to help and got tangled up with all the wires. He spent several hours with loads of boxes around him with bits of wires sticking out of them and I thought he was crying at one point. I tried to help but he seemed to be cross still so I went and sat under the desk just in case.

The Postman

I'm feeling a little let down this morning! My new best friend Postman came and The Owner did his usual thing of putting his head in his hands and moaning. I think it must be some religious thing because he always says the same mantra. "How much?" Over and over.
After him bringing me treats last week I thought he was my friend, but I did my best little dance over by the bucket where The Owner keeps my biscuits. Not a thing! He's not my best friend anymore! I shall plot my revenge!

The Dead Badger

I've been sent under the desk and I suspect I'll be sent to the boot room when I get home but oh boy it was worth it! The Owner's friend Annie came round and offered to take me for a walk with my little friend Phoebe this afternoon. On the hill I found a dead badger, they are my favourite!
The Owner wasn't around to get jealous and Annie didn't seem to mind, until I got into the car when she went a funny colour. So I rolled in it! But I think I smell particularly good now! I don't think The Owner is quite so sure.

The Fight

We had a fight last night, The Owner and me. He wasn't going to let me into the house until he had washed me down. I mean, with a hosepipe!!!!! He thinks he won and tells me I smell nice and fragrant now, but you should see the kitchen! He smelled a little damp and musty for the rest of the evening as well! I must find a way to get back up there and do it again. Because I can! Alright!

Being Left at Home

Oops! I've been doing my doggy best to make up for the damage to the kitchen last night after the bath (hosepipe) and I think I have just undone it all! It's been raining here today and I've just been outside in the garden doing what doggies do best in the garden. I came rushing back trying to show him how pleased I am etc. and put my paws in the middle of his chest as I jumped up at him. He's got muddy paw prints in the middle of his chest now! He's going out tonight, although I guess not in his clean white shirt from the way he has just thrown it in the washing machine and I am getting the feeling I won't be going with him somehow. Perhaps I can drag his jumper out from behind the fridge and lay on that again for the evening. If he didn't like the paw prints on the shirt he won't like the jumper when he finds it!

The Night Out

I did go out last night with him! Going out is my favourite! Dunno what happened but that funny thing on the wall started making a noise, I think it must have been upset coz he picked it up and cuddled it to the side of his head and talked to it for a while. When he put it down he was walking around singing and he seemed to have forgotten about the paws on the shirt incident.

Then he put me in the car and we went to the pub, pubs are my favourite! He met a nice young lady and I liked her, she kept telling me how nice I am and made a real fuss of me. In fact she made a fuss of me most of the night and left The Owner to enjoy his pint at the other end of the table. Not sure what I did but he definitely had a bit of a strop with me on the way home. Perhaps his beer was off!

The Small Boy is coming!!

Off to collect Small Boy now, this is my favourite! I get to play in the river for an hour whilst The Owner has a pint and then I've got a whole weekend to see what I can get away with whilst getting Small Boy the blame. It's nice to have someone else to shoulder some of the onerous responsibility for blame that I have to carry.

The Riverside Pub

Oh such fun, I managed to get The Owner wet from both sides! The first one was usual, retrieve rock from river......place on bank behind The Owner......shake vigorously. At this point The Owner shrieks with delight (I think) as well as the people on the next table. Next came my 'Pièce de résistance'. He didn't see me run under the table and drop a rock, so I shook myself vigorously just to let him know I was there. You should have seen the inside of the car when he got me home. The Owner is out there now with his Dyson cleaning it. It is raining this morning; he doesn't appear to be happy!

The Postman's Revenge

Oh dear! I was in the garden earlier, when Postman came. I saw his van and bent on revenge for not giving me a Bonio the other day, went right up the top of the garden and waited for him to get up to the front door. Then I launched my charge! Down through the cherry orchard, round the trees, past the satellite dish, heckles up baying for blood.

Wrong Postman! The relief was on today. Postman wet himself! The Owner had to help Postman clean himself up and I'm in the boot room again. Well how was I to know?!? He drove the same red van! I'm thinking I'm not going to be taken to the pub this lunch time!

The Visit to The Pub

The Owner must have forgotten about Postman already coz he did take me to the pub! I like pubs they really are my favourite! I have to be on a lead in there, pub rules, and The Owner had the lead round his wrist when he went to the bar and got a glass of wine for himself and an orange juice for Small Boy. Some nice lady said hello to me as he picked up the glasses so I went to say hello to her. Next thing was, he starts to throw all the drinks from the glasses in his hands all over the floor and blamed me! I think he must be suffering still from the same bad drink he had last time we went to the pub. I may have to stop him going I think, if he can't behave himself. Dinner's late this evening!

It's my Birthday!

Birthday? Is it mine? Do dogs do birthdays? Perhaps that explains why The Owner was wandering around annoying me the other day with that ruddy Moonpig theme tune! He does love me! I've never had a birthday before, I thought it was only hoomuns did them. I will be especially nice to Postman today!

The Hot Tea on the Lap Routine

I only forgot myself twice over the weekend; first time was at the pub, as already reported. The Owner, having done the washing and the lawns decided a cup of tea and what he calls "a quiet hour" watching the funny looking very noisy cars going round the track on the telly. I mean, too noisy! And where would you put your K9 in them? He always finishes up shouting at the telly during his "quiet hour" anyway! Small Boy got his coat out which usually means going for a walk with him. I don't do walkies with small boys, only The Owner! I forgot myself and jumped on The Owner's lap to escape. He was on the settee that I am not allowed on and he had a mug of hot tea in his hand. An easy mistake to make I felt! Tea everywhere and a lot more shouting but not at the telly this time! I took myself off to the boot room out of the way!

The Last Delivery

Postman came this morning, to the office. I was expecting the usual head in hands mantra thing from The Owner "How Much!?" etc. But Postman had one of those grinning faces on and I thought he must have brought me at least The Owner's Moonpig card. He handed The Owner a letter and he made him sign something and then they started talking. The Owner started waving his hands about and talking even louder and Postman left without giving me a Bonio even though I was doing my little dance by the biscuit bucket. The Owner put me in the car and we had to go and collect his mail from the post office in town. It seems that after my little incident with the wrong Postman on Saturday, Postman won't deliver his mail and we have to go and get it. I'm keeping a low profile at the moment. So far he is blaming the Post Office for having a "Bunch of wimps" as postmen. It may not stay that way!

The Birthday Drink

"So", he said opening a beer can; "It's your birthday! Tell you what, try some of this", pouring the contents of his can into a glass ashtray. I, forever gullible and never one to turn down anything I can eat or drink, indulged him.

For the next couple of hours my legs would do absolutely nothing that I asked of them in an orderly fashion and this morning I have an army of gun dogs with heavy boots on thundering around inside my head! Does he wake up feeling like this every morning? No wonder he is always grumpy!

The trip to see Peter Boro

I've been out with The Owner for the day today, in the car. Cars are my favourite! He was up really early this morning and put his smart clothes on. He normally leaves me behind when he wears them, says I get him covered with hair. Well covered with hair works for me! Then he said "Come on we are going to see Peter Boro", not sure who he is but we did drive a long way.
I don't think Peter Boro could have been in coz he only stayed a while and talked to several people and then drove me all the way back again. I reckon Peter will be in trouble when he catches up with him!

Collecting MY mail

The Owner still hasn't blamed me over Postman not delivering to us anymore. But when we went to collect our mail today he got into a right row with the sorting office hoomuns. I had got more fan mail! Addressed, as you would expect, to Jack Labrador, they wouldn't give it to him coz he hadn't got any ID on him for one Jack Labrador.

Argue as much as he could that I was just a dog, actually he said a rude word when he said 'just a dog' but I pretended not to hear, they insisted that it must be given to the addressee. So he told them that Jack Labrador was out in the car if they insisted. So postman was sent out to give the package to me. It was the same one I had made the mistake with last weekend! Postman wet himself again! Not sure they will be delivering to us again any day soon!

The Owner has his "Happy Head" on!

Not sure what is up with The Owner today. He was up early! It's been rather unnerving as he has been nice to me all day so far. I thought I even saw a smile on his face when he went to collect his mail this morning from the sorting office.

We saw Postman whilst we were there; the one who wet himself yesterday when he brought my fan mail out for me. He was hiding behind a heap of mail bags when we got there making strange noises and smelling faintly of urine. The Owner went straight over and shook his hand and wished him a good day. After yesterday I'm not sure even I would have shook Postman's hand, I saw what he did with it!

I'll keep you informed!

The nice Vet

Hah! That's better, he's grumpy again! Normal service has been restored! I now know why he has been so happy today; the joke has been on me. It's been the day for my annual visit to Vitnery Hoomun and he seems to find it funny what they do to me with that thermometer.

Having a small problem with lack of descending in the little boys department, she has to have a quick check round to make sure all is in order, which I have to say is not an altogether unpleasant experience. If I wince a bit on the walkies later I may get taken back for another go another time. Now the laugh is on him as he's had to pay the bill, so he's all grumpy again. The equilibrium has been restored! Now, where's the boot room? Think I may make myself scarce!

Last night's takeaway

Why does he do it? The Owner I mean. Last night I ventured back in from the boot room as I hadn't heard him start cooking his dinner and I normally get given a Bonio when he has his dinner. Bonio's are my favourite! He's fidgeting! Then he jumps up grabs his keys saying that a nice pizza, a bottle of wine and a video are what's called for tonight. I've never had pizza but I'm sure they would be my favourite.

When he gets back he's got beer, kebab and a video. Even I wouldn't touch one of them kebabs! Every time he goes to the pizza shop he gets as far as the kebab van and loses his way. Now, as usual, he keeps running upstairs holding his belly. He'd have been better off having some of that dead badger on the hill he tries to keep me away from! Look out! There he goes again up the stairs again.

The Spilt Tea

I'm in the boot room already this morning! I had my breakfast and went up the garden to do what doggies do best in gardens. Breakfast is my favourite! It's raining outside and when I came in again The Owner had picked up his Sunday paper after having rummaged through the big heap that comes through the door on a Sunday morning and made a mess, then settled down with his cup of tea on the settee that I am allowed on.

Well that's what I normally do! Climb up on it with him and snuggle down for a cuddle while he reads the paper and rants a lot. Unusually he isn't ranting at me so that's why I like it. I was only a little bit wet from the garden! He jumped as if in some kind of protest at my apparent dampness, I jumped to get out of his way and only slightly knocked his mug of hot tea. So now I'm in the boot room and his trousers and the cushion covers are in the washing machine. He won't want to wear those trousers when they come out, even I can see they are going to be a pinkie shade of orange!

The Pink Trousers

Feeling inspired by his need to clear up the spilt tea earlier this morning, The Owner started looking behind cupboards and under things tutting and muttering about dust and cobwebs as he went. There's only him and I here and I'm terrified of that damn vacuum cleaner so quite who he thought he was tutting about escapes me. Unable to get out in the garden there then followed a day of frantic activity with a duster.

I tried to help but I wasn't appreciated so I sat and watched. Things were going well until the washing machine finished. I knew it would happen! He now has a rather fashionable pink pair of trousers which he tells no-one in particular that they were wearing thin anyway. I think they were the ones we had to drive to Bath to get only two weeks ago! Fortunately he got fed up with cleaning before he got to the boot room; I was worried he may have come across his jumper I have been using as a blanket to lay on.

Hiding The Jumper

The Owner's cousin came to see us today; he's from a very long way away! They kept talking about Oz, not sure but I think that may be near Swindon. Whilst they were all busy down the bottom of the garden with the barbie I thought it was time to use a bit of K9 cunning and drag The Owners jumper upstairs and hide it under Small Boys bed ready for when he comes up next weekend. Should divert the flack I hope.

The Jumper discovered

Tee hee, my little ruse worked! The Owner spotted the corner of something poking out from under the bed and when he investigated he pulled the rest of the jumper out. Fortunately there were so many paw prints on it they blended into one so nothing obvious to link it to me. Snigger! He is having a rant as I write and is threatening to ring up small boy and let him know what he thinks about the whole matter.

Another Ooops!

There's been a bit of a problem it would seem. Something I hadn't allowed for in my plans. The Owner has called Small Boy to tell him what he thought about the jumper etc. and somewhere in the conversation Small Boy mentioned a seemingly insignificant fact that hardly seemed worth a second thought (I hoped). Apparently The Owner was actually wearing it when he last took Small Boy home!

I am now at the back of the cupboard under the stairs, he'll never think of looking for me behind the Dyson! I could be here for some time!

The Wet Leg

I spent the night at the back of the cupboard under the stairs, thought it safest. Come breakfast time, hunger and a bladder full to bursting point forced me to reveal my whereabouts and I came skulking out of my hiding place. The Owner was stood there by my food dish with his hands on his hips frowning. This was not going to be my most auspicious start to a day!

I did my very best walking to heel all the way to work this morning, I think The Owner was pleased with me a little and when we got there another hoomun was there already, I have seen him with The Owner at the pub. From a quick sniff at his leg I deduce he has a lady K9 at home that I would really like to know so I forgot myself a little and sent her a scent message as us dogs do. The other hoomun soon started complaining bitterly about a wet leg.

I'm up in the calf sheds if anyone wants me!

Ah, Badger!

Feeling a bit delicate this morning. Went for walkies with The Owner earlier and finally got to that badger up on the hill. I resisted the temptation to roll in it but thought that a quick munch on a bit of its leg wouldn't hurt. It keeps repeating on me now, perhaps I was a little hasty and should have left it a bit longer before sampling!

I'm not under the desk today instead I am laying in the door way, The Owner thinks I am doing so to enjoy the sun. Truth is that as the door is open, if I am half outside he can't notice the rather dodgy affect the badger appears to be having on my digestive tract! Hopefully it will soon pass!

Ooops, excuse me again!

The Lawn Mowing

The Owner has been outside this morning giving the lawn what he describes as a light trim. In as much as you can ever give two feet of grass a light trim! It did liberate some of my balls and other toys that I had long forgotten about and one or two other things I probably shouldn't mention here.

Yesterday's badger munching, is still having a profound effect on my bottom and being one who prefers a little privacy when conducting ones ablutions I opted for the long grass as yet uncut. Besides, what he had already cut looked far too clean and nice to do anything on. It would appear he didn't notice it before he ran over it with the rotary mower and there followed much bellowing and changing of shirts etc. I have found a nice cool spot up in the woods behind the barbie out of the way, the cricket match is on over the lane and he has cracked open a beer already so I'll stay up here until time or alcohol has dulled his memory!

The Cricket Match

After a while I noticed The Owner come creeping back from the cricket match with an empty beer bottle and return to the field a while later carrying a whole pack of full ones. I thought some of the nice people dressed in white must have known me because they kept shouting at the top of their voices "How's Jack!" At least I thought they were!

So I crept out from behind the barbie and joined The Owner at the cricket match to see who was asking after me. It all went well until one of the nice men in white hit his ball straight towards me, so I though he wanted to play and I picked it up and took it back to him. He didn't seem pleased and chased me off the grass. The Owner was laughing loudly and so now we are both banned from the cricket pitch!

The Owners Dads Barbecue

We went to see Owner's Dad yesterday. Owner's Dad has a cat. Now, I like cats but I do sometimes find that cats don't understand me! I didn't see Cat for quite a while after we got there and the barbie was in full swing. There were tables loaded with little pots and jars of stuff and a big plate of burgers and sausages that I particularly had my eye on.

But I couldn't find the opportunity to get one knocked to the ground without drawing attention to myself. The Owner kept telling everyone not to feed me saying, "He prefers his dried food when he gets home". I mean who is he trying to kid? Anyway, Cat appeared eventually and came to join the gathered throng and jumped up on Owners Dad's lap. It was at exactly that point that Cat must have seen me and changed direction rapidly using its claws to grip on Owner's Dad's lap and then launch itself straight across the table, through the plate of burgers most of which landed right in front of me on the floor. Owners Dad stood up rapidly, grabbing his groin and protesting about claws and pain and stuff, knocking the remaining pots down as well. I tried valiantly to clear the mess up for them; cat hasn't been seen since! I reckon he'll be in the boot room for a week when he shows up again! The Owner was sent down the KFC for replacement food. I must team up with Cat again!

The Bloomin' Roses

The Owner was around the garden till quite late last night sniffing at the roses and standing back and admiring etc. Enough to make a dog feel quite nauseous! He came in as dusk settled over the cottage with pollen dusted all over his nose and then started sneezing. He had the nerve to blame me and my hairs for his condition! Cheek!

Knowing that it was the pollen dust that caused The Owner's sneezing last night I set out this morning to help rectify the problem and wee'd on all the blooms. It took quite some doing with just the one bladder full of wee, but I managed! He came out the front door and made a bee-line for the rose blooms again and stuffed his nose straight in the first one he came across which just happened to be one that I had watered earlier. He started pulling funny faces and "Phewing" a lot. I did check it later but it smelled ok to me. I think he's just getting choosey!

The Return of The Big Yellow Machine

The man with the big yellow digger is back on the farm digging more holes. Knowing that on his last visit my attempt at watering his holes in my own particular style was less than welcomed and also bearing in mind the amount of water which sprayed from something deep in one of his holes, I opted to keep well clear.

Postman is about to make his first delivery since the last regrettable incident and I had already had that warning finger wagged at me a few times. Well, Man in Yellow Digger was driving down past the office when Postman came up the track, so I ran out to greet him hopeful of a Bonio. Man in Yellow Digger swerved in what I felt was a very exaggerated fashion. Now we have a big hole in the side of the office, Postman has gone home to change his trousers again and Farmer has given The Owner a letter which appears to be addressed to Bill. It can't be a very nice letter to Bill as The Owner has his head in his hands again and appears to be crying. I can't help feeling that they are all blaming me! I'll be in the calf shed if anyone wants me!

The Lady Chocolate Lab

Went out with The Owner last night to a hall and there were lots of people there listening to two lady hoomuns. I thought the chances of a Bonio were quite high, and then I saw her, across the crowded room, a lady Labrador, chocolate, it was love at first sight! I thought The Owner would have at least got me close to her so we could have a good sniff as dogs do when they meet.

I always try and do the right thing for him and act all cute and cuddly when he sees another lady hoomun so that he can get the chance to talk to her! Then I noticed what the problem was going to be. Her owner was a lady hoomun, blonde and skinny, just the type he usually plays up to. So he told them all my embarrassing little mistakes and made her laugh lots. Lady Chocolate Lab didn't want anything to do with me afterwards, how embarrassing was that? He was singing in the car all the way home, I think I heard him say he was seeing her again next week sometime. That gives me time to plot my revenge! If he wants an embarrassing dog, I'll give him embarrassing! I've taken myself off to the boot room, part in protest and part to get away from his singing.

Off to my Favourite Shop

I think today is going to be a good day! He has been unnervingly happy since the other evening. We are off to my most favourite shop ever today! The one where he gets the big bags of dried food for me. After the last bag which I managed to get tipped over and so had to clear it up myself (and get Small Boy the blame for it) the last one didn't last so long as normal. This would ordinarily have brought on a whole load of huffing, sighing and grumbling, but this time he seems happy about it! He gets my Bonio's from there too; Bonio's are my favourite, had I mentioned that? He tells me he is going to get me a present from there as well, I don't think I have ever had a present! Do K9's do presents? I think I'll go and get in the car now, just to be sure.

The Shopping Trip

Well, I'm not sure if equilibrium has been restored or not. The Owner is still wandering around the place singing..... badly. But we do need to find another shop to be my favourite shop where we get my food from.

We have a big box of Bonio's and an even bigger box of Markies, as well as my sack of food. He bought me one of those retrieve dummy things like Lord Bath used to give me to work with and a funny ball thrower thing and a big new cushion and another dog whistle. That makes four whistles he has, although I am not sure how many times he would be able to whistle from the same mouth!

It was when we got to the checkout that it all went horribly wrong. It seems that the price they charged him for my feed was a pound different to what was marked on the shelf as some hoomun yoof had not changed the label on the shelf, but he had to prove a point and call the manager. Remind me never to go shopping with The Owner again!

Chaos at The Barbie

Last night The Owner took me to another barbie. Before we went he had a barf, I hate barfs! Then he sprayed stuff all over him, he smelled funny after that. When we got there we walked in and I was hopeful of a tasty morsel or two and then there she was, across a crowded garden, through a sea of hoomun legs, Lady Chocolate Labrador!

So I found the best stick I could and picked it up and took it over and gave it to her. She picked it up! That was it! She loves me! I thought I'd impress her further by doing my silly run round the garden, it always makes The Owner laugh and Lady Chocolate Lab started to follow. This was starting to go well although I did notice The Owner wasn't laughing much! Well how was I to know that Old Lady Hoomun was going to be trying to carry a tray of burgers down the patio steps as I came around the corner pursued by my new love interest? We were both sent back to our owner's cars and our owners were asked to leave so they drove to a pub. The Owner and Lady Chocolate Lab Owner sat at a table in the pub garden laughing and drinking and doing hoomun stuff for a long time but we were left in our separate cars. I wonder if she was sent to her boot room when she got home as well.

The Great Upstairs!

Yesterday The Owner took me round to see Lady Chocolate Lab and we had great fun running around her garden while The Owner and Lady Chocolate Lab Owner were sat in the garden watching and laughing and doing hoomun stuff.

Then we all went inside and we were allowed to go upstairs! I've never been upstairs before, I didn't think K9's do upstairs. I have now realised why The Owner kept me from going up there at our home! Lady Chocolate Lab Owner has a nice soft bed, I know because we climbed on it and curled up in a nice warm duvet! And she doesn't have a boot room! I think I might try that at home next time The Owner is out!

The Builders Biscuits

The Owner has got Builder Hoomun in to do some work to the cottage; the window sill on the kitchen window has rotted. I'm just grateful that I can't quite manage to wee that high or I'm certain I would have got the blame for causing the rot!

I thought Builder Hoomun and me were going to get on well at first; he sat down on the bench in the garden to drink the cup of tea The Owner had made for him and put some biscuits on the bench for me. I thought "What a kind man!" So I took them! Seemed perfectly reasonable to me! Builder started bellowing loudly and chased me round the garden. He's going to get indigestion, running around like that when he's eating and drinking! I had planned a day with my new friend Builder Hoomun in the garden but I think I'm going down to the farm to find The Owner now.

The Builders Mess

Well I have kept right out of the way today. Builder has been in again and he's knocked most of the window out in the kitchen and there's now a big hole there. There is dust everywhere in the cottage and muddy footprints all over the kitchen carpet.

Small Boy once made a mess like that with a kitchen cupboard door and everyone got the blame so I made a point of coming down to the farm to find The Owner and staying where he could see me most of the day, just so I didn't get implicated in the mess brewing at home. I wonder if it's safe to come out yet.

The Romeo Dog

Man, those roses stink! The Owner will be hanging out the same window later on stuffing his nose in them and waxing lyrical. Yuk and Phew!!!

The Jehovah's Witness

We were sat there watching the telly with some noisy motor bikes whizzing very fast round a track. I think The Owner must have known one of them coz he kept shouting at this one called Moto G.P. how he wasn't worth the money or something. But someone called Jehovah must have had an accident somewhere, as these people came knocking at the door saying they were witnesses to it.

The Owner didn't seem pleased to see them and seemed quite grateful that I had rushed out barking and stuff. He even forgave me for knocking his glass over in my rush to go and bark at them which was a first. That would normally mean a while shut in the boot room! When I burst through the door they were stood there looking at the sky saying 'Save us!' I did look up but couldn't see anything!

The Ditch

Last night me and The Owner went to the pub, pubs really are my favourite! There was lots of people there all dressed posh, ladies with funny dresses on and men with suits like The Owner wears when he goes to Lundun sometimes. I think it was a wedding or something, do K9's do weddings?

Well he started showing that picture of me up at the window to everyone, which I was a bit embarrassed about at first until I realised all the lady hoomuns thought I was cute and made a fuss of me. No Bonio's though! On the way home, walking again since you ask, it was dark, a car appeared in the distance and suddenly The Owner was gone! Couldn't see him anywhere! Then I heard him grumbling, he had stepped sideways to get out of the road and fell in the ditch, well more of a stream really and Car Driver Hoomun stopped and helped him out of the ditch again, all wet and horrible. It was a long squelch home after that, as he tried desperately to reason with himself that it was someone else's fault.

I do sometimes wish dogs could laugh!

The Builders Holes

Well, talk about double standards! We went home for lunch today, The Owner and me. When we got there, Builder was just finishing putting the window and its frame back together. I thought "That looked nice", and went on a quick patrol up the garden to check to see if Builder had left any sandwich crusts round by the bench from his lunch earlier.

When I came back they were both stood around a hole they had just dug discussing things with a certain air of gravitas. Then before you could say "Bonio's five times a day would be nice, please" they've got shovels and forks and a big metal bar and there are holes everywhere! They had hose pipes squirting water everywhere and of course The Owner being of a, frankly, childish nature, just had to squirt it at me as well and then laugh loudly. I just hope they fill them all in before tonight, Lady Chocolate Lab is coming round this evening and I really don't want her to think I would behave in such an infantile manner. I may find a way of shutting him in the boot room tonight as a punishment.

The Owner's in the boot room!

Oh peace! For a while anyway. The front door was open and yet he locked the back door to keep Builder out, why, escapes me as there was a stonking great hole where a window should have been in the kitchen wall. Now, Small Boy has been telling him that the latch on the boot room door keeps falling off for a long time, but of course he isn't going to get a new one and put money in the tills of B&Q.

Incidentally there is a burger van at B&Q and Burger Hoomun is a really nice man and always gives me a sausage (when The Owner isn't looking). So tonight the wind blows the boot room door shut with a bang whilst The Owner is in the boot room doing heaven knows what...... and the latch falls off! No surprise there then! Ok, so it may have been helped to bang shut a little by an exuberant tail swishing! So there he stayed until Lady Chocolate Labrador and Lady Chocolate Lab Owner arrive. Eager to see that all the seats and cushions were going to comfortable enough for them I took the opportunity to try all of them. The Owner did look quite pathetic when they arrived and let him out. He has been milking it ever since telling anyone who will listen about an incident in his early childhood when he was imprisoned by a bully. Yeah!?!?! Once upon a time....

The Holes in the Neck

What to tell you about first? Should it be the lump on the back of The Owner's head or the bite marks on my neck from Lady Chocolate Lab?

Well the evening had been going swimmingly once we had got The Owner to shut up about being “incarcerated in that awful tomb!” Well hello, that’s my boot room you’re talking about there, where I get sent for everything and for anything!

Lady Chocolate Lab Owner and The Owner were talking and drinking and doing hoomun stuff so I thought maybe now is the time to get a little closer to Lady Chocolate Lab. So I snuggled up nicely on MY cushion with Lady Chocolate Lab and started to sniff her ear a little, gently I thought! Then I got a whack across the nose from The Owner and Lady Chocolate Lab bit me on my neck! I now understand why The Owner always says that women are unfathomable! So I took myself off to the boot room, sorry, “That awful tomb”, as a precaution leaving Lady Chocolate Lab curled up on MY cushion!

Wounded I am! The Owner, predictably, thinks it’s funny of course, keeps making jokes about not drinking too much in case I leak! He has no sensitivity!

The Bandaged Head

The lump on The Owners head, I forgot to tell you about it! The Owner’s friend Annie turned up at work the other day and I did my best sad eyes look staring at the lead as she always takes me for a walk. A pushover in the presence of such K9 talent! So we went for a walk whilst The Owner got on with some printing stuff for her.

Someone has removed the badger from up on the hill which was a shame as that ought to have been getting quite edible by now! I was so excited when I got back as I always get a Bonio that I went running through the door. The ink had apparently ran out whilst The Owner was printing and he was in the stationery cupboard behind the door. Well I didn’t know!!!! I ran in, the door hit his bum; he stood up, (far too quickly as it happens) and hit the back of his head on the door catch! Well I thought it was only a little bump! Clearly I was wrong judging by the amount of fuss he has been making ever since. I met a lot of people that I have seen before at the hospital on previous occasions. He came out with stitches and a plaster but has since opted for the full head bandage, inevitably. We were sat watching a program about King Tut last night and I thought he was looking a bit like one of them mummy things! I escaped trouble as Annie was there and he didn't want to appear grumpy. I think I may save up some of my bigger accidents for when she is there again!

Old Reg the Paper Boy

I was in the garden nice and early on Sunday, Sunday mornings are always fun, they're my favourite. We get a lot of cyclists in funny coloured clothes pedalling by on Sundays and I can have hours of fun hiding behind the hedge waiting until they get right outside and then let fire with the big guns. It always causes a wobble or two!

I have found that if you wait until they are just saying to each other "What a lovely cottage!" and other such yucky stuff, that it has best effect. One day I will manage to get one of them to wobble enough that they fall off!

Well, I had patrolled checking for badgers and squirrels and stuff like that and I was just setting myself up ready for the cyclists, when old Reg the paper boy turned up...... on his bike! Well how was I to know it was him?!?! I heard the bike and settled in anticipation of the right moment to make my move for best effect and then launched forward with heckles up..... I think The Owner has to go and collect his own paper on a Sunday morning in future; and Reg seemed a little uncomfortable in the trouser department and walked his bike down the road whilst continually adjusting them as he went.

The Flower Bed

Me and The Owner went to one of his friends for a barbecue the other evening. I like barbecues, people feed me stuff when The Owner isn't looking. The Owner's friend is particularly good at doing that! Near the barbecue there is a big wall all the way round what I took to be a flower bed. The wall is just above head height for a dog of my stature.

There was another dog there called Barnaby, he's a funny looking thing if you ask me, little tiny legs and a really long body, a lot on his mind and intent on telling the world all about it! Well I was enjoying a good sniff around the back of this 'Flower bed' when I heard someone drop a sausage on the floor. Well, I was not about to let Barnaby get it and with his short legs he would have to go all the way around the outside of the flower bed. Me being a little more athletic, if I may be so bold as to say so, I opted to go a more direct route, up and over the top. Well no-one was more surprised than me to find that the 'Flower Bed' was in fact a big fish pond with a big net over it! The net stretched enough to let me fall in the water but I could not get grip enough on anything to continue my journey to the fallen sausage! All my legs were through the holes in the net and I was stuck, helpless and humiliated! To make matters worse they kept calling him a sausage dog from then on and me the non-sausage dog! The Owner still keeps bursting out laughing whenever he sees me and trying to imitate me stuck in the net. I think he looks more like a camel, he smells like one as well!

The Pack of Sausages

The Owner went creeping off down to the burger van earlier this morning hoping no-one would know he had gone. I like going down there coz The Lady Burger Van Hoomun always gives me a treat when she sees me and The Owner isn't watching. When we got there she had just received a delivery of fresh meat and stuff.

The Owner jumped out of the car and left the door open. Thinking he had left it open for me I jumped through from the back of the car and got out as well. The Hoomun Burger Van Lady was busy talking to The Owner so I went exploring around the back of the van. In one of the big boxes was a fresh catering pack of sausages! Assuming she must have thrown them out I picked them up and took them back to the car. A little later The Owner came back to the car and we drove back to the office. I opened the pack on the way and tried to select the best place to start on the string of sausages, there was miles of them! When we got back to the office The Owner opened the back of the car to let me out and had a bit of a funny turn. It seems that sausages were not what he was expecting to see in the boot with me. It also seems that Lady Burger Van Hoomun was not what he was expecting to see driving up the track behind him either. She did seem a little more animated than when we saw her only a few minutes earlier. I am beginning to suspect that I wasn't supposed to take those sausages as The Owner has gone to the shops to buy some more. I think I'll take myself off up to the calf sheds for a while when he gets back, just to be sure!

Hoomun Yoof!

Yesterday I was up round the back of the dairy where I had found a particularly good heap of badger poo to roll in. Now I know what you are thinking, isn't he lucky to have found it, but unfortunately much as I try and persuade him differently The Owner never seems to quite understand!

Well, I had got the shoulder sufficiently smeared to impress The Owner, I felt, when I went back to the office to show him. When I arrived there a Hoomun Yoof had arrived for an interview. I'm not sure what is wrong with the view we have already across the fields with my friends the cows, to the church and Robbie Williams house. Anyway I went rushing in to greet him and introduce myself, but neither him nor The Owner seemed particularly pleased to see me. Maybe it was just at an awkward moment in the discussions I thought, so I persisted with my jumping up and rubbing against the legs routine, when Hoomun Yoof ran outside holding his nose and mouth and making some very strange noises! The Owner lent him a pair of his trousers which was quite comical I thought as Hoomun Yoof could have got into just the one leg! I guessed that my latest attempts at converting The Owner to the delicacies of badger poo failed when he started chasing me with the hose pipe and yard broom with a particularly angst ridden look in his eye. I'm a bit disappointed with Hoomun Yoof as he never gave me a Bonio from my bucket before he left!

The Lavender

The Owner's out in the garden doing stuff with that rose which he informs no one in particular has 'Gone past its best' and not a moment too soon if you ask me! Now it's the lavender down the front path! Oh heaven help us! Yuk and double phew! He's out there now weeding around them "To make sure we see them at their best".

I tried to distract him by lying across the middle of them on my back but that didn't seem to be appreciated so now after a morning poking around with them he smells like those two little old ladies up in the village. I can tolerate them coz they have always got a biscuit for me and then we are on our way again but he is with me until it wears off and one does have certain principles you understand. I think I might have to wee on them later to make them smell a bit better. I wee'd on one earlier and I think he suspected when he got to it in his weeding as he gave me a very strange and accusing look. I thought it best I came in at that point and let him get on with it. Besides, that bit of nice steak he got out of the freezer earlier looks like it may be nearly thawed out so I suspect it may need guarding....just in case!

The New Lavender Bushes

Oh man was I in trouble on Sunday! After much rummaging in the lavender beds he came in stinking like those two old ladies in the village and announced we needed more lavender to make up for those that didn't make it through the winter. More!!!? So we got in the car and off to the garden centre we went. He bought several more lavender plants and an ice cream each.

I don't think he noticed the one I had already stolen from a small child who was just not quite careful enough. After devising some kind of torture chamber in the back of the car by surrounding me with lavender bushes we head for home except we got as far as the pub when he announced that we would stop for just the one! That was always bound to end in us having to leave the car behind and walk home! Sat out in the garden and who should come round the corner but Lady Chocolate Lab and Lady Chocolate Lab Owner. I was a little wary at first as the puncture marks from her last visit were only just beginning to heal over but we were soon bounding round the gardens in a frantic and lust fuelled game of chase again. Another brute of a dog arrived in the shape of a big black lab although his Owner didn't let him off his lead but I still felt the need to do a little scent marking, just to be sure, and rushed around weeing on things until my bladder was nearly empty. That was where it all went wrong! How was I to know that big purple thing in the middle of the lawn was Lady Chocolate Lab Owners hand bag? The Owner appeared quite vexed by the whole thing and rushed around with handfuls of tissue and smelly sprays trying to clear up my efforts. I went and stood on the bank out of the way and watched whilst the rest of the pub garden laughed. Lady Chocolate Lab came and joined me on the bank and I think I even saw her Owner laughing a little which only made The Owners mood blacker. When we got home I opted to find the spot behind the barbie in the woods. I think that was far enough out of the way!

Cooked lavender

The Owner found every reason imaginable not to walk back for his car yesterday, opting instead for the lazy way out by waiting for someone to arrive who had a car and was heading back past the pub and was fool enough to give him a lift. After a day in the hot sunshine the inside of the car was like an oven, in fact he had to put a pair of gloves on to touch the steering wheel. What a wimp!

When we eventually got the steering wheel cooled down a little, enough for him to drive home, he suddenly remembered the lavender plants in the back. I was sat with them; I didn't need to remember them! One thing for certain, they won't need drying out at the end of the summer! So this afternoon we have to go back to the garden centre for more plants. This is the garden centre who foolishly guarantees their plants will last for twelve months and I suspect The Owner will be trying to claim some free replacements. Although how he thinks he is going to swing that one escapes me! I can't help but think they might notice that the plants he will present to them as evidence will have the same consistency as cooked lettuce!

Thrown Out of the Garden Centre

Why did someone tell The Owner about the garden centre's offer to refund or replace any plant of theirs which did not survive? We went back, four cooked lettuce plants formally known as lavender (Yuk & phew!) in hand and brandishing his receipt. The very nice young lady on customer service saw me and found a dog biscuit from somewhere, I liked her!

She immediately said that they would replace them... well I wouldn't have done! Was he satisfied? No, not a bit, he wanted something extra for his time and petrol! So The Owner demanded the manager. I didn't like her quite so much as she didn't have a biscuit for me. Lady Manager Hoomun told him that he ought to think himself lucky as she could quite clearly see he had left them in a hot car and she wouldn't have replaced them! She told him to take his replacement plants and go. He had a hysterical moment - She called security. Just when I had managed to think another biscuit out of nice young lady on customer service desk's pocket and into my mouth, he gets us thrown out! As we drove out of the car park, Lady Manager Hoomun was stood at the door with her hands on her hips and a yoof was being sent across the car park with a paint pot in his hand towards their big name board, I suspect to modify their guarantee to exclude cooked lettuce plants. Can anyone recommend another good garden centre as I think we are going to need to find one!

The Cushion

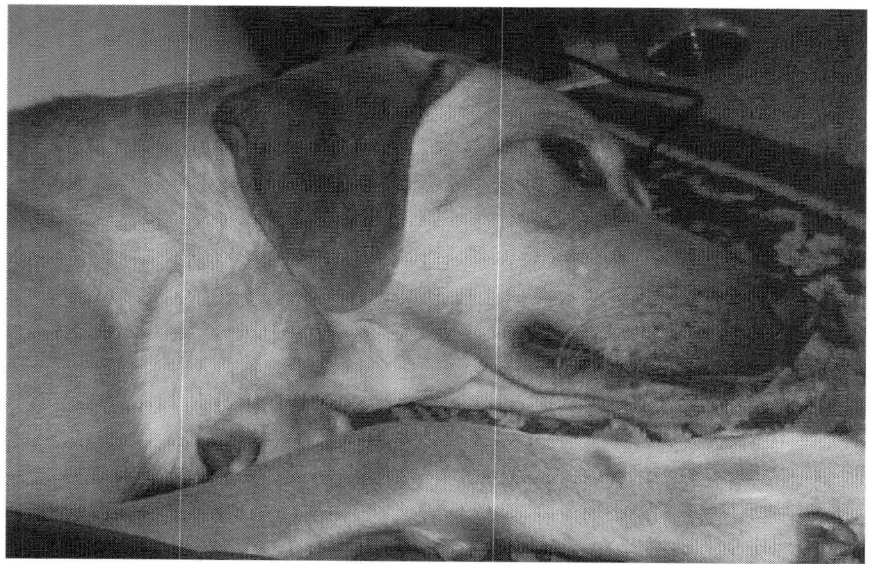

If he comes creeping around here again t ruddy camera of his when I am asleep I am going to lose my sense of humour!

AnotherCushion

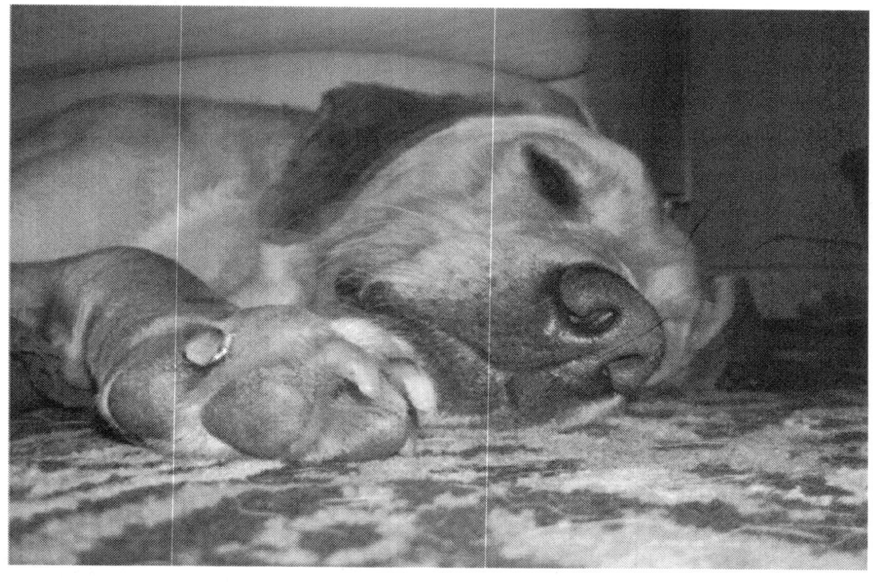

Oh now I get it! This is all about me pinching his velvet cushions off the sofa and snuggling up on them!

Monkey Dog

Oh revenge is so sweet! Me and The Owner went to work this morning and on the farm they were looking after a skinny strange looking dog with very long legs, I think they called him 'Monkey'. Mmm, I think that says it all really, clearly no breeding!

Anyway, his lady owner turned up to pick him up and came up with MY dish in her hand. How did she get that?! So Monkey dog goes and wee'd up MY post so I had to go and wee on it as well. Then he goes and wee'd on the gate, so I had to go and do it as well. So he then wee'd up the corner of The Owners office wall! Well I thought The Owner would have said something about that, at least I was beginning to hope he would coz this Monkey thing dog can wee a lot higher than me! Nothing to do with prowess, just he had longer legs than me and I was starting to struggle to wee high enough so I had to be cunning. Lady Monkey Dog Thing Owner had left her posh car door open so I went and wee'd on the side of the car and he took the bait and went and wee'd on the same spot, except he wee'd higher. Tee hee! All over the car seats! Oh Boy was he in trouble, I'm glad she's not my Owner! I went and sat back in the office under the desk and felt a certain kind of smug satisfaction. Serves him right, he looks like a camel anyway!

The Beach Towel

Yesterday was warm, I understand that. Hoomuns like to lie around in the sun and cook themselves. I understand that as well. But, hey, so do dogs! He comes wandering out looking like heaven knows what with his sun hat on his head and with very dodgy cheap sunglasses. I think he bought them about three years ago at the petrol station and they have only one arm left. The other one fell off after the first week and too tight to buy more, he has to have his head on one side when he wears them to prevent them falling off! A pack of beers under his arm and a towel draped over his shoulder. I think it best we don't discuss the shorts here! The towel is spread on the ground and I try and climb on but whenever

I do he chases me off. I try and lay down beside him and he chases me off! I had to lie on a heap of dead leaves in the end whilst he, The Owner, lords it on the towel! Later in the day he starts pulling buckets of water out of the well to water his plants, including the smelly lavender. Well I could have done that! Predictably, one of those buckets of water had to come my way didn't it? So dripping in water, while he wasn't looking, I went and curled up in the middle of his towel. Later, watering finished, he came back to his towel, opened another beer with a satisfied sigh and laid back on the towel. A moment later he shot up again and threw his beer everywhere complaining loudly and I was in trouble, but oh boy was it worth it!

Early Mornings!!!

What's on my mind? I'd like to know what's on The Owners mind and this morning I can't think there was too much! There I was, happily snoring to myself (the noise keeps the badgers from pooping outside the back door) dreaming of Bonio's. Had I mentioned that I like Bonio's?
It was still dark when I heard him come crashing down the stairs and start fumbling around in the kitchen. He was going to have to put the light on eventually and it's a lot easier on his temper if he does it sooner rather than later. I thought we must be going somewhere; nothing else normally gets him out of bed that early. He gets himself dressed, in clothes straight out of the washing machine, Yuk, he must be sleepwalking! Then he gives me my breakfast, at 3:00 in the morning, so I forgave him immediately. Then he shuffles off down to the office and begins furiously banging away on the keyboard. He is giving me a right old headache with all the noise! When the dairyman came out to go and get the cows in for milking, just after the sun came up he thought we were being burgled and came across to check, pitch fork at the ready. It won't last, by 11:00 he'll be falling asleep over the keyboard and wake up with red marks across his forehead spelling "QWERTY". I think he must be sickening for something! Maybe he might forget he's already given me breakfast, if I try my little dance and just see what comes my way. It may work! This could be a very long day....

Caffeine poisoning!

Well, it was a long day, I was right about that and I think today could be just as long for a different reason. By 06:00 his first report and demo of a software system was on its way to someone, not sure who and I'm not sure he did either from the confused e-mail he has had this morning.

By 09:00 he was starting to feel the effects of dragging himself out of bed so early. He seemed to reason that he could do the early starts when he was driving so there is no reason why he shouldn't be able to now! Hello?!?! That was ten years ago! Time is a bitch when it comes to clouding the mind over what we can still achieve. I used to be able to outrun any dog around here a couple of years ago but I couldn't out run the jaws of Lady Chocolate Lab when she took exception to my amorous advances the other night! By 10:00 he was starting to fall asleep over the keyboard with the mouse in his hand and then coming to with a jolt as his head started to fall. The mouse jolted as well and moved files and folders all over the place. He still can't find some of them. Then he started on the strong coffee! By lunch time he had so much caffeine in him he couldn't keep his hands from shaking! Now this morning he has to explain away the rather manic e-mails he was sending to everyone all afternoon and the sometimes embarrassing misspellings of several crucial words in them! Last night he had to explain why he managed to send three pints and two packets of peanuts scattering all over the bar, all on different occasions, where his hands were shaking so much. Fortunately he has come down off the manic ceiling and I am today looking forward to the first Postman's delivery for a while. I must behave! I must behave! I must behave......

More Stinking Flowers

Oh man that garden! The rose (Yuk and phew) is in another flowering apparently but it has got a bit cunning and only flowered up high where I can't pee! The lavender (double yuk and phew!) is stinking the neighbourhood out and round the back of the cottage the Jasmine is in full flower but that is on the shed roof and try as I might I cannot get to pee that high and believe me I have tried! So many smells in the same garden and not one of them good! He, The Owner, is wandering around in heaven spouting nonsense about the 'perfume'! I am keeping a low profile today whilst I scheme and plot a way of damping down the stench from these flowers of the devil! Meanwhile I will content myself with peeing all over the lavender (double Yuk and phew) whilst I work out my next move!

The Badgers Came Visiting

Oh dear! He has not had a good start to the day! Well I've been trying to tell him for ages that there are badgers in the garden at night and despite his admonishing of me for digging little holes in the lawn, it isn't me!

Last night they kept me awake with their grunting and snuffling around the back door to the boot room.

All night they were out there carrying on like a load of hoomuns at a barbie. This morning, I feel like I haven't slept a wink, mainly coz I haven't, and The Owner comes bouncing down the stairs all fresh and perky. Let's me out of the boot room and then opens the back door for me to go out for my wee before breakfast. Well I'm not going out there, there may be badgers still about and I may be brave but I'm not stupid! Rolling in their poo is one thing but actually meeting one, face to face, not going there! He was intent on me going for a wee and was trying to evict me from the back door and I kept digging my heels in and sitting down or rolling over on my back. Anything but have to go out there. So he strides purposefully outside as if to show there was nothing to be afraid of and puts his bare foot straight in a dollop of badger poo left just outside the back door. There then followed much 'yucking' and 'phewing' as he tries to scrape it off his foot and from between his toes and tries desperately to find someone to blame for his predicament. I'm guessing that I am not going to find a way of persuading him on the benefits of rolling in badger poo just yet!

Working From Home

We've been home this afternoon, me and The Owner. He spent all morning telling everyone that he was going to be working from home for the afternoon. I wondered what that meant exactly but soon found out. We got throught the door and he quickly changed into his old gardening clothes, poured himself a very large glass of something and went and sat on the patio.

After he'd finished that he went rummaging in the back of the shed and emerged with a triumphant smile on his face and a gallon of fence treatment in one hand, the label of which was so old it had "By Appointment to His Majesty The King" on it and an old brush in the other. I am thinking that this was not quite what he was implying by "working from home". So he starts painting the fence with this stinking paint stuff and I go indoors for a lay down. I keep checking on him every once in a while, just to make sure he's doing it right and after a while he comes wandering back in with an empty glass in his hand, presumably looking for more wine. Suddenly there is a right rumpus going on in the kitchen! He's shouting and using words that would make his mother blush! So I went to investigate. Well I have absolutely no idea how all that smelly fence paint stuff got all over my tail!!!! But I do however; have a very good idea how it got up every door and cupboard in the kitchen and dining room. I think I'm going up to the woods at the top of the garden and hiding behind the barbecue for a while.

Psychic Jack

Does anyone like octopus? Throughout the latter parts of this foopall ,since The Owner realised that this strange looking animal had gained some fame for predicting outcomes of foopall matches a long way away, (I think they must be playing near Swindon somewhere) he's been putting down little boxes with funny colours draped over them and a Bonio inside and taking pictures as evidence.

He's tried ringing every newspaper in the area looking for one who's daft enough to believe I can predict who puts most balls in the net thing and do the silliest dance afterwards. Hey! Two boxes, two Bonio's, no problem! Nothing clever about that, get the closest one first and then on to the other as quickly as possible before he changes his mind. I'm very good at predicting F1 results, Moto GP, horse races, cricket, hockey, and the odd game of scrabble and tiddlywinks as well. Bring on the Bonio's!

A Sporty Weekend

Well what a weekend of "sport" we've had! He sat there yesterday afternoon watching the noisy cars and I sat with him as I tried to understand what was going on. Ok, so he had a Bonio in his pocket which was the main reason for my attentiveness but I did watch the cars as well.

Now as far as I could understand, these very noisy cars, so loud that they had to wear these big hats, (presumably to keep the noise out) drive for about a hundred and fifty miles and get right back to where they started and then jump about with great excitement that they haven't really got anywhere! Try as I might, I could not see where their K9 would sit in those funny cars! With that done and still mystified, I thought the cricket over at the cricket pitch would have been his next target but no, I was wrong! The pack of cans of beer I had spotted in the fridge was not for the cricket but for another game of foopall on the telly. He's videoed me selecting a Bonio from a coloured box and is claiming I predicted the result and that is being sent to the papers this morning. I am guessing he is going to delete the ten other videos where I "predicted" the other team would win. There was so much shouting at the ref going on that I couldn't get to sleep so I went over and watched the cricket, a much more peaceful game I felt and I was also wary of bringing the ball back for them after the somewhat negative reaction I had the last time I tried. So I curled up and enjoyed a good snooze. When I woke up they'd all gone! All alone in the middle of a very large field I was, and it was getting dark. The foopall was finished when I got back and so all the shouting was finished, his beer cans were empty and he was asleep! Mind you I think the shouting was a little quieter than the snoring so I stuck my nose in his ear. He woke up quite quickly and got all grumpy. Equilibrium restored!

That annoying little grey thing with an attitude!

If I hear one more time that grey thing say to me "Hey Dog, don't you think I look cute, there will be one more thing on the lunch time menu than previously planned!

Running Aground

We're having a great time on our holidays, me and The Owner... well I am anyway! Lots of pubs alongside the canal and I love canals and rivers, I love pubs as well.... I also LOVE BONIO'S, had I mentioned that?

There's only me and him on the boat thing but he just has to get the biggest boat on the canal, it was so big, if I ran from one end to the other and back again I didn't need a walk that night! The man at the boat yard wasn't very convinced when he told him that the rest of his party was joining us that night. We stopped at nearly every pub along the canal and there were quite a few! Rounding a bend there was a pub in sight, it was crowded with Lady Hoomuns so I thought we would definitely be stopping, I don't mind as Lady Hoomuns always feed me tit bits. As he came round the bend he went in real close to the bank so I thought he was mooring there, so I jumped off! How was I to know he'd just got it wrong and ran the boat into the bank and got it stuck?!?! It took him ages to get it off the mud again. There was lots of noise and revving and he was making a lot more noise than the engine! I kept out of the way and sat on the bank and watched as all the Lady Hoomuns were laughing at him. I opted not to jump back on board with him when he got it going as it was going to be a bumpy ride for the rest of the afternoon, so I ran along the bank. It was tiring but I felt it was safest!

Through The Long Bridge Thing

Well The Owner stood at the back, leaning on the railings on the boat with his big mug of tea in his hand trying to look like he was in control of everything. Then there was this big bridge looking thing coming up, actually it was more like a hole in a cliff face really where the water went through and it had trees and stuff like that way on up at the top. But he chugged resolutely forward, towards the hole.

I couldn't help but think that maybe the chimney thing coming out of the roof near the back of the boat was a little too tall and that it might be why everyone else seemed to be taking their chimney things down before heading in! Well, it was very dark in there and I couldn't see a thing, except a little dot of light a long way off, which seemed to be where we were heading. The noise was very loud and very strange inside and I couldn't really make any particular noises out, but when we emerged the other side after a frankly less than perfect passage through, I noticed the chimney thing laying along the roof and over where, until a few minutes ago, The Owner had been standing and the railing he was leaning on was now bent! There, beside me, was the mug of tea spilled all over the floor, but The Owner was nowhere to be seen! Well who was pointing the boat? Me apparently! I knew pointing the boat had something to do with that stick coming out of the floor of the boat which The Owner seems to spend most of the time, when travelling, leaning against in a nonchalant manner, and which I would wee up at any and every opportunity. He seems to believe it will impress everyone and anyone! But what to do with it? Moments later there was a big bang and a lot of shouting at the front end and everything came to a standstill. I did venture to have a quick peek around the front but I was a bit concerned as I appeared to have pointed it into the bank.... through another boat….. which was now sinking and its Hoomun seemed particularly vexed about it! Then The Owner came wading out of the hole in the cliff through the water, with a big lump on his head. I went and hid coz I reckoned I was going to be in so much trouble, but the other Hoomun kept shouting at The Owner and then started hitting him! Someone called the Hoomun police and I thought it was going to be the dog pound for me. But I liked Hoomun Policeman as he had a pocket full of Bonio's and I like them, so it all worked out well in the end!

Lady Hoomun Policeman and her Lady Chocolate Lab

Well we got The Owner out of the hospital, the other Hoomun Boat Owner out of the police station, our boat re-floated and a big crane in to lift the other boat out of the water where it had sunk. That was really impressive! Dangling on the end of a big piece of string high in the air, leaking water from the many holes that I think I may have caused and put on the back of a really big lorry to taken to Shorance.

Not sure where Shorance is exactly but I heard The Owner say that it would be repaired in Shorance. The best bit was that somehow I didn't get the blame for not pointing the boat properly. There was a Lady Hoomun Policeman who came and asked him lots of questions about what happened and wrote it all down. I really liked her as well coz she had a pocket full of Bonio's too. I haven't tried to get a Bonio from the Hoomun Police around home, perhaps they get issued with Bonio's as well as other stuff? That evening Lady Hoomun Policeman turned up where we were moored, near a pub since you ask, without her uniform and guess what? She had a Lady Chocolate Lab as well; and Bonio's! Me and New Lady Chocolate Lab ran up and down the bank, in and out of the water having great fun whilst The Owner and Lady Hoomun Policeman sat and drank and talked and other Hoomun stuff until they went back to the boat for more drinks and stuff. Well I've been planning this game for a day or so, but I've just had no-one to play it with. If you run across the roof of the boat and drop over the side and onto the little deck, in through the window and across the table, out the other side and back on to the roof again to do it all again, it just looked perfect for a game of chase. So I got Lady Chocolate Lab to follow as I dropped over the side and on to the deck and launched myself through the window to the table. This is the point where the evening went downhill a little for me! Well how was I to know he had biscuits, cheese and stuff and glasses of wine all over the table? They weren't there when last I looked! I managed to knock them all on the floor, which was no bad thing as I could then clear them up, but The Owner didn't seem to share my enthusiasm for my new game. I also heard a very large splash outside as Lady Chocolate Lab missed the deck and went over the side. The Owner wasn't impressed about the table and even less impressed that he had to get in the water and rescue Lady Chocolate Lab. There isn't a boot room on board but there is an engine room, a little smaller than I am used to but I think I could be here for some time to come.

His Special Mug

I was a little concerned that The Owner may have forgotten where I was this morning and started the engine with me still in the engine room. I needn't have worried, he was not about to turn down the opportunity for a good scowl and frown with his hands on his hips as he lets me out. He is of course milking it over yesterday's events.

He's been sitting there with a piece of dead cow draped over his eye as he remembers his Grandmother doing that for a black eye. By this morning his eye was quite a peculiar colour after his little argument with the other Hoomun Boat Owner yesterday. It did give me a bit of a funny turn when I saw him with the dead cow on his face as I came back from my morning wee over the mooring ropes. After trying hard for a bit of sympathy for a cold he hasn't got, not brought on by his late evening dip in the water last night, we got under way. He was not about to run aground for the third day running so he set a very purposeful course down the middle of the water and everyone else, if they knew what was good for them, had to navigate around the side of him. There were several little altercations with other boat Hoomuns who felt he was being a little too confrontational, but I knew him better. He hadn't got warmed up yet! He had bought a special unbreakable cup which apparently could keep a drink hot for hours, from the shop beside the pub before we left this morning. So he put it proudly, full of hot tea, on the shelf at the back of the boat beside the railings where the chimney thing had fallen. Well I was never very happy with the way he had wedged the chimney back in place with twigs after it got knocked over! When he came across someone who was a bigger bully than him and made him get over towards the side of the canal he had to go under a low tree. This managed to dislodge the chimney which fell down again, with a big thump just beside where I was snoozing. I jumped up (well who wouldn't?) and managed to knock the new special mug into the water. He thought about putting me in the engine room and thankfully chickened out and settled instead for grumbling and moaning loudly. For me, I felt the boat wasn't quite long enough but I still went and curled up right at the front of the sharp end. I think I may stay here for the duration today.

Early Morning on the Canal

What a lovely morning I've had, just a shame The Owner got into so much trouble over it. Not my fault this time I might add! I was curled up in the early hours of the morning under one of the lazarettes (now aren't you impressed how I am picking up the boating language?). It was barely light and certainly before the sun came up.

I became aware of movement in the galley, so I went to investigate. It was The Owner, making tea, and already dressed in his shirt and shorts. He tells me that as it was such a lovely morning he thought he would get up and "see the morning in". I'm not sure how he arrived at that conclusion as he hadn't even looked out of the curtains at that point, but I went along with it. He took his mug of tea and went and sat on one of the seats in the bow (more technical terms!). So I sat up there with him. He was right, it was a beautiful morning! The mist was rising gently from the water and forming an eerie sea of mist on the fields from which the cows appeared almost to be hovering. The odd moor hen called from the canal bank somewhere. The gentle hum in the distance of the pumps in the dairy and otherwise, peace and tranquillity enveloped the emerging morning scene. I sat beside him watching the scene and catching the odd sniff on the almost imperceptible breeze as he gently and absent mindedly ruffled the fur on the back of my head. After his second cup of tea and when the sun was starting to burn off the mist from the field, announcing the arrival of a new day, drowsiness started to get the better of him and he started to fall asleep again. So he took himself off for what he described as "a little lie down". All that was left of that pleasant hour was a ring of tea on the deck where his cup had stood. I curled up back under the lazarettes; the next thing I heard was a loud banging on the roof of the boat and a very aggressive, official looking chap was getting very agitated saying, "It's 11 in the morning and this is a night time only mooring area! People should not be drinking so much they can't get up in the mornings if they want to be mooring on my canal bank!" As far as I know The Owner only had a tea and an orange juice last night. The Owner emerged, bleary eyed, from the cabin wondering what all the fuss was about and got a fixed penalty notice slapped straight in his hand from Horrible Man, (that wasn't what The Owner called him) from Inland Waterways, who went off up the path tutting loudly about people shouldn't drink so much they can't get up in the morning. The Owner has been talking grumpily to himself all morning since then.

Back Home

We took the boat back yesterday and only had the one argument with someone who, The Owner felt, was moored where we should be and he had a minor discussion with the boatyard man who by now had heard about the sinking. The Owner threw all our stuff into the car and spun the wheels in his hast to get out of the car park. Not sure why coz I'm sure I saw him pay.

He only grumbled the once at the staff in the motorway services forecourt on our way back, about their standards of training and how they "Couldn't make a decent cup of coffee if their lives depended upon it!" We virtually crashed through the front door and he fell straight into his favourite armchair, turning the telly on and opened a beer before his bum had even hit the chair. He settled back with a sigh of relief as the very fast and noisy cars started racing very fast back to the same place. This was clearly the reason for our chase all the way home! I still don't understand the rules but then neither did the bright red cars apparently. He gave up in disgust at that point and with a fresh beer or two we went over to watch the cricket. I was very good and even when the red ball rolled right to my feet I didn't pick it up! I wanted to go up on the hill and check out that dead badger, another week on since I last visited it and it should be getting quite interesting by now. But we had to do this bonding thing and sit and watch the cricket 'together'! There was also a deer up in the woods before we went away which warranted another look by now I felt. We had a spell of this bonding once before but after a good roll in a dead badger we soon got over it.

The Disappearing Pond Water

There has been a theft in the village while we were away! I managed to get out for a bit of solo rambling around the farm today, just to check on one or two things..... like dead badgers and stuff. I thought I would be a bit clever, not wanting to upset The Owner as he is in such a good mood since we have been back, so I went and visited the dead badger up on the hill first and thought I would round the trip off with a quick splash around in the pond on the way back.

Imagine my surprise, SOMEONE HAS STOLEN THE WATER! I did have a good root around but it definitely isn't there. Now this left me with a bit of a problem, a very smelly shoulder and nowhere to wash it off. I thought if I bounded through the door and went straight behind the desk he wouldn't notice. The Owner didn't say anything when I got back and I thought I had got away with it, he soon got up and went outside and I breathed a sigh of relief. Yup, definitely got away with it! Then he called from outside, so I went rushing out as it was about coffee time and that always means its Bonio time, but he closed the door behind me quickly and then produced the hose pipe from behind his back.

I felt he was a little harsh with the way he used that stiff broom as well!

And Now The Water Trough!

I am beginning to suspect foul play here at the moment. Yesterday it was the pond water, STOLEN!!!!! I can still not find any suspects; it seems to have just vanished into thin air. Then today I went for a little ramble about the farm after lunch, I don't get any lunch but apparently The Owner deserves some, and I made a bee-line for my first option of a little aquatic adventure. Imagine my absolute horror! Empty! Not only empty but disconnected!!!! I run the risk here of wearing out the exclamation mark key if I'm not careful. I will keep you informed of any developments.

Another Water Trough

Some of my confidence has been restored; I have found another water trough that still has water in it. I did check inside to make sure that there wasn't a bung ready to be pulled out or even some kind of syphoning device but I think it is all clear. Obviously the water thieves haven't found this one yet!

The Water Tanker

I think I may be on to something here. I was out this morning on a short patrol around the farm. Well really I was just trying to keep out the way because the water cooler man called this morning to the office and he surprised me as I didn't hear him drive up the track. The Postman a bit later in the morning had a piece of my mind and all in all The Owner didn't seem too pleased with me so I opted instead for a quick trip around the fields. I was just having another quick sniff around the pond looking for the water when what pulled up but this thing. I can't think that he was up to any good so I hid in the hedge and watched for the rest of the morning. He's been back twice since and drags this great big pipe out and puts it under the manhole cover. Not sure what's going on down there but it can't be any good. I'll keep you informed!

The Incident of the Smelly Hosepipe.

I have been regarding The Owner with a particularly suspicious eye today after 'Mo the Wise' suggested the smell from the manhole where I think the lorry may be stealing the pond water from may be significant. He was clearly not wanting to arouse my suspicions that he may be behind it as he pretended to be busy at the computer all morning. When his Hoomun friend turned up for coffee I let myself out and went and sat in wait for the lorry to come back for another load of pond water that I suspect he may be hiding down the manhole. I didn't have to wait long before the lorry tanker turned up to steal another load of water and Tanker Driver busied himself with his very large hose down the manhole. I crept forward, very stealthily through the bushes and waited for my moment. It smelled far worse than The Owner could possibly have managed so I suspect he may not be behind it after all. Just as Tanker Driver was pulling his hose out of the man hole I leapt forward, defence of my village and its pond was my only motive, with a loud bark I broke cover. Tanker Driver swung around in a sort of terror and I got covered with the contents of his pipe. Oh the smell!!! Yuk and phew just doesn't cover it! I spent an hour lying in the cattle trough to try and wash away the smell. Now, I still smell and the cattle won't go near the trough. The Owner is going to wash me down with the hose pipe next and for the first time ever I am looking forward to it! I think that may not be the pond water down there after all!

Talking Cows!?!?!

We had a gentle wander in to work this morning, out of the gate, down past the cricket pitch and past The Manor where I always stop to wee up the wall. I consider it a small statement for the workers against the capitalist elite.

In the paddock the other side of The Manor is a small field where are kept a couple of dry cows, not sure what a dry cow is as they look no different to the rest, but that's what The Owner says they are. They were stood by the railing fence this morning, waiting for us and so The Owner said "Morning Mrs Cows", as we walked past. "And Good morning to you!" came the response! The air of surprise was palpable at that moment; as it dawned on us both that cows don't speak! They say also that dogs can't type but I, of course, have proved that wrong. So was this another of those watershed moments in the history of animal communication skills and another step further into the strange and surreal world of The Owner? With almost a tremor in his voice he stepped tentatively up to the fence and asked "Are you well this morning?" Ordinarily I pour scorn on his chat up routine and he usually gets me to break the ice with his Lady Hoomun Friends, but to be fair, what do you say next to a cow in a field that has just wished you a good morning!? "Very well thank you, and you?" came the response. The Owner was suddenly looking very peaky, with an ashen looking face and a rapidly developing stammer. "Um, not too bad - under the circumstances", came his rather feeble reply. I was feeling none the more confident about the developing scene, so I stood behind his legs and peered tentatively around the side of him. "Don't you think the dahlias are extraordinary this year?" came a further show of intelligent banter from the cow. But with that the rather jolly figure of the Lady Hoomun Gardner from The Manor popped up from behind the stone wall behind the cows. Somewhat relieved and yet taken aback by the turn of events, all The Owner could manage was a rather feeble "Quite so!" as he turned and shuffled off further in the direction of the office. When he got there he fell into his comfy chair and poured himself a very strong coffee and has been silent ever since! I didn't even get a Bonio!!!!

Maybe I'll Visit The Badgers

Walking to work yesterday morning The Owner was keeping a very cautious eye on those cows still, I don't think he is quite convinced about Hoomun Lady Gardener being behind them talking to him yet. Whilst he was trying to get them to answer him again with more of his intellectually stimulating repartee I went and had a quick check in the pond.

There was water in it!!!! But when we went home again later it was gone again. I am sure Hoomun Tanker Driver is behind it somehow, I'm just not sure how he is doing it. One thing is certain; I am not going to get near him again when he has that big hose with him. I can still smell it on my fur from the last time. Maybe if I go and have a roll around up near the badgers set that may be enough to mask the smell a little.

Vic's Visit

Oh Lordie, I am in so much trouble this afternoon! The Owner was sat at his desk absent mindedly munching on a sandwich. There was me wishing his leg would fall off or something as he hadn't given me a Bonio whilst he was eating. He says it ensures I understand who is boss if I eat after him. Huh! I know who is boss!

Well, a car pulled up outside and then it all went quiet again. The door burst open and a man dressed completely in black burst through the door! Well I was terrified and The Owner didn't seem to be any happier than I was, so I felt it my duty to protect him and leapt over the desk with a lot to say on the matter. Well the man in black fell to the floor whimpering, so I felt I had made my point. I think his name was Vic R. but I didn't quite catch his last name. The Owner picked Vic up off the floor and sat him on a seat and all Vic kept saying was "Oh Lord Bless me!" and "Oh my goodness!" The Owner gave me a particularly hard stare and made Vic one of his special coffee's that he only has once a day. Then Vic asked for another coffee and then another, which I felt was starting to make mountains out of what was only a little woof. After a while and when Vic's hands seemed to be shaking quite badly (and I know this coz it took three attempts to get his keys in the car door) Vic was on his way. The Owner said I was going to hell for that one. Didn't quite understand what he meant by that and I am not sure where Hell is, perhaps its near Swindon somewhere, by the way he spoke about it I don't think it was going to be a very nice place so it probably is near Swindon. Either way I think I'll go up to the calf sheds for the afternoon, just in case

The Small Boy visits with Strange Woman

Last weekend Small Boy came and spent the weekend with us and he brought his mother who I think is called Strange Woman. At least that's what The Owner keeps calling her. The woman was a whirling dervish! If it wasn't screwed down then it was put in the dishwasher or washing machine, if it was screwed down or too big for her to lift then it was vacuumed and polished!

She was getting far too close to some of my toys for my liking so I took my favourite little red dragon soft toy and hid it upstairs where I'm not supposed to go. This morning it has resurfaced! It is the morning of The Village Church Fete when traditionally old ladies draw battle lines over a Victoria sponge and The Owner likes to wear his special Village Church Fete white shirt and cream coloured trousers with his blazer. So he gets them and washes them for the occasion. You're ahead of me here aren't you? My little red dragon is a pale imitation of its original self and The Owners shirt and trousers have a distinct pink tinge to them. Fortunately Strange Woman seems to have got the blame! He's jumped into the car and rushed off to town to get something to remove the colour which in itself is going to cause further problems as the Tesco Driver Hoomun Yoof is due any minute and after last week's shouting match over the missing Bonio box (Tee hee, got away with that!) I don't think he will be feeling much like waiting at the gate for The Owner's return. The day could worsen yet as he will be looking for his funny straw hat later and I know that is behind the tumble dryer in the boot room, half chewed and full of fluff and cobwebs. I'll keep you posted.

The Village Fete

The Owner arrived back from the supermarket in town clutching a little packet of something which he threw in the washing machine, along with his pink shirt and trousers and one or two other bits he'd turned pink as well. Then he opened the door again and checked through it all for anything that may have been a colour other than white then closed the door again.

He looked at it for a while longer, holding his chin, and then opened the door and checked for a third time, just in case. With the washing machine gently whirring in the corner the phone rang, it was Tesco, ringing to say they were sorry for their driver being late getting to him and she could be another half an hour. About half way through I saw a light bulb come on as he suddenly remembered the delivery, so he made much of how he had "been waiting in all morning for her to turn up" and "is this the way they treat their customers" etc.. Tesco Driver Lady Yoof turned up and was severely 'tutted' at for his inconvenience and immediately forgiven when she knocked his delivery charge off the bill.

We went to the village fete this afternoon and he refused to take his blazer off because of a very pink shirt, even though it was too hot. The Hoomun Lady with the breath that could de-scale a kettle from a hundred yards was having a big argument over what was the correct filling for a Victoria sponge with the two old sisters from the Old Rectory, so that hadn't changed since last year, they were arguing about it then! Vic R. was there with his family and I still cannot work out what Vic's surname was. The Owner was joking with him about his dog collar but my one is not white like that. I went and sat behind the burger van hopeful of a morsel or two and was not disappointed and even more so when the two sisters and the lady with the breath that could de-scale a kettle etc. worked their argument up to such a pitch that they were throwing cakes at each other. I of course volunteered to clean up after them. Oh the tranquillity of village life!

The Large Wine Glass

We've been out for most of the day; The Owner took me to a car boot sale this morning. Not sure why as he already has a boot on his car which looks perfectly good to me, but I went along with it. He went from stall to stall arguing with all of them about whether or not he could buy it cheaper, new, at the supermarket.

I made a little mistake early on in the day by weeing up the first post I came across. Well I was bursting! I didn't know it was an antique hat stand, whatever one of them is! We had to scuttle on down a few stalls quick to get away from some people who were just a little less than amused by my efforts and watched us for quite a while with their hands on their hips. A bit unnecessary I thought! All was not lost though as we found a burger van, it was not the Hoomun Lady Burgervan Owner that I know but she was ok as she gave me a sausage when The Owner wasn't looking. He seemed particularly pleased when he found a wine glass, which he told anyone who was daft enough to listen, was built to hold a whole bottle. On the way home we stopped in Tesco Shop and he bought a bottle of wine. Now usually he has a couple of empty bottles at home with expensive labels on that he fills from a plastic bottle that costs no more than £2.99 for a litre and then takes it out to his guests and lets them watch him pour it into his decanter. But, today he bought one that was worth lots of money, more than a whole month's supply of Bonio's. When we got back we went and watched the cricket over the way and then came back and he started to prepare some mouldy cheeses and some slices of mouldy sausage (Yuk, not touching them myself!). He fed me and I went off up the garden to the woods at the top to do what doggies do best after a meal and then came rushing back down the garden feeling relieved and well pleased with my efforts, round the corner and straight into the table he'd put out. His expensive wine, in his new glass, was on the table........... and is now all over my back! I am now in the boot room, with the door shut! He is indoors somewhere drinking more of his cheap plonk from his cheap glasses. Don't think I will be getting a Bonio tonight somehow.

I've Got a Hangover

You may recall how yesterday I was doused in a bottle of what The Owner described as 'the finest of wines' and I was left in the boot room to clean myself up a little. Well this morning I still have a pretty pink patch on my back and side and to cap it all I have a bad headache and I don't feel well! Is this what you hoomuns have to go through after you've drunk some of this stuff? Can't imagine what would have made anyone think this was the result of a good night out. I feel grumpy as well so heaven help Postman when he arrives, I may have an opinion on the matter!

The Garden Gate

Tonight, by the time we got home from the office, you'll be pleased to know I am sure, I was feeling a lot better after my hangover. When we got in, The Owner fed me and I went up the garden to the woods at the top, to do what dogs do best in the woods after feeding. Ever mindful of my little "Ooops!" yesterday I made a very cautious return to the cottage taking particular care when passing the patio table. Things were going well I thought. After a while The Owner decided it was time for my evening constitutional across the fields and I was REALLY excited after having done very little all day but feel sorry for myself. We got to the front gate and The Owner opened the latch. Now I know the gate opens inwards but I forgot myself and burst forth and now the gate opens outwards. Well it doesn't really open either way now, it just sort of lays on the floor, propped up on one edge. Does anyone have any gate hinges they don't want?

The Cow with a Calf

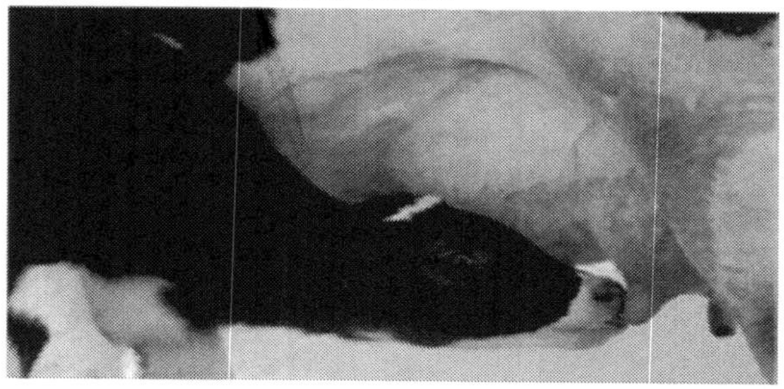

It is raining here ever so hard and apart from The Owner getting very wet on the way home for lunch because he didn't believe the forecast and take a jacket with him to work this morning, I actually quite like the rain. You understand that my concern about The Owner's well-being is only borne from the knowledge that he will get wet, then cold and then grumpy. The down side of all the rain and stuff is that all my efforts at weeing up post, trees and other bits and bobs all get undone as it gets washed away. So on the way home I nearly ran out of wee and only just managed to find enough to do the tree on the front path to the cottage. It was a bit of a struggle!

On the walk back, given the fact that it is still raining and everything had been washed away again, I was unable to repair the damage and so at the moment my territory is largely unprotected. This leaves me feeling quite vulnerable. So the walk back to work was a more straightforward process than I would normally have done; until I got to the paddock by the old barn! Can we have a few dramatic chords at this point? In the paddock is a cow with two young calves, only a few days old, so I wandered up the grass bank for a closer look at mother and child. Then I saw it! What on earth is going on here? Is this even right?

The Owner's Evening Visitor

Last night The Owner had a Lady Hoomun come to see him. I've seen her before in some of the groups of his friends but he told me that this was a "Private matter". When she turned up I did my best to make her feel welcome by rolling on my back and doing the silly run, out round the tree and back and other stuff like that.

The Owner made them both a mug of tea and they sat down. Well this was normally my time for a fuss so I rolled over The Owners lap and stuffed my nose under his hand to try and attract his attention. So The Owner shut me in the dining room. It was obviously a misunderstanding so I went through the kitchen and stuffed my nose on the back door of the boot room and went outside and round the cottage and in the front door and back to where The Owner was sat. It seems that it wasn't a misunderstanding as I was promptly put back in the dining room and both doors were shut this time. Harrumph! After a while The Owner came in to make another pot of tea and so let me go up the garden, he had obviously forgiven me I felt, so I went quickly up to the woods (because I needed to, alright?!) and then came running back down, across the patio, through the boot room, through the kitchen, through the dining room, down the hall way building speed all the way and then did my silly run twice round the living room carpet. I thought that would make him smile a bit! I did notice he looked quite peeved so I went faster. It would seem that the cards and paper across the living room carpet didn't require muddy paw prints, or reshuffling, and were apparently quite important. Neither did the two tea mugs require knocking over. Lady Hoomun left soon afterwards, I guess, although it is a little difficult to hear properly what is going on in the rest of the house when you're shut in the boot room.

Dunking Your Toast

We got off to a bad start this morning. The Owner came banging down the stairs first thing and put the kettle on and then let me in the house. He fed me and then set about making himself some toast and put lots of butter on it. So far it had gone well! Then he went to pour the tea into his cup, picked up the pot in one hand and the tea strainer in the other......I couldn't help but think that he may have been better off putting both of those things over the cup but instead started to pour the tea over his toast. It took him several seconds to realise what I thought was a very obvious mistake!

There then followed several minutes of cursing and swearing and very noisy cutting of more bread. The toaster which can be very temperamental, clearly had recognised the gravity of the situation and co-operated when the bread was put in and the buttons were pressed. Once the toast was made for the second time and the tea poured, into the cup this time, The Owner shuffled off upstairs with it to bed again. Perhaps hoping it would be better starting the day again. I went outside for a quick patrol and discovered it was raining very hard, puddles everywhere! After a while I thought I ought really to try and bring a smile to his face after such a bad start to the day so, even though I am not allowed to, I went upstairs on my return to the cottage and clambered up on to his bed to let him have a cuddle. I thought that was one way to make him feel a bit better. He didn't seem to appreciate the trouble I went to and complained very loudly about muddy paws and wet fur. In fact there was nearly as much swearing as there was when he poured the tea in the wrong place. You just can't help some people can you? I think I will leave him to it.

Another Early Morning

He, The Owner, is beginning to worry me. This morning when it was barely light he comes grumbling down the stairs and starts clattering around the kitchen trying to put the kettle on. Eventually he has to give in and put the lights on and the earlier he does that the less pain he inflicts upon himself and the better my day will then turn out to be.

It's not the kitchen light that worries me but why is he getting up so early? Toast toasted and tea made and poured into the cup this time and not over the toast, he then starts grumbling coz Reg the Paper Boy hasn't been yet with his papers. I am on best behaviour where Reg the Paper Boy is concerned after the last incident. The Owner was presented with a laundry bill and told in no uncertain terms that he wouldn't deliver any more if I acted up again. Eventually Reg turns up with the paper and after a brief conversation about the mornings being the best part of the day The Owner made himself another cup of tea and settled down to read his paper. I don't think he had got through the headlines on the front page before his eyelids where starting to become a little heavy. I curled up on the far side of the room out of the way because I knew what would happen. Within a few minutes his hand went momentarily limp as he slipped into sleep. I say momentarily because that was the hand he had his tea in and when the hot tea spilled over his lap it suddenly wasn't very limp at all. Not yet seven in the morning and already he is on his second change of clothes! Even though I was on the other side of the room he still gave me half an accusing stare. I just hope he learnt his lesson the last time and doesn't put the cushion cover in with his trousers again. Although I liked the pinkish orange colour his trousers came out! It's now eight o clock and he's already asleep again and snoring loudly. I think I'll take myself for a walk this morning. It could be another very long day!

The Squidger's Demise

This morning was quite a sedate affair, nothing out of the ordinary. I got fed, then let out up the garden for a quick patrol of the perimeter and then back in doors where The Owner had made himself a cup of tea. I did my quick little dance to see if I could elicit a dish of sweet tea for myself but to no avail as The Owner grumbled off to the living room and sat down.

He picked up the TV remote which he rather childishly refers to as "The Squidger" (see, I was right, it isn't a real word! The spell checker doesn't like it) and switched on the TV to watch the BBC Breakfast News. Normal behaviour is to grumble at the presenters about "poor diction" or "slovenly standards" and to shout angrily at any politician who feels brave enough to show their faces on the screen and this morning was no exception. He even became extremely animated when "That Slime Ball Peter Mandelson" appeared on the screen. The morning was normal! Then he said those words which have great significance, "Ah Well"! Now that can mean any of many different things and the skill comes in working out which and therefore an appropriate course of action from me. This morning the "Ah Well!" I took to me mean he was going to get ready for work which was a cause for great excitement as it had been raining overnight and there was much weeing up posts to be done, so I jumped up and ran across to where he was sitting and put my paws on the edge of the seat. Unfortunately that was where "The Squidger" was and I managed to change channels as I knocked it off the seat. That was a mere inconvenience but it was the plop that followed which caused the problem as it dropped into his mug of tea. The Squidger seems unable or unwilling to do anything now and he is stuck on the CBBC channel until we can go and get a new one. I get the feeling that Sponge Bob Square Pants is not going to cut it for this evening's entertainment. I may opt for the spot behind the barbecue for snoozing this evening. Is it due to rain?

Badger

First thing this morning The Owner did his usual routine. Come down the stairs (grumbling to himself) put the kettle on, (still grumbling) put the tea in the pot (more grumbling), let me out and then feed me (lots more grumbling, this time about the price of dog food) and then whilst I go up the garden he shuffles off to put the telly on and grumble at the BBC news team.

This morning it was still stuck on CBBC so there was a lot of grumbling going on. I went up the garden as normal and imagine my surprise and pleasure when I came to realise that a badger had left a dollop of poo especially for me in my garden! So I rolled in it, all down one side and went rushing in to show The Owner. He didn't seem at all impressed when I came in; he ruffled the fur on my shoulder and got it all over his hand. Well he wasn't supposed to do that!!!! He sent me outside after that and I had to walk downwind of him to the office. When we got there I had to sit outside whilst he did his computer stuff and had a cup of tea, I felt sure he had the hosepipe in his mind for me! Postman is on holiday so we have Relief Postman this week. To be fair, I didn't see him come up the track so hadn't time to prepare a suitable repost. Suddenly there he was and made a big fuss of me. He was far too polite to say anything but I don't think he was too impressed with the badger poo that was now all over his hands and as he retreated down the track he was seen to be looking at his hand and then trying to wipe it on his trousers. I was set about by The Owner with the hose pipe soon after, I think he derives far too much pleasure from that hosepipe and the yard broom! Later in the day The Owner's mate came in for a coffee and was complaining about how the post today had a very strange smell about it and had we noticed. I felt it was time to slip unnoticed out of the door and go on a quick patrol around the farm.

The Hussy Comes to Visit

The other night, just before we went home for my tea, Keeper Hoomun from the farm, who is my mate, arrived to go and do his evening patrol of the farm. No need for him to do it as well, I do enough patrolling for the both of us but he seems to need to feel he's doing something constructive. On this occasion he had brought his little spaniel bitch who smelled particularly gooooood! Well, god forbid! The bitch was all over me!

The Owner had to drag her off me!!!!! I kinda wished he didn't but you know how these owners get sometimes. So he took her back and put her in Keepers car and then had to drag me home. Man, did he grumble that night. I just wanted to go back and see if she was still up there looking for me! The following morning, when it was time for work, now I know what you're going to say, "let him open the door first", but I was so keen to get down to the farm and wait to see if the hussy turned up again that I ran straight into the front door as soon as The Owner put his hand on the latch to open it. I did have to stagger a bit whilst I regained my composure before I was ready to meet the world. Of course The Owner had no sympathy, he kept going around with his finger pressed against his nose and laughing at me. I think he looked like a camel! I spent the rest of the day watching in case she came back to see me. My friend Keeper Hoomun is not so much my friend now, he turned up to patrol the farm the following night without her! Well he can patrol his own farm himself without my assistance from now on; I think he walks like a camel too!

The Water Table

Forgive the slight blur on my picture but I thought it lent itself to a better image of frantic action, which there was! I was becoming a bit concerned about the continued lack of water in the pond and particularly after listening to The Owner the other night so I felt a more thorough search of the pond for the leak was in order.

One evening last week The Owner was looking out of the window, glad that the rain was providing a further excuse not to get out and cut the lawns, when he sighed as he poured himself another very large sherry and said, “Well at least it will lift the water table enough to help the ponds!”. Now I’ve sat and thought about that and I’ve snoozed whilst contemplating that, but try as I might I cannot get my head around it. How on earth do you build a table out of water?!?!? And how will that help the pond?!?!?!? And how do you lift a table made only of water???!?!? I think I need to select a particularly succulent Bonio and take to my bed for another nap whilst I consider this further. Still haven't found the leak in the pond though.

Stairway to heaven

Well it wasn't raining when we went in!

Abandoned at the Cricket Match

Yesterday, as previously reported the weather was good here and The Owner took some cans of beer and went over to watch the cricket. After the suggestion of a hoomun friend of his he grabbed one of the picnic chairs left after a barbecue at the cottage in preference to sitting on the floor and fidgeting through the entire match.

Armed with his new best friend, the picnic chair, and a pack of Fosters, he deposited himself just outside the boundary under the tree to watch the match. It was not long before these early mornings he has been inflicting on himself (and me) started to take their toll and his eyes became as heavy as his beer can, which he dropped as he fell asleep. It was a good match with plenty of boundary shots and other stuff and I had learned my lesson from previous matches and despite the fact that I think the home team really needed my help I refused to pick up the ball and take it back to the bowler for them. To be honest, The Owner saw none of it after slumber overtook him completely. They finished their game and The Owner was still sat in his picnic chair, under the tree, sound asleep surrounded by the foam from his fallen can of beer. They packed up the wicket and cleared all the boundary markers and The Owner was still sat in his chair asleep! So they all laughed loudly as they jumped in their cars and rushed off up to the pub to celebrate another sound defeat and left The Owner still in his chair and still very much asleep. Well that left me with a dilemma, should I go with them up to the pub and try and scrounge a morsel from an empty crisp packet or two, should I stay loyally by his side and run the risk of copping the flack when he wakes up with a stiff neck and is looking for someone to blame, or should I go home and see if I can sort myself out some tea? I opted for the tea at home option but after an hour and the clouds were beginning to gather on the horizon I thought I ought really to go and check on him. Anxious not to get too much flack I sat by the gate into the field and waited. The gathering clouds having gathered; were now looking for someone to dump their contents upon and settled upon The Owner, and they dumped in some style. He eventually came round and realised that the rain was near monsoon levels so shuffled off home grumbling, dragging his chair and beer cans behind him. The good thing was he then fed me! Two meals in one night! Result!

There's Water in the Pond

It was only moments after five this morning when he came grumbling down the stairs. How do I know this? Coz HE has to have the old grandfather clock boing boinging all night long "To add a sense of time to the cottage". He has a nice little digital clock on the cooker that adds all the sense of time you need to the cottage and it does so quietly!

HE can't hear it from his bedroom; however this piece of torture equipment is right outside the boot room door. Tick tock tick tock boing boing! I have already planned to wee up it enough to cause it to rot and then fall over. A bit long term I know but you have to be a bit subtle sometimes. Anyway, he grumbles around the kitchen and makes a cup of tea and then goes for the next stage in his morning ritual of shouting at the telly whilst watching BBC Breakfast News, except it's too early even for them, so he falls asleep. Well that made good use of the early start then didn't it! When he did eventually wake up again he spent far too long getting ready, all I do is a quick shake and wipe my ears with my paws and we're ready to face the world. After more rain last night and yesterday there are so many posts to wee up as you would imagine. I was having to pace myself for fear of running out before we got to the office. As we passed the pond I noticed that someone had thrown a bottle in during the night and I marked that down for exploring later in the day and carried on. I was half way towards the farm when it suddenly dawned on me, it was floating! The bottle was floating! There was water back in the pond! There was room for more, agreed, but I think Tanker Driver must have come back in the night and put some back. I frankly don't believe all that nonsense from The Owner about tables made of water, it was definitely Tanker Driver and I shall be hiding in the hedge today and watching for him to return with more water. I will keep you informed!

The Hussey

My goodness! We've had days of rain and I have been getting quite wet sat in the hedge guarding the pond, waiting for Tanker Driver to return. Then this morning, on our journey in to work (I call it a journey, but for The Owner it is really more of a shuffle) there it was! In the bottom of the pond! A foot of water! I feel I should have heard from the boot room if Tanker Driver had been during the night. Maybe I just slept too soundly? I will try to keep my ear to the ground and listen better tonight. Earlier this afternoon whilst The Owner was shouting at his computer screen about the England cricket team's shortcomings all was otherwise quiet. When without warning and giving the impression of a whirlwind, The Hussey launched herself through the door at me. The bitch is possessed! She came through the door and jumped on me, flinging her every womanly wile upon my person. The Owner jumped to my rescue in his biggest display of activity all day (he will have to go and have a lie down now) and tried his best to protect me. Keeper came flying through the door as well and grabbed The Hussey and dragged her from me. It was all very messy for a while and I now have a soggy ear. It just ruins my coiffure!

Nieces Visit

The Owner's Niece came to see us yesterday, not sure how she managed it, she came up from the south and arrived from the north end of the village! So Niece brought this funny Black Little Girl K9 with her and I just couldn't work her out at all.

I took Black Little Girl K9 for a walk around the farm, to show her some of the things she may have found interesting like badger poo and stuff like that and was she interested in it? No not a bit! I took her up the hill to my big black bath and showed her how to get in and how to splash around and stuff like that and particularly how to get The Owner very wet when you leap out again - not interested! I thought she may have been interested in a bit of cow poo rolling. No, not interested! However she did rather like eating the cow poo which Niece was particularly disgusted with and I thought may have been sick, not tried that myself though. I think she may need a bit more instruction yet in the art of being a Labrador.

The Blue Van Man

Aha! Now I am getting the picture! The water level in the pond was down again this morning when out on patrol, but look what I found there! With that long hose thingy on his trailer he MUST be the one behind the disappearing water. I have yet to work out what it does, that hose trailer on the back of his big blue van, but I am feeling quietly confident I have found the culprit. I am not sure what the significance is of his van being blue. The Owner has a somewhat disparaging opinion of white vans generally and shouts at them a lot. That is until the White Van Man gets out of his van and walks back to speak with The Owner and it is at that point that The Owner starts looking behind him and tutting loudly. I need to find out if he has an opinion on Blue Van Man but I am beginning to suspect that when I unveil him as the water thief, the whole village will have an opinion on the matter. I will keep you informed!

My confrontation with Blue Van Man & Tall Trailer Hosepipe Hoomun

Well I think I made some significant progress today. There I was shuffling back up to the office after lunch, actually it was The Owner who was doing the shuffling, and I was flitting energetically from sniff to sniff, but what's new? Back at the office The Owner was brewing for another shouting match with the computer screen and the water cooler which he seems to think may

have sprung a leak, so I guess there then follows at some point a shouting match with Lady Water Cooler Office Girl, but that may yet happen another day. In order to get away from the noise I took myself off for a quick patrol and particularly to keep an eye on the pond. Well you could have knocked me down with an empty Bonio box! Behind me, yes behind me was the blue van, with a manhole cover up and a hose pipe in it and two men doing things! Well this needed further investigation so I went closer but they saw me. I think they were trying to divert my attention when Tall Hosepipe Trailer Hoomun gave me a Bonio. Well of course I had to accept but I kept a very watchful eye on them. It appeared to me they were putting water in the manhole but it didn't get very full and I checked the pond later and it did appear to be empty again. This detective lark is quite complicated; I think I may have to go back to looking for dead badgers and deer. I can feel a headache coming on. Speaking of which I need to go and check on The Owner.

The Owner goes Walkabout

It was a normal start to the morning, that is to say normal for this household. Before the sun came up I heard Old Reg the paper boy throw The Owners Sunday paper at the front door from the gate, he's done that since I mistook him for one of the cyclists in brightly coloured shorts and top who frequent our road on a Sunday morning and provide me with great sport. Then I hear the loo flush upstairs and The Owner comes grumbling down the stairs to put the kettle on. Everything was perfectly normal. He sat there reading his paper shouting at no one in particular with some angry or witty repost depending upon the type of story he was reading. Normality would then have involved a second mug of tea, a rant at The Andrew Marr show and then we would have gone for our walk around the farm and a further attempt on my part to educate The Owner on the subtleties of badger poo rolling. But this morning, first mug of tea finished, he put his boots on. I thought we may be in for an early walk and then go out somewhere, that's what normally happens when he puts his boots on before his second mug of tea on a Sunday. But without as much as a bye or leave and without putting his trusty tatty Barbour on, he shuffles off through the misty morning field….. without me! It's now been raining for over an hour and I still haven't seen him come back. His behaviour has worried me more than a little of late and this even more so!

The Owner hasn't returned!

It's now nearly lunchtime and The Owner hasn't returned! I notice he has closed his bedroom window, the first time since I have lived here with him and there's only two pounds on the electric meter. I daren't go and patrol looking for him in case he comes back. It's pouring down with rain, but I will stand firm and await his return.

He Wasn't at The Pub

I have been to the pub to look for The Owner and got thrown out of there for not having a lead (pub rules) and a stroppy boxer dog wanted to pick a fight with me. I have breeding I do, I don't do pub brawls! The Owner wasn't there, so I came back to the farm to see if he was at the office but that was all locked up and quiet as a mouse inside. I am getting very worried now; he has missed his second mug of tea, breakfast, his mid-morning sherry and now his Sunday lunchtime drink at the pub!

The Last Post.....

I've been on a patrol all around the farm, followed where I last saw The Owner heading through the morning mist and have come back home. Not a sign of him! The house is cold and except for the noise the electric meter is making all is quiet. I know The Owner does something to the meter when it makes that noise but I have no idea what or even if paws and claws can manage it! I'll go on another patrol later and see if I ca

THE OWNER – MY PART IN HIS BREAKFAST

We Have Electric

Yesss! We have electric! Owners Daughter came to see me and gave me some Bonio's and some feed so all is nearly well with the world again... well my world anyway. I've been ok; they took me in at The Manor which was good of them but those shiny floors? Oh man! The paws go one way and legs the other every time I tried to walk across them.

I'm afraid the hereditary ancestral aspidistra was a victim to my slight instability on polished floors. After apparently 100 years with the same plant they were due to replace it I would have thought. More later, much to do now I have electric. Has anyone seen The Owner? He still hasn't been seen!

I'm Back!

Thank you all for your concerns and welcome back. It is a very troubling time, has anyone seen The Owner? His tea mug still sits where he left it, with green mould now growing out of the top of it, well I can't work the dishwasher! I have patrolled daily across the hills in search of him, well ok there is a very interesting badger carcass up there to be fair, but The Owner is my primary cause for concern at the moment.

I have been unable to report from The Manor; it appears that Manor Hoomun and Lady Manor Hoomun don't do computers. I did search the downstairs for one but was unable to find anything. There may be one upstairs and although The Owner doesn't normally let me upstairs here, I didn't fancy my chances there either. Nothing to do with Manor Hoomuns rules, just with the amount of polished wood on that grand staircase I didn't fancy my chances of getting to the top and staying the right way up! I also didn't fancy my chances of remaining a welcome visitor if there was any repeat of the famous ancestral aspidistra incident either. You should see the size of the boot room in there as well! I was completely spoilt for choice as to which corner I should drag my duvet into for my bed each night. You could have fitted the entire cottage in there!

Oh Lordie! Manor Hoomuns grand kids came to see them today. Where is The Owner when you need him???

Gazette & Herald

Local Man Reported Missing

14:34 Tues 7th Septeber 2010

Compton Bassett residents are being asked to keep a careful eye on their walks around the area for any clues to the whereabouts of a reclusive neighbour, usually seen with his dog at his heel wandering the farms of

Does this explain anything? Has anyone seen The Owner?

The Dirty Concrete Pond

The Owner has still not come back and I begin to wonder if it was just one too many of my unusual smells or something. Now that I am a part time resident at The Manor I feel a little more able to include the grounds in my patrols of the farm and I have something rather interesting to report.

Over the back end of the gardens, near the marsh that The Owner was always at great pains to keep me away from I have found a big concrete lined pond...... full of dirty water! Now, I have a dilemma! Is my new part time host really the pond water thief? Has he really been taking it from the pond all along and not as I had reported been due to Tanker Driver Hoomun or Blue Hose Van Hoomun? I need to watch this very carefully but without making my suspicions public, until I can be sure.

Lilly's Pond

Harrumph! I am back in the boot room at the cottage tonight, I thought it best! I had been fed - in The Manor. You notice how I capitalise the name just to add an air of gravitas. So having been fed, I went for a leisurely patrol of the gardens so as not to arouse suspicion over my suspicions about the pond water showing up in the concrete pond at the far end of the gardens.

Manor Hoomun was down there when I arrived and I could hear him talking to no-one in particular (much like The Owner did) about Lilly looking good as he prodded about at the edge of the concrete pond. I'm not sure who Lilly is yet but he clearly had affection for her. Unaware of who the other wild residents of the gardens are yet, I crept closer and managed to disturbed Hen Fesant who made a frightful row and scared me half to death and so I ran, mainly in panic. Next thing I knew I was floundering around in the concrete pond which I now understand to be Lillie's and I appear to have got the blame for taking Manor Hoomun with me. He was spluttering loudly as he climbed out in a much exaggerated fashion with pond weed draped over his shoulder and a pretty pink flower perched delicately on his head. Never mind that, I was covered in mud as well, although I was clearly going to get no sympathy at all. So I opted to take myself back to the cottage to my proper boot room after having first stopped to collect my duvet from The Manor and drag it back with me. Has anyone seen The Owner? Life was never this complicated before he went. Perhaps it was the badger's poo?

The Ming Vases

I was up early this morning, anxious to make amends for the misunderstanding at Lilly's pond last night. Another reason is that I couldn't sleep for the taste of pond water in my mouth! However, my morning patrol of the farm and surrounding areas went well and I came back more than a little damp from the heavy dew.

I went and sat by the main door into The Manor and awaited Manor Hoomun or Lady Manor Hoomun, whichever was the first to rise. It was a very pleasant hour sat in the early morning sunshine, steaming gently as I dried. My thoughts were mainly with The Owner, trying to work out why he had gone off like that and where he was now. He didn't even have a jacket on when he left! I was snapped back out of my little world of thought as I heard Lady Manor Hoomun descend the main staircase inside and open the door with a cheery "Good Morning Jack, do you want your breakfast?" Some people ask the silliest of questions, but eager to offset any negativity for dunking Manor Hoomun in Lilly's pond last night I scuttled inside in a very excited fashion. Doh! The polished wooden floors! I forgot them again! A major slide across the large hallway leaving claw marks in the polish as I went saw the ancestral aspidistra take another dive and two old Chinese looking vases which apparently belonged to Ming were only slightly broken in half as well. Not sure what all the fuss was about, they were old anyway and The Owner bought one just like it for a tenner from B&Q. There was also another little vase looking thing which went down as well and smashed into loads of bits. You should have seen the amount of dust and stuff which came out of that one! Lady Manor Hoomun seemed particularly upset about this one and kept calling it Uncle Eric, strange kind of a name to give a vase if you want my opinion! I get the feeling that I have been banned from that part of the house.

The Maze

Sorry for my absence for most of the day yesterday, it was an enforced one over which I had little control. I now realise that Old Reg the Paper Boy is also the one responsible for cutting the hedges in The Manor. Until now I had only ever been aware of the noise of the hedge cutter at this time of the year and not who was behind it, my view being blocked by a hedge twelve feet high.

Down the bottom end of the gardens is a big patch of hedging in the middle of the lawn, which I now understand to be called a maze. Inside it somewhere, making a great deal of noise was Old Reg the Paper Boy and his hedge trimmer. On my morning patrol I thought I would venture in to see if he needed a hand with anything. Well ok, my main motive was that I know he doesn't have any teeth and so I reasoned there may well be the odd crust when it came to sandwich time. So fearlessly, (only because I had no idea of what lay in front of me) I ventured in. Well I never found Old Reg the Paper Boy, nor his sandwiches for that matter. Neither did I find my way back out, not until Manor Hoomun came looking for me as the sun was starting to set and I thought I was in for a long cold and lonely night stuck in the maze. As I walked back across the lawns with Manor Hoomun he was chatting politely about how bright the harvest moon was. Bloody Harvest Moon! Bloody Maze! Bloody sandwiches! Bloody Old Reg the Paper Boy! Bloody Everything! I'll be in the boot room in the cottage if anyone wants me!

Police Hoomuns are in the Village

There have been Police Hoomuns all up and down the village today asking all kinds of questions about The Owner and I have to say I am not particularly impressed with the kind of questions some of them were asking! And even less so with some of the answers that were being given! I have made notes, expect reprisals!

They came and called at The Manor this afternoon and asked Manor Hoomun several inappropriate questions whilst stood right beside me. “Has he exhibited any strange behaviour before?” His whole life has been one long episode of strange behaviour but that’s not for them to say and I was about to give them a swift nip for their cheek when Manor Hoomun waved a cautionary finger at me. He is already becoming far too knowledgeable of my ways; I may have to throw the odd spanner in the works to unsettle him from time to time. When Police Hoomun suggested that maybe The Owner might not have been of sound mind it was just too much and I just had to do something. Nipping him on the butt was already forbidden by Manor Hoomun so I watered his rather large boots; no one had forbidden me from weeing on him had they? I had to empty most of my bladder before it soaked through but I felt a point had been made.

Police Hoomuns Conclusions

Well yesterday we had the brightest of Wiltshire Constabulary combing the village and asking all kinds of incisive questions. Most of them were ridiculous and some were very insulting towards The Owner and I had to have an opinion on the matter.

One Police Hoomun had to go and requisition a new pair of boots from their stores after I wee’d over them after I was forbidden from giving him a quick nip for a particularly disparaging comment about The Owner. Later they called in Police Dog (Hello! Nearly three weeks after The Owner disappeared?) who rushed about full of self importance barking a lot, until he slipped his collar and then we had a good game of chase around the cricket pitch much to Dog Handler Hoomuns distress. At one point he was so red in the face as he bellowed at Police Dog I thought he was going to explode. It was a good game but I suspect he may be sent to his boot room when he gets home. Today they have issued the result of their extensive enquiries, “The Owner is missing”. Well that has cleared up any doubt then. We can all rest a lot easier on our Comfy Cushions now then can’t we? I think I may need to extend the range of my patrols a little in search of clues as to his whereabouts. Has anyone seen The Owner?

Uncle Eric

Manor Hoomuns family came to The Manor for lunch yesterday, so in fear of getting further dressed up by the grandkids I made an early morning departure to go on patrol and widen my search for The Owner. Often on a Sunday he would go to the cafe up by the main road, so after a quick canter up across the downs I arrived and sat outside by his favourite table, watching in case he came for coffee.

It was all going well, although The Owner was still nowhere to be seen, with people coming up and saying hello, until some old lady told Cafe Owner Hoomun that there was a stray dog outside! Me, a stray dog! I have breeding I do! She walked like a camel anyway. Cafe Owner shooed me off so I wandered back to The Manor which is when things took a bit of a turn for the worse. I sat in the boot room out of the way, kept myself to myself until nearly lunch time when the smell of roast beef dragged me out. An ageing Aunt I have not met before was sat there nursing this strange looking cat thing that growled at me, I chose to ignore it but it persisted, so I wandered off between all the legs of those drinking sherry in the hallway including Vic R who I haven't seen since the Church Fete. I took a very careful route across the floor to avoid sliding into the ancestral aspidistra when Strange Cat suddenly launched itself at me and slid across the polished floor leaving claw marks as it went and straight into the stand at the end where Uncle Eric's mortal remains have been placed into a new urn. His eternal rest being unexpectedly disturbed for the second time in only a few days!

The Owner has been reported seen working in Crewe B&Q wearing bright orange overalls and going under the name of 'Bob'. I'll keep you informed.

Cows in the Herbaceous Border

Oh, this morning had a certain warmth in the air from where I was stood. Nothing to do with the weather you understand. That warmth which comes from the certain knowledge that there is going to be a lot of doo doo flying around and most unusually, there is little, if any, coming my way.

I had been for the morning patrol quite early this morning, for no other reason than the cottage is beginning to get quite cold without anyone to drive the heating controls as I cannot reach that high; so I came back to The Manor to await breakfast. Lady Manor Hoomun came down and threw back the curtains to look across the manicured lawns and flower beds, at least those that the badgers haven't dug up already. Her gaze settled immediately and perhaps predictably upon the rather large arse of a cow which was on the patio depositing another half a ton of manure across the patio furniture. I say another because it had already done so over the sundial which I fear will not be telling any time at all until a serious amount of shoveling had taken place. The roses which were enjoying a last flourish of flowering activity (yuk and phew) were eaten to the stalk by the teeth and digestive tracts of about forty ruminants who had taken the opportunity presenting itself after the somewhat inadequate gate closing skills practiced by Cowman earlier that morning. Two of them had taken the opportunity for a quick soak in Lilly's pond and were getting quite tangled up in the aquatic foliage. The cowman was summoned to remove his charges from the herbaceous borders watched over by Manor Hoomun and Lady Manor Hoomun who stood with a suitable frown and hands on hips whilst he did so. I, not wanting to miss out on the opportunity presenting itself from someone else's misfortune, found a suitably disapproving look of my own to add to Cowman's discomfort. I feel today is going to be a good day! Has anyone seen The Owner please?

Party Organiser Hoomun

I think this weekend may be one to be avoided at The Manor and I shall keep a low profile and stay in the cottage. Tesco Hoomun Yoof came today and made a delivery, now when he delivered to The Owner he would unload a few boxes. Inside one of them somewhere was always a Bonio (had I mentioned that I like Bonio's?).

So I overcame my natural suspicion of him and allowed him or sometimes a her onto the premises. Well today Tesco Hoomun Yoof arrived at The Manor and unloaded the whole van full! I did check to see if there was the odd Bonio in the boxes somewhere but could not find one. So he has gone back on my list of people to be suspicious of and I felt justified in having a quiet low grumble at him as he passed by. I felt I had made my point. With that much food delivered I am guessing that it is not just the two of them this weekend. A strange lady who I think was called Party Organiser Hoomun arrived and became very theatrical as she unpacked all the goodies from Tesco bags, still no Bonio though so I may have to have an opinion about her as well before long. Now, the point of my story, you remember the cows getting into The Manor gardens and two of them getting into Lilly's pond? Well since then the pond has dropped its water level quite a lot and there have been several meetings with Cowman and Manor Hoomun down there. There has been a lot of pointing and arm waving and a not insignificant amount of shouting going on, I think there may be more to follow on that story. But, significantly, the water levels in the village pond have risen as Lilly's pond levels have dropped! I am beginning to suspect that maybe they are connected and that Manor Hoomun may have been behind the whole event after all. I will keep you informed.

Fan Mail Arrived

Postman has delivered again. To me!!!! My secret admirer has sent me doggie chews again.... to me!!!! All we need now is his grumpiness to return and the equilibrium has been restored. Has anyone seen The Owner?

The Christening

Well today I have a new best friend! Yesterday was a busy one round at The Manor when Party Organiser Hoomun turned up and was very theatrical again. I think I ought to refer to her as Theatrical Party Organiser Hoomun from now on. She was as theatrical taking all the goodies out of the cupboards as she was putting them in the cupboards when Tesco Yoof delivered them in the week.

Then these nice men turned up and put up an enormous tent on the lawns. I say nice men because they all gave me the crusts from the sandwiches that Lady Manor Hoomun took out for them. Enormous Tent smelled a bit musty when they had put it up so I tried to help make it smell a bit better by weeing up the door post but it was not appreciated and they all chased me off. All the family turned up just after lunch for a "Christening". Not sure what one of them is so I tagged along when they all went off to try and get some idea what a christening was, and whether I should have an opinion on the matter. When we got there, guess who we met? Vic R was there and wearing a long white dress too! He kept flicking water at me and saying things like, "Bless you". Well I wasn't finding this at all funny and thought that an opinion may have been in order but before I could express it he picked up one of the grandchildren and started pouring water over her head. She sure as heck had an opinion on the matter and they couldn't shut her up! So they all went back to The Manor and stood around in the tent whilst Theatrical Party Organiser gave everyone sandwiches in a very theatrical manner. It was when some of the Hoomuns were standing up and talking at great length to everyone else and everyone else was applauding politely that my new best friend made an appearance. A badger from the set in the paddock came under the side of the tent, presumably looking for sandwiches and cakes as well and caused a right old rumpus with kids running and ladies standing on chairs and men trying to be all heroic (as long as it didn't involve getting too close to Badger). I did my bit to save the day and went along and cleared up the spillages as Badger was causing them and I was getting all the praise for being brave. As he is now my newest best friend I think I shall henceforth refer to him as Adge The Badge, I managed to get him blamed for one or two other of my indiscretions at the same time as well. I thought it right to return the favour and as Reg was away I went and left the potting shed door open so he could get at the bird nuts and judging by the shouting from down there this morning I think he may have found them. They keep telling me The Owner has been found but I haven't seen him as yet, but I will keep you posted.

The Green Canvas Bag

The weekend had been going swimmingly, new best friend, offloaded a load of misdemeanours on to him. Met Vic R again, The Owner is rumoured to have been found. Party last night which I got fed at and another party tonight.... and that's where it all went wrong!

Having a background of being bred as a gun dog and being trained on Lord Bath's estate (had I mentioned that?) The Owner used to keep me in trim by sending me on a ridiculous chase after a canvas bag stuffed with heaven knows what. Well tonight, round at The Manor, they had all had a little to drink and were throwing stuff for me to retrieve and then rewarding me with little treats of sandwiches and caviar and stuff like that. Not sure about the caviar but the sandwiches were good. I did try some of that fizzy stuff in a dark green bottle but the bubbles went up my nose and made me burp.

Anyway, it was an easy mistake to make I thought. There was this little green canvas bag, a little bigger than I am used to I admit but it was green and canvas so I picked it up and ran off across the lawns with it. Yes, I know there was a bit of rope attached but I thought it would sort itself out and everyone was laughing at me and cheering me on so I ran faster with it. It's funny how you don't notice " Go Jack Go!" change to "oh no Jack no!" and then to "NO JACK NO!!!!!!!!!", when caught up in the fun of it.

Well, when the nice men turn up to take the tent down in the morning they won't have a lot to do now but the caterers may have to wait for half an acre of canvass to be lifted up before they can get at the remains of the food.

I'll be in the boot room at the cottage if anyone wants me!

The Hospital

The day started well, the sun was warm as I had a quick patrol of The Manor gardens and went down and found my new best mate

Adge the Badge. There was a rather inviting dollop of badger poo down near the set, just ripe for rolling in, but I resisted.

I've only had a quick roll just the once since I have been part time living at The Manor and frankly it wasn't worth it. Dinner was thrown outside in my dish and I was not allowed to cross the threshold and The Owner isn't there to hosepipe me down to make me clean again. Now I know that ordinarily it is a bone of contention between The Owner and me but after having to put up with it for three days my initial delight was starting to wear off. Anyway I was sat on the front steps to The Manor steaming gently in the morning sun from the dew when I heard Manor Hoomun come down the stairs to let me in. Then he said something strange, "Someone special wants to see you today Jack!" Well I thought maybe Robbie Williams was coming down from his house but then Owners Daughter turned up, fetched my lead from the cottage and after having a cup of tea with Manor Hoomun and Lady Manor Hoomun during which there was much serious conversation, she put me in her car and off we went. Now I like cars, they are my favourite, but I haven't been in one since The Owner went off, so it was nice to see the village and places like that from a slightly higher vantage point again. She took me off to town and to the hospital, not the hospital where The Owner has been when he gets bandaged up from time to time but a different one. I'm not really too sure what's going on here, this is a strange place, but I have to turn the laptop off now while we are here so I will have to tell you more later.

The Owner!!! I've Found The Owner!!!!!!!!!!

Well I have to report yesterday as being a little strange. First, Owners Daughter turns up and takes me out in her car. Now I like going out with her in the car coz I get to ride in the front seat with the window down which The Owner never allowed me to do. We turned up at a strange hospital in town and met Daughter Diesel Dog Owner there as well.

Small Boy would have made the entire family, but he wasn't to be seen and I couldn't hear any loud crashes or bangs so he presumably wasn't there at all. Then I get put on my lead and taken into the hospital. Now, in The Manor you remember the trouble I had with slippery floors? Well this place had floors like mirrors and try as I might I could not stand up properly and immediately managed to separate one old lady from her wheel chair and another from her Zimmer frame which did have a bit of a comedy element to it but no one except Diesel Dog Daughter found it funny and Nurse frowned at her a lot as she picked two old ladies up and re-attached them to their various devices. We walked down a corridor and, oh mercy, found a carpet to walk on as we entered a room. Oh dear! More shiny floors! There in the corner, sat in a chair, was a man wearing a bath robe. Well he looked like The Owner, but The Owner doesn't have a robe at all and this one wasn't grumbling so it couldn't be him! Then Station Nurse came in, not sure why she is called Station Nurse because I didn't see any buses or trains on the way in, Man In The Corner started grumbling at Station Nurse when she told him that he had some visitors. He is grumbling! It is The Owner! What's he doing in hospital? Don't care! So I did my silly run around the room....... forgot the slippery floors............oh dear! Many nurses were called to put them all back in their chairs and re-attach them all to their various devices and a gardener was also called to re-pot what to me looked suspiciously like another ancestral aspidistra. But it worked! The Owner was laughing and Owners Daughter was standing there looking at him with her hands on her hips and frowning as she does when he does something she doesn't approve of. Diesel Dog Daughter was asked to leave with me then but The Owner came outside with me and walked around the gardens. It was great fun as he threw sticks for me! I'm not sure that he should have thrown them that close to the greenhouses though. There was a very large crash came from one of them, not sure if it was from the stick or whether Small Boy was there after all. I'll let you know.

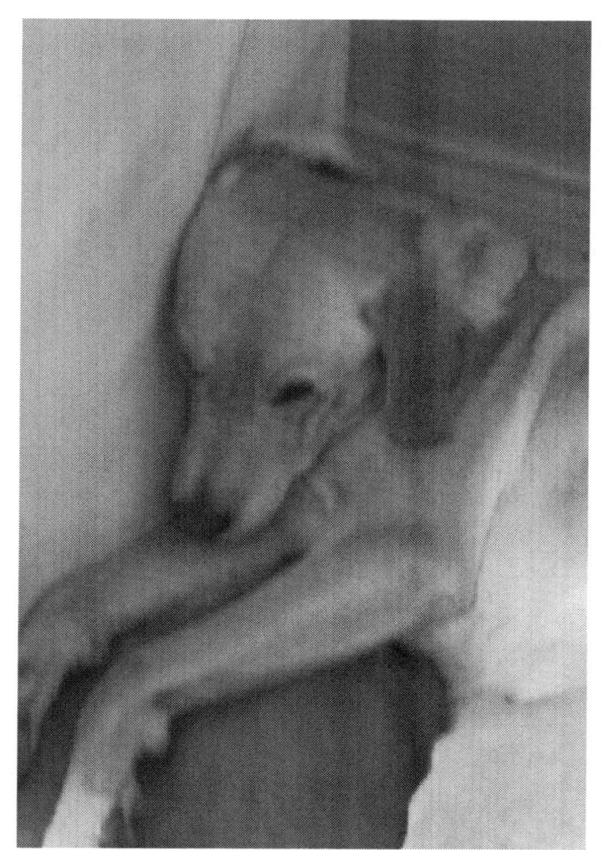

Ah! Sunday Mornings!

It's Warm in the Cottage Again

This week has been a cold one outside, but guess what? I have been warm!! Owners Daughter has been staying whilst she gets the cottage ready for the return of The Owner. I have been up to the hospital every day with Owners Daughter to see The Owner which has been fun, we have been out in the gardens walking and throwing sticks and fetching them.

He throws, I fetch, there has been a break in his training but we are doing well again on the "He throws - He fetches" training when I get fed up and wander off in search of a crust from the gardener's lunch behind what remains of the greenhouses. We have been restricted to throwing soft toys now, as there is only one greenhouse left and the man that supplied the pot plants inside the hospital has withdrawn from the contract until after The Owner has been sent home again. One old man who has lived there for ages and never spoken to anyone has laughed at me every time I try and cross the shiny floor and he even spoke today. He said "Oicumerejack!" not sure what language he speaks, he maybe from Devizes. Owners Daughter has been cleaning up at home which was a good thing coz she is a little easier to deal with than The Owner when they find his jackets and jumpers in my bed in the boot room. Bad thing is, I now have to ask to go out as she keeps shutting the back door, grumbling about the cold and the draught. I've managed perfectly alright with the door open these last few weeks! I think she comes from Bournemuff so she may not be used to the outdoors. But now I think about it she does grumble a lot, must get it from The Owner!

Silent Grumpy Man

This week has been a bit hectic with my new found purpose in life. Owners Daughter has been here and has taken me up to the hospital to see The Owner every day and The Owner seems to be a little less grumpy now.

Silent Grumpy Man who sits in the corner is now not so silent and laughs loudly at me trying to cross the slippery floors. Silent Grumpy Man is not to be confused with The Owner who is also Grumpy but grumbles a lot and so cannot be considered silent, indeed neither can Silent Grumpy Man now. And you wonder why I get confused sometimes?

I have found if I jump out of the car quick before Owners Daughter can get a lead on me I can run round the back of the ward and stand at the big glass doors that lead into the room where The Owner sits. Someone will let me in and that way I only have a few yards of slippery floors on which to cause mayhem. The Owner then takes me for a walk around the gardens along with Silent Grumpy Man who doesn't say lots just laughs loudly at everything but that is an improvement apparently. Towards the end of the week Strange Lady in Wheelchair has also been joining us on our walks. You may remember I was introduced to her on my first visit when I knocked her out of the wheelchair when I slid on the floors. Old Lady Zimmer Frame still keeps well away from me. Strange Lady in Wheelchair likes to pretend to throw sticks for me. Oh how we laugh at my antics as I search in vain for a stick which we all know is on the floor behind her. The first time I don't think she really knew where it went as she seemed genuinely surprised when The Owner bent down and picked it up from behind her. But realising she was on to something here she kept doing it. The Owner smiled and picked her stick up for her, Silent Grumpy Man just laughed loudly at it and I had great fun jumping around in a heap of leaves that Gardner Hoomun seemed particularly vexed about, having just swept them all up. Owners Daughter just stood there with her hands on her hips frowning a lot at the daily growing ensemble.

The Big Green Electric Box

Well you could have knocked me down with an empty Bonio box!! I had been out on a post lunch patrol and as always I ventured past the pond just in case there was water back in it. I had to stop and do a double take of the situation. Where the manhole cover is that Tanker Driver Hoomun has, I believed, been emptying the pond from, were two vans and a lot of wires and switches and stuff. Electrician Hoomun and Electrician Yoof were busy putting a new big green box full of electric in beside the manhole. Clearly the problem had been that the old box had run out of electric! Silly me had been blaming everyone when no-one had thought of checking to see whether there was any electric left in the old box. They seemed alright to me anyway as they both gave me a bit of biscuit for my troubles. I will keep an eye on the situation and report back.

The Dummy Stick Throwing Routine

Small Boy was brought up to go and see his Dad (The Owner) at the hospital, which had its advantages. I managed to offload the last of my little indiscretions prior to The Owner returning!

We were both taken to the hospital and I hopped out of the car quickly before Strange Woman could get the lead on me. Some people are so easy it is almost embarrassing really. So I took Small Boy with me round to the window into The Owners ward, I take this route because I don't want to slip and slide too much on the floors and I have a certain sense of responsibility here and I knew that this would also limit the possibilities for Small Boy to have an "Ooops" moment. The Owner saw me and jumped up quick to let me in and then saw Small Boy. Now I am not sure what goes on here coz his eyes started leaking again, the same as they did when I first turned up and pretty much when everyone turns up really. The Owner managed to stop his eyes leaking and Silent Grumpy Man uttered his only language again "Oijackcumere" and laughed a lot then we all went out for a walk around the gardens. The Owner, Me, Small Boy, Owners Daughter, Strange Woman, Strange Woman in Wheelchair and today for the first time Strange Woman with Zimmer Frame. She has always given me a particularly wide berth since my first visit when I managed to divest her of several surgical devices after sliding on the slippery floors. Small Boy decided to help and made a frame to carry these surgical devices for her out of some bandages, sticking plaster and a bedpan but not to worry; we found a carrier bag to put all the leftover bits in. The process roughly goes that they all pretend to throw a stick and drop it behind them and laugh loudly as I pretend to look for said stick in large heap of leaves that Gardener Hoomun has raked up again from last time. They have fun; I play in the leaves.....,. It works! OK! I did have to share my heap of leaves with Small Boy this time, but I managed.

My weekend resolution which I shall carry forth for ever more, NEVER, EVER, TRUST A HOOMUN! Owners Daughter was upstairs doing whatever she does in the mornings before she "faces her public" as she tells me every morning. When suddenly she calls down the stairs, "Jack, come on, come up here"! Well The Owner doesn't let me up there normally so she immediately went up in my opinion as I bounded excitedly up the stairs. When I got to the top she invited me into the bathroom and then closed the door behind me. What was she doing?!?! She told me what a good boy I am, well I know that already, and then picked me up! What is she doing I thought. Are my legs not working? They were when I ran up the stairs! Oh no no no no no no no no no no no no no no no no no no no no no no no no no! That smells of lavenders! Yuk & Phew! She put me in the bath and washed me, told me I would smell nice afterwards. Well she was lying, I smell of lavender now (Yuk & Phew!). My only consolation in it all is that I got out twice and that bathroom is now going to take more than a little to clean it again. She thinks she has bought my loyalty again with two Bonio's. I of course took them from her, but if anyone wants me I shall be round at The Manor in their boot room!

Tesco Delivery Yoof Visits

Oh I'm so sorry for not getting round to reporting on progress recently. I have been rather busy with my new found fame at the hospital, getting several, who had not had a lot to say to the world for several seasons and many reasons, to start to talk again.

The Owner and I, on our daily walks around the hospital grounds had acquired such a following of late that on one occasion, when I was there, when the nurses were changing shifts, the ward sister got quite panicked as she thought all her patients had done a runner! She came running across the gardens looking somewhat flustered, then looked relieved and at once became very firm as she chased 15 people back into the ward. This was all very amusing and a bit perplexing for those concerned as only 12 of them were patients; the other three were just waiting for a bus and came across to see what the fuss was about. Last night Owners Daughter found his card and account details for Tesco and placed an order. The order wasn't quite as large as the one they had round at The Manor when Theatrical Party Organiser was there, but it still took up most of the van when Tesco Hoomun Yoof arrived to deliver. That was when the day took a down turn! He came with a mate to help him move the boxes and his mate got a big trolley thing out of the van. Now I know The Owner always has a box of Bonio's in one of the plastic boxes for me, had I mentioned that I like Bonio's? So I got very excited and started running around the garden in a very excited manner. I would make a high speed appearance from round the corner of the cottage and dive through the hedge, down into the ditch and then round to do it all again. I thought that might attract some of his attention and I may get a Bonio out of him. Had I mentioned that I like Bonio's? I decided to alter my course slightly on this one trip and thought that a quick once around my tree that I wee up may have been enough to get a Bonio out of them. When I rounded the corner there he was, right across the path! So I opted for the only route I could see, which was between him and his trolley. Well it was too late and I was going too fast to try any fancy manoeuvres and even this one didn't quite work. It seems that there isn't actually room for me between his legs and the trolley! Owners Daughter was already standing with her hands on her hips by the time I worked out which way was up again. But to be fair to her there was a few bags of shopping which needed clearing up and Tesco Hoomun Yoof was complaining bitterly about the state of his trousers and that he had to sit all day in them. He left with another pair of The Owners trousers and a length of baler twine to hold them up with whilst Owners Daughter put all the shopping back in bags. Well if she looked more at what she was doing and not glare at me she might get on a bit quicker! I think I am going to be in the calf sheds at the farm if anyone wants me.

Bonio's!!!!! My Favourite

She does love me! Well, after the little debacle when Tesco

Hoomun Yoof last delivered and also considering there was no Bonio's for me I was beginning to think I was not loved! Sniff! When out of the blue, another Tesco delivery with the same Tesco Hoomun Yoof at the wheel! He did avoid the trolley which caused the problem last time and I, for my part decided to avoid rounding the corner of the cottage at too high a speed to avoid any untoward interaction this time round. Well you could have knocked me down with an empty Bonio box! Just look what Owners Daughter had bought me. Well, OK, so strictly speaking The Owner bought them but he doesn't know that. I am a happy pooch today!

Standing Guard

Now I'm getting worried that another hoomun in my life has gorn orf! Owners Daughter has been gone far too long for going and collecting Owners Dad. Well at least comparing it to the time it takes The Owner to do the journey. I shall stand guard and wait.... inside the porch! Well it's raining out there, I'll get wet paws!

The Owner's Day Visit

Eventually Owners Daughter returned; I suspected at first that she had been off doing some shopping. The Owner was always mumbling about women and shopping, not sure what it entails but I know there are always a lot of bags involved and I thoroughly approve because I can run around for ages in amongst all the paper and have a good time.

Anyway, she got out of the car with a load of bags in her arms so I began to psych myself up for the unwrapping process. Then Owners Dad got out of the car so she had clearly managed to get to his house and back OK. I was hopeful that he may have brought Owners Dads Cat with him, last time I teamed up with him I benefitted from the proceedings with a large plate of burgers and sausages. I know it was unintentional on the part of Owners Dads Cat but, hey, get it where you can!

There was another shape in the car I could observe as I bounced around with great excitement round the lawn, the car layby (including the puddles) and the muddy garden path. Then the shape moved and got out of the car..... surely not......it couldn't be........ it was!!!!!! It was The Owner!!!!!!! I was a little concerned at first as he spent a little time looking in the direction of the field where he had disappeared all those months ago, but I tried really hard with my welcome dance around the garden then as he came through the gate I forgot myself and jumped up. Oh dear! Muddy paw prints in the middle of his chest on his clean white shirt and he sat back in the muddy puddle by the cars. Owners Daughter was frowning loudly, if you're asking me how you can frown loudly when frowning is to all intents and purposes a silent process then you haven't seen Owners Daughter frown! Hands on hips and a furrowed brow; I was expecting a lot of grumbling from The Owner as well but he just laughed and rubbed my head and got up and wandered in to the cottage with water dripping out of the seat of his pants. The Owner is home! Only for the day but he is home,

Clearing the Decks.

Allow me to refresh your memory at the slightly bizarre scene when last I wrote. The Owner, having been found living under the arches near the weir in Bath (thank you for the tip off from the Bath Grime busters) was taken into the hospital with the shiny floors. Owners Daughter and Owners Dad arrived one weekend with The Owner!

Now this is where it gets weird! I got all excited (well who wouldn't?) and jumped up at him and left two muddy paw prints in the middle of his clean white shirt and pushed him backwards and left him sitting in the muddy puddle. Now ordinarily this would have induced a session of grumbling somewhat akin to that experienced by the citizens of Pompeii just before Vesuvius buried them all! All that happened was that he smiled at me, rubbed the top of my head and got up and wandered in doors dripping water from the seat of his pants! There were a lot of very loud frowns coming from Owners Daughter at my little indiscretion but a kind of benign approval, even amusement, from The Owner.

I found it very unsettling! His general demeanour didn't change much all day, unlike his shirt, trousers and underwear which had to be changed straight away because of the muddy puddle and paw prints. He also smelled strangely of hospitals unlike the more normal, slightly musty aroma of his crusty old Barbour jacket. At another moment of excitement I picked up one of my little treasures from my bed to give him, which just happened to be the remains of his straw hat that he always wears to the village church fete that I stole in a moment of madness earlier in the year. Owners Daughter grabbed it quick from me and looked stern saying "He doesn't need to see that, not today!" So I did capitalise on the moment and produced several other little misdemeanour's that I had been hiding, waiting for a suitable moment to dispose of and all were grabbed quick by Owners Daughter with the same phrase "He doesn't need to see that, not today!". All were put in the bin for me, which was a very satisfactory outcome and I managed to clear the decks completely!

I have never seen The Owner so laid back nor have I ever seen him allow Owners Daughter to fuss around him and mother him quite so much without it eliciting the normal resentful grumbling. It was nice to see The Owner again for that day and again on the following day, but I would rather he just got on with being grumpy again, I know where I am with him then. More to follow but have to let Owners Daughter have the pleasure of turning the computer off again to save the planet.

The Demented Badger

Well last weekend, after several day visits from The Owner, he came home for good. Not only was Owners Daughter here, as she has been for the last few weeks, turning stuff off or down all over the place, but Diesel Dog Daughter turned up with Diesel Dog and Very Strange Woman. Very Strange Woman is not to be confused with Strange Woman who comes up with Small Boy. I know what you are thinking, "His life can get complicated can't it?" Well you're not wrong there! Anyway, I took Diesel Dog out in the garden to show him the best bits to roll in and stuff like that. All he would do was run up and down the woodland path like a demented badger! Then The Owner came out to see what was going on and sat on the seat to watch. Diesel Dog came over to see what he was doing and I'm afraid I had to show him that The Owner was my owner and not his. I have learned not to wee up The Owners leg to claim territory so did the next best thing and sat on the seat with him.

Returning to Work

I am very concerned! I am beginning to suspect that there may be some kind of plot by sinister forces going on. It started with the water in the pond going missing (Still dry, even though they put a new box of electric by it!) and now I am beginning to suspect something may have happened to The Owner!

You may recall before The Owner went away that I was predicting a row with Water Cooler Office Lady because the water cooler had sprung a leak. Today was the first day that Owners Daughter has allowed him to go back to work. It was really nice to wander down to the office this morning, a patrol I have missed for some months now. There were a lot of sniffs I have missed for far too long and many posts that required weeing up and tufts of grass and other stuff like that on our patrol. We got here and it was like opening some vault, lots of cobwebs and a general silence that suggested that nothing had been happening there for quite a while. There was also an empty water cooler, a smell of damp carpets (for which I will not be held responsible on this occasion) and a big puddle in the corner (also nothing to do with me). He dials the number for Water Cooler Office Lady and the conversation is along these lines...... Hi Karen (Dunno what he calls her that for, I know her name is Water Cooler Office Lady!) How are you?........ That's so good to hear..............Yes; we have a problem with the water cooler.......... No, next week will be fine...............I'll leave it in your capable hands.......No, thank you!....................Click!

Well you could have knocked me down with an empty Bonio box! He would never have turned down a good opportunity like this for a row and I suspect Water Cooler Office Lady thought so too as she rang straight back to check it really was actually him that had called. He has been like this since he came back from hospital. He looks like The Owner, he has The Owner's voice, now we have got rid of the smell of hospitals he even smells like The Owner (a mixture of cheap cologne and stale Barbour jackets), but, but, but..... I think he has been swapped for a space alien!!!!

The Snow Fall

Look, please, I've done my patrol; I refrained from weeing up the neighbour's kid's snowman (as instructed). I am cold, I have wiped my paws on the mat, now can I please come in? I know you've lit the wood burner and there's a little square of carpet in front of it with my name on!

Diesel Dog and The Sherry

Well his good mood is still surviving, despite the kind of provocation certain to have induced a serious grumbling session formerly. Small Boy arrived and immediately set to work with the old "Snowball down The Owners Neck Routine".... not a grumble! In fact he seemed to enjoy it and retaliated with much laughter and merriment.

I am not really grasping this whole snow thing here; you go outside and throw loads of frozen white stuff everywhere, roll in it (and I remember what I left underneath that snow) get wet trousers, jackets and gloves, freezing hands and feet; then tell everyone what fun you've had! It is clearly a hoomun thing! Just leave me with a square of carpet and a stoked up wood burner and let me know when you come back indoors!

Diesel Dog Daughter came up again with Diesel Dog and Very Strange Woman. Snow and a big garden and Diesel Dog had to do more demented badger running, up and down the path across the back of the garden. Now this is something else I am just not getting! What is it about that path that he has to run up and down it like that? I must have a go myself, but not until the white stuff has gone! I don't mind sharing my square of carpet in front of the fire but I don't share my cushion and you may remember I had to have an opinion about that when last they visited. It clearly worked as Diesel Dog didn't try and evict me from it unceremoniously like last time. However I thought The Owner was going to start grumbling again when he was having his daily glass of sherry when coming in from the cold. He sat down on the floor and put his glass beside him. Diesel Dog was patrolling the living room carpet and as he passed, dunked his tongue in the unguarded glass. The Owner just laughed! Although it was funny, the faces Diesel Dog pulled at the taste of The Owner's cheap sherry. I have seen the faces The Owner pulls at it sometimes and he is used to the taste! I don't think Diesel Dog will be trying any of The Owners unguarded glasses left within reach for a while.

Snowballs at Jack

Come on Jack, they said. Come and have a picture taken beside the snow man, they said. Before it melts, they said. They all stood around smiling (I thought) with their hands behind their backs. So never being one to turn down a good opportunity of having ones picture taken, I obliged. That was when I realised that the benign smiles were actually evil, menacing grins, as they all produced snowballs from behind their backs! If anyone wants me I'll be indoors by the wood burner and if that gets too crowded I'll be over at The Manor in their boot room by the boiler!

Niecin Bournmuff

Further evidence of The Owner's reformed personality emerged last night. We shuffled home, that is to say, I bounded athletically whilst The Owner slid precariously from frozen puddle to frozen puddle.

When we got there he dived in to the post box by the door and retrieved several brightly coloured letters and a couple of startled spiders and a big brown envelope. Normally brown envelopes are left unopened for a couple of days and then opened, resulting, usually, in the head being held in hands whilst shouting "How Much!" Today however it was opened immediately, producing several smaller brightly coloured envelopes. I have seen this kind of trick done before and then the smaller envelopes are opened and several more coloured envelopes are produced and then everyone claps wildly. However they were addressed to various people including one to The Owner and me. That was three cards I have had now! He told me they were sent from Niecein Bournmuff. I'm not sure if I have met Niecin Bournmuff yet but she sounds like she is from a very long way away, perhaps near Swindon somewhere. When he opened the envelope there was loads of little silver bits which went all over the carpet! Normally, the fact that my name was on the envelope would have been enough to have made it my fault somehow so I quickly turned for the boot room as a precaution, however he laughed! I am kinda getting used to this un-grumpy The Owner now, but I have to confess I don't understand it.

Thoughts on Christmas

This hoomun Christmas thing has left me a little confused. Christmas eve we went home from the office taking particular care to keep The Owner out of the ditch after sharing just one too many glasses of port with Dairy Man Hoomun and when we got back home he dived into the post box on the wall. One of these days he is really going to fall in that thing!

But...... he produced a big parcel from its depths..........for me!!!!!!! I think I am going to enjoy Christmas I thought. This was from a place called Oztralya! Now, I have never been to this place so I guess it must be the other side of Swindon. But I had MY OWN Christmas card and little pressie and he didn't even grumble when more of that sparkly stuff fell out on the carpet!!! Anyway, Christmas Day saw us going to work until Dairy Man came out with another glass of port. The Owner disappeared and left me in the office with my Christmas pressie from Oztralya and a bit of festive tinsel. I wasn't quite sure what the significance of the tinsel was, so I ate it. It was quite a strange experience to see it lying on the ground behind me when it came out again and I think The Owner may have worked out where it went! On Boxing Day he was a bit poorly and the day after he was very poorly! He kept saying it was something to do with the flu. Now I'm clearly not understanding something here, coz I kept looking up the chimney and the flu from the wood burner seemed to be working perfectly! He was making lots of strange hissing noises as he breathed as well. He has clearly got fed up with that game now so things are back to normal again. Still no grumbling though!

There's Water in the Pond

You will remember, I am sure, how the water in the pond disappeared suddenly whilst we were on holiday last summer. There have been several who have been under my suspicion since and we have had several false starts when I thought there may have been water coming back, but all to no avail. The pond has stayed resolutely free of water! I have even suspected space aliens of being behind it!

Now, strange things do happen around here! All of a sudden, a week or so ago, we went to work in the morning slipping and sliding through the snow and ice, and when we came out that night it had all gone! Every last bit of cold stuff had been taken away whilst we were in the office for the day. But who could have undertaken such a herculean feat?

The pond, I'm sorry I digress; I have been using it as a bit of a race track recently. Wee up telegraph post, then run down through the dry pond and up the other side and wee up Dairy Lady Hoomuns car before The Owner has seen what I am up to and I do the same thing in reverse going home at night. Last night it was dry as normal when I ran through it. This morning The Owner got up at a silly time and I was worried that he may have been planning to wander off across the fields again and not be seen again for several weeks so I took his boots and hid them behind the ironing board. He never uses that anyway so I thought they would remain undiscovered behind there. He didn't wander across the fields so I needn't have worried but when he came to look for his boots I had to find a way of sneaking them back in. If he had looked behind the ironing board he may have found some of the other little treasures I have hidden there since Owners Daughter went home again and that would probably have started my day badly. His boots on and smelly Barbour Jacket round his shoulders we started off down the road for the office. Now I was so pleased he hadn't wandered off and we were going for our normal patrol before the office, so I wasn't really looking where I was going. Post wee'd up and on at break neck speed through the pond for Dairy Lady Hoomuns car...... (Splutter!) Who the hell filled the pond over night?!?!?! It was full to the brim! Unfortunately, I was in the middle of it! The paint is wearing off the exclamation mark key on the keyboard the amount of times I am using it on this report!

The Damage Caused by the Hounds

Yesterday the hunt came around the farm, hounds and horses everywhere! The Owner kept me in the office with him, out of the way, which I was more than a little relieved about. But going home last night, what destruction! All my weeing posts and tufts of grass etc. all wee'd up by hounds!

Well I didn't have enough on board (as it were) to put right all the damage. I did try but it was just a token effort. So at about four this morning I started taking on water and emptied the big dish The Owner puts down for me. When he got up, I resisted the temptation to go up the garden for the customary mini patrol and wee and instead took on more water. By about half past eight (our normal time of going to work) the pressure was getting quite intense but I took on more water to be sure and went and sat by the front door waiting. What was going on? He made himself a second cup of tea and sat down again! Why does he have to choose today to go in late? We eventually went in at half past nine and to be honest; walking was a little uncomfortable by then. But I persevered and just about managed to get all the damage put right, my territory is once again protected.

A night by the Fire

Don't know what has got into The Owner tonight. Candles lit, fire stoked up, and he sits there, on his own with a glass of wine in his hand and a silly grin on his face. I'm not bothered personally; I've got the carpet by the fire! Happy days

The Owner Visits the Pond

Let me just say from the start, I am in the boot room, door closed. I can throw no light whatsoever on The Owner's behaviour last night, he sat there all evening crunching on a burnt pizza (of which he gave me none), slurping at his wine glass periodically, burping, then spouting Shakespearean sonnets to no-one in particular.

It wasn't the usual over indulgence of wine, as when I did a quick patrol of the living room carpet this morning for crumbs, I happened to notice that the bottle was still half full. This morning on patrol he stopped near the pond and after a while stepped up to the edge, threw his had back and looked at the sky as if about to compose the sonnet that Shakespeare forgot to write. To be fair I was looking for an opportunity to accidentally nudge him off balance but nature has a wonderful way of intervening at these moments to create that for which you yearn. He hadn't taken his blood pressure pills this morning before we left and throwing his head back like that caused him to have a dizzy moment and lose his balance and fall straight in the pond. When he surfaced, looking a little silly with that weed on his shoulders, I was the first thing he saw and so by association it must have been my fault!

I am now in the boot room, there is a trail of water spreading across the kitchen floor emanating from a heap of sodden clothes and two boots and The Owner is upstairs lounging in a hot bath. I think there could be more grumbling when he gets out as I can hear the heating pumping but the radiator is cold; I fear he may have forgotten to order any oil again. This could be a very long day!

No Oil = Cold House

This is the second night running! Fire lit, candles lit, the rest of that bottle and a book. The good thing is I get the carpet in front of the fire again, which is just as well as the heating oil did run out as HE forgot to order it and the rest of the house is cold.

The Floaters

The nerve of some people! On patrol this morning to work and just wandering past the pond looking for a suitable post to unload the bladder on, (I can't manage for quite as long as I used to since the overload required to cover up the destruction of my territory caused by the hounds last week), when you could have knocked me down with an empty Bonio box! Just because a piece of wood will float there is no need to prove it by throwing it in MY pond! The Owner has been in once this year which he will probably reason is enough for him and so it will fall to me to drag it out I suppose. Such responsibility I bear!

My Entanglement with Farm Owner

It's been a very difficult day here! When The Owner and I wandered to work this morning, through the frosty grass, we noticed that the road as we approached the farm was getting very icy, well I did anyway as there was a decided loss of traction and I don't think it was appreciated much when I managed to knock Farm Owner to the floor in a particularly daring power slide as I rounded the corner into the farm!

It would seem that the drains on the farm had blocked over night and all kind of matter had backed up and lifted the drain cover and flooded across the road and then frozen. No harm done I felt! He got up and removed the odd bit of soggy paper from his jacket and went about his business grumbling a little about dogs being fenced in or something. When we went home for lunch I did my usual trick and as soon as the door was open I burst forth into the sunshine. Well not all the ice had thawed where the sun hadn't got yet and I found that bit quite quickly. Ok, so it may have been a little unfortunate that Farm Owner was going home for dinner at the time and I now realise what the other stuff that went with the soggy paper was, as it had now thawed and reverted to its original state. Personally, I think Farm Owner made just a little too much of the whole thing when I knocked him over for the second time today and I could see absolutely no merit in him rolling in that stuff like that! If I were his owner I think I would have made him wait in the boot room until he had cleaned himself up a little! If I had left little dollops, well big dollops actually, like that all over the place I think The Owner may have had an opinion on the matter. So I'm not really understanding at the moment why it is that I am confined to the tack room over this! It's dark now; I hope The Owner hasn't forgotten about me..... It's awfully quiet out there.

Hellooooo!!!

The Owners New Found Drinking Friend

Well he came back yesterday evening....... eventually! I suspect that he had been to the pub as he smelled strongly of wine and brandy. So did his new found drinking companion Farm Owner who also had the faintest whiff about him of something a little less pleasant, although I had better say little about that as I feel I may come in for a little flack about how the odour had been acquired.

We wandered back up the road in a particularly round about kind of way, presumably to avoid the ice and other frozen detritus which still spews forth from the manhole cover near the office. It must be much worse than I feared as he walked from side to side of the road all the way back to the cottage. He was also singing loudly which was a wholly unpleasant experience and I think he had stumbled upon a completely new way of using the voice in melody and harmony. He basically said all the words on the same note and just varied the volume louder or quieter as required. This morning he is a little quieter and has mercifully stopped his singing and is instead growling quite a lot at anyone who comes anywhere near him. I think I may try my luck at getting another breakfast at The Manor; it may be safer to spend the day down there. Nearly forgot! I have a new friend today who refers to me as Posh Jack. I think I like this. Being recognised for one's breeding has its benefits. Had I mentioned I was born on Lord Bath's Estate?

On Birthdays

This weekend has left me with one or two little conundrums! Firstly, birthdays. Why do hoomuns celebrate birthdays and why do they always cheat when it comes to telling everyone how many they have had?

Now I know that when I have a birthday The Owner tells me that it goes up in sevens. At the weekend it was Pub Landlady Hoomuns birthday and so on Sunday lunchtime we went to wish her a Happy Birthday (and for The Owner to have more drink!). I distinctly remember last year and I remember how old she told everyone she was, so why was everyone trying to make her feel better by telling her that she was only one year older? I know she should have been seven years older! My second conundrum was Burns night. Why do hoomuns celebrate someone getting burnt? Every time The Owner gets burnt on the wood burner (which is often) he doesn't do any celebrating. He dances around the living room carpet a lot holding his hand or his knee on these occasions but as far as I know he doesn't celebrate the anniversary. He would probably be celebrating every night if that were the case! Nevertheless he went out on Saturday night to celebrate Burns night and that was probably the strangest event I think he has ever taken me to. There were men there wearing skirts!!!! And everyone was going round saying things that I didn't understand and then laughing loudly as if at their own jokes. As for that man wearing a skirt with some animal under his arm that was wailing loudly!!! To be fair, if he was blowing loudly through a stick in me I fear I may have a less than favourable opinion on the matter myself. When The Owner got home he kept rushing around the house holding his belly and his mouth making some very strange noises and was still doing the same the next morning when I got up for my breakfast. It all seems very strange to me!

Oil Delivery Man and the Snake

It was a strange morning yesterday looking back on it. We got up first thing in the morning to a cottage as cold as could be, still no heating oil, and The Owner went to the fridge to get his milk for his morning tea. It was at that point that I heard the closest thing to a grumble since he has returned that I have yet to report. He thought that the fridge had broken down.

Well if anyone were to ask for my opinion I could have told him it was still working. I am the one who has to put up with it whirring and gurgling all night long as it stands right beside my bed. Now as I understand it, the fridge is designed to keep its contents at a constant low temperature. However, if the temperature outside it i.e. in the boot room is lower than the fridge is normally set to, it's going to feel warm in the fridge!

Now I have to point out, in my defence, that I have never been there when Oil Delivery Man comes to deliver. He puts some oil in the tank and then comes to see The Owner in the office and they then have a cup of tea and talk about lorries and diesel and stuff whilst The Owner pretends to know what he is talking about and then The Owner pays Oil Delivery Man some money and after he gives me a Bonio, he goes on his way. So generally, I like Oil Delivery Man! Yesterday morning I heard Oil Delivery Man's lorry turn up quite early and I was still at the cottage, so I went out the back door and round to the front to say hello. When I got there all I could see was a huge black snake disappearing after him around the corner. Well he was my friend! So I felt he needed protecting and so I launched myself upon this snake with great enthusiasm. It struggled and pulled to try and get away so I bit it harder and tried even harder to pull it away from my friend. Just as I managed to bite a bit of its skin off it gave up struggling and Oil Delivery Man appeared looking a little flustered from round by the tank. I thought he was going to be so pleased at my efforts to protect him. However The Owner was summoned and I get the feeling that once The Owner has bought him a new hose we may have to get a new Oil Delivery Hoomun. Well how was I to know?!?!?! It was a very quiet day at the office apart from some very loud stares from The Owner periodically.

Dog Lady Opposite's Unexpected Visit

Well, we have oil, and after a lot of swearing at the boiler, we have heat as well. Which means he will have to put away the milk and butter from the kitchen work surfaces where they appear to have taken up residence in recent days.

So on his awakening this morning he comes down the stairs wearing very little and singing and telling no one in particular how warm it all is indoors today. Frankly, I preferred it when it was cold and he had several shirts, jumpers and fleeces on. Apart from when he went looking for his 'special fleece'...... Well I needed something a little extra in the boot room coz it was reeeeeely really cold at night!

Some mornings Dog Lady Opposite comes over, if she is taking her pack out for a long walk, and takes me with them. I like that coz I get a Bonio when we get back and a rub down with a warm towel. Have I mentioned that I like Bonio's? Anyway, whilst he is flouncing around the dining room telling me how warm it is indoors and extolling the virtues of the very efficient new boiler (the same one he was swearing at yesterday!), Dog Lady Opposite bursts through the front door to get my lead and take me with her! There then followed a very bizarre scene. The Owner stood in the middle of the dining room with a cushion, the only thing he could grab at such short notice, covering his embarrassment. Dog Lady Opposite looking him only in the eyes. Both carrying on a conversation about gravel extraction (the topic of much village conversation lately), as though this was perfectly normal behaviour! I suspect the heating may be turned down a little tonight somehow!

The Space Aliens stole my post!

There has been little worthy of report these last few days. Get up - get fed - go on patrol - come back - go to work - pond still full - come home - get fed- sleep and then do it all again the next day, until yesterday. Well the day started normally enough and as we came home for lunch there was a white lorry parked near my telegraph post with some complicated looking thing on its roof.

I claim ownership of the post only in that it is the one I always wee up, which applies to most telegraph posts and fence posts and anything which isn't moving at the time I guess. I regarded the two hoomuns in the lorry with particular suspicion. Mainly because they didn't throw me any crusts from their sandwiches as we passed. But in the fullness of time how right I was! I am beginning to suspect further space alien activity here. We went home and The Owner made himself a sandwich as normal, and then proceeded to devour the whole darn thing! He never even so much as drops a crumb that I might have a sniff at! When we started our shuffle back down the road to work you could have knocked me down with an empty Bonio box! The white lorry was gone..............and so was the telegraph post!!! All that was left was a deep, round hole just a little larger than the post was. I had a quick sniff but could think of nothing to explain it other than the lorry must have been a spaceship and it is clearly fuelled with telegraph poles! That is what I think happened! So I wee'd in the hole to be on the safe side anyway and went back to the office for a quick snooze whilst I considered the matter.

I've Got a New Post I Have

I need to report that the telegraph pole has been replaced - with a new one - with not a drop of wee on it.

A situation which I did my best to remedy but my effort was not appreciated by the space aliens in the white lorry with the funny stuff on the roof. Well, they hadn't quite finished filling the hole up with dirt before I got to it. It may have had something to do with my aim being a little off as well, but I believe that was just a side issue. I think they may have been a little miffed that I got to wee up it before they did; you never know with space aliens!

Lady Chocolate Lab, Again!

Last night The Owner went out and I only just managed to squeeze in to the back of Noisy Car Owner's car. There was barely room for a box of Bonio's in there! So we went off out and when we got there I thought I may have recognised the place from before, although in the back of the car, with paws and gear sticks going where paws and gear sticks were never intended to go, it was difficult to be sure.

So when Noisy Car Owner and The Owner got out, I unfolded myself and got out of the back of the car. There were some lights there so I could now see that the reason why it was difficult to find where the seats were in the back was that there were no seats! Is this more space alien theft? Not sure yet! We wandered in to this building and I still felt I had been here before at some point and then I realised, there were women everywhere with tea cups and biscuits. I think I am going to like this place! Then I realised where I had recognised this place from! I have been here before; this was where I met Lady Chocolate Lab! There was the same two ladies at the front telling everyone stuff about Aunts, Uncles and Granddad's etc. and one of them even told The Owner about his Granddad although I didn't know The Owner had one of them, I've never met him. Then the door at the back of the room opened..........and through the forest of legs...........looking as good as ever...............was............Lady Chocolate Lab and Lady Chocolate Lab Owner. I was beside myself with excitement! They told The Owner that they would throw us both out if I ever did that again! Even The Owner was behaving a little strangely at the sight of Lady Chocolate Lab Owner. When we went home later we had to go back in Noisy Car Owner's car so I'm not sure if Lady Chocolate Lab is going to come and see us or not.

The Builder Hoomun on a Wet Day

You may have noticed that it was raining yesterday. I know this to be true because when I came in from my first early morning patrol (which is little more than a dash up the garden to relieve the pressure slightly before demanding my breakfast) The Owner was particularly anxious that I didn't get too close to his short fat hairy legs.

I feel it my duty to rise to such a challenge and managed to rub a lot of the rain drops on my coat against his legs. That which I couldn't get onto him I stood behind him and shook off, half of it went up his back, to his shrieks of delight, and the remainder went up the door and wall. I have such simple pleasures in life! I am not digressing yet as the rain is important to my story. It was a wet day in Compton Bassett and I was settling down under the desk having chosen to defer my main morning patrol, hopeful of a morning spent snoozing in the warm and dry, when the door burst open! Well, I say burst, but in reality it is becoming more of a fight with a sticking door which the uninitiated can easily lose. I suspect what followed was something to do with Manor Hoomun (The Owner's landlord) losing just such a fight with the door the previous day. There followed much drama from Manor Hoomun and a long sit down in the comfy seat and a very large measure of The Owners brandy he got from the airport on his trip abroad recently. This was followed by much telephone action and the arrival yesterday morning of Builder Hoomun, the one who did the work down at the cottage last year. The door was wide open and lots of banging and scraping as sawdust and rain covered everything including me! Well he was working away near my biscuit bucket, which also got covered in sawdust, so I tried very hard with my little 'give me a biscuit' dance. To no avail! So I tried a bit harder. Still to no avail! Then he shouted something like "Geroutoftheway Mutt". I have no idea what it meant but I gather from his general demeanour that I wasn't popular with him. So he chased me out of MY office! I didn't think that was a good thing to do so I ran around the back of his van and wee'd in his tool bag and then went up into the calf sheds out of the way. A quick sniff round unearthed something rather unpleasant and very organic which even I would not have rolled in so I took that down and left that for Builder Hoomun in the back of his van. I feel a point was made!

Recycling Lorry Driver's Journey Home

Last night was a very strange hoomun type of experience for me when The Owner and I went to the pub. Unusually it didn't involve The Owner falling in a ditch or the pond (still got lots of water in that). We had to escort Recycling Lorry Driver home from the pub!

We were sat there minding our own business, wearing my brand new lead (pub rules) that the Owner made by tying several odd scraps of baler twine together just before we came out, as I tried to use my powers of suggestion to get people to throw me the odd scrap of food from their plates. Not one! Not a sausage or even a little bit of fat from a juicy steak! Mainly coz The Owner kept telling them all that I preferred my dried food when we get home! Has he been sniffing something again?!?! Let me think..... dried food.... juicy steak......Hummmmmm No, definitely the steak! I was beginning to wish all of their armpits were infested with the fleas of a thousand camels when Recycling Lorry Driver announced to the world, or at least that bit of it which was prepared to listen to him, that he was going to walk home with us. The Owner made some lame excuse that he was going to take me for a quick walk over the fields on the way back but Recycling Lorry Driver was having none of it and he wanted to walk back with us.

The Owner always says that, I have no idea why because we always walk straight home to light the fire and put the telly on but it makes him sound energetic I guess. Anyway we got outside the pub and The Owner was talking to Recycling Lorry Driver and he just said Ooooooh! Aaaaaargh! And when we turned to see what he was Ooooooooooohing about, he was gone! Nowhere to be seen! Vanished! And not even a ditch in sight! His bag was still on the ground where he had been standing but he was gone and I was beginning to suspect the same space aliens that emptied the pond, but The Owner noticed a foot with a boot attached sticking out of the hedge and after much tugging we got the rest of him back through the hedge. The Owner had to hold him up all the way back to his place! I had a great responsibility in all this as well, I had to carry Recycling Lorry Drivers bag home. I don't think I am too keen on this kind of hoomun behaviour and I shall find something disgusting to do when next asked to carry a bag, just to make sure. It was far too heavy for a dog with breeding such as myself. We had to stop at every fencepost or gatepost all the way home. Not for me to wee up them you understand, but for Recycling Lorry Driver to be ill over. I think I'll avoid those posts when next on patrol that way for a while. You can't be too sure can you? I did notice this morning that his van hadn't moved, perhaps he fell through the hedge into the field from his garden path. I'll check later.... or maybe tomorrow, in case he has been ill again!

Diesel Dog Visits Again

The Owner was giggling to himself all morning and every time he looked at me there was great mirth and laughter. The kind of laughter you get when everyone else has noticed something you have done or are about to do and you haven't yet. The kind of laughter which usually precedes me making a fool of myself again.

All he would say was "Your world is going to get turned upside down today Jack m'boyo" and then much more laughter. I did check in the mirror several times but there was no evidence of breakfast or dead badger stuck in my teeth. You may recall that the weather was warm and the sun was out so I curled up quietly on the prickly mat in the porch and dreamed of running and woofing and stuff like that. Nearly woke myself up several times! I heard a car pull up outside but assumed it was Postman and thought I would have one more quick snooze in the sun before getting up and launching myself down the garden path to protect my territory when there was one hell of a commotion going on and this demonic demented badger launched itself through the gate and up the garden path, over the top of me and on into the kitchen. Having taken a quick trip around the kitchen it emerged with two empty tuna tins in its mouth and looking suspiciously like Diesel Dog. As I came more to my senses I realised it must have been as Diesel Dog Daughter and Very Strange Woman were also getting out of the car. This means an afternoon of manic running up and down the back garden path for no apparent reason I guess. I have to warn now that any attempt by Diesel Dog to climb onto my cushion will be met with an opinion, although fortunately at the moment he seems more intent on bringing all the empty tuna tins from the recycling box back into the house, hotly pursued by Diesel Dog Daughter and Very Strange Woman.

The Demise of The Tennis Courts

Yesterday on my early morning patrol up the garden I saw Big Yellow Digger Driver go down the driveway to The Manor. But breakfast was beckoning and had to take priority so I made a mental note to self to include The Manor gardens in my mid morning patrol, not out of nosiness you understand, just a need to know everyone's business.

Now I know that Manor Hoomun is away at the moment as I heard him tell The Owner the other day, but I reckon he is going to be terrible mad when he gets back and I really wouldn't want to be around to see it. Behind the hedge at the back of my garden is The Manor tennis court. It doesn't get used so very much these days but it does have high fences all around it and is very useful when Manor Hoomuns grand kids come round in the summer, it's like a big play pen for them and it keeps them out of my way. Last summer whilst The Owner was heaven knows where and I was living round at The Manor I did manage on one occasion to round up a few more and then kick the gate shut on my way back out. It was very peaceful for a while, if you could ignore the screams from the grandkids shut in the tennis court, until Lady Manor Hoomun came to see what the commotion was about. I was always a bit suspicious of that young one as her bum rustles when she walks and then even more so when she told Lady Manor Hoomun it was me that locked them in. Lady Manor Hoomun gave me a particularly withering stare! I digress. Big Yellow Digger Driver. When I got round to see what he was doing round there you could have knocked me down with an empty Bonio box! He had driven through the fence and was digging up the tennis court!!!! Manor Hoomun may well be sending him to the boot room when he returns! I didn't stay around for too long just in case he came back and thought I may have been in some way responsible. I took myself straight back to the office and under the desk out of the way for the rest of the day. I didn't get much sleep yesterday, it was all very worrying!

World Book Night

Last night being Saturday night, The Owner, when he left the office turned left out of the gateway and headed to the pub. He had also grabbed my lead on the way out of the door which is another good clue as to what is going to happen. He has found my proper lead now so I don't have to use that 'New one', he made from a number of bits of bailer twine all cobbled together. I have to use a lead when we go there (pub rules) but oh that was so embarrassing! Doesn't he understand I have breeding? Imagine what would have happened if Lady Chocolate Lab had turned up and seen me wearing that!!!! Fortunately we have the good one back again so all is well. We were sat there minding our own business when I had a fear that Strange Lady with the Bags, (who you may remember from before when she took up residence in the bus shelter by the village hall), was coming through the door. This hoomun and lady hoomun from down near our end of the village came struggling in with a suitcase full of books and spread them out over one of the tables. Now, The Owner usually uses books for throwing across the room at me, or at least he did before he was in hospital when he was grumpy, so I kept a particularly wary eye on Book Hoomun. Well it would seem that it was World Book Night last night, (I'm not sure if that is good or not yet) and Lady Book Hoomun told everyone who couldn't escape quickly enough all about it and insisted they take a book home with them. Well I was beginning to suspect a lot of K9 cruelty across the area last night with the number she was giving out to other hoomuns but it seems that there is another use for them. If you choose, you can read with them as well as throwing them across the room at the family K9.

Good job I had my glasses with me really!

The Very Important Business Meeting

Last night we had to go out for an "important business meeting". To the pub since you ask! Now I have never been on an important business meeting before, I usually get left at home or in the car outside, so I didn't quite know what to expect. It seemed to consist of some bloke coming in and saying to The Owner "Right mate?" to which The Owner replied "Right John?" They then bought each other a drink and sat and talked a lot of nonsense for an hour and then two more drinks - each - and then more nonsense talked. By the end "Right John?" had changed to "You're alright John!" only said in a rather slurred fashion which I am unable to convey properly in the written word. Then, oh the embarrassment! With him lolling over the bench unable to sit up straight and telling everyone in the pub how he loves them, in walks Lady Chocolate Lab and Lady Chocolate Lab Owner! I couldn't hide or disassociate myself from him as I was attached by a lead. Oh the embarrassment! He gets up to buy Lady Chocolate Lab Owner a drink, puts his hand in his pocket to get some money out and drops all his change on the floor. Tells everyone in the pub "It's alright!", like they cared anyway, bends down to pick it up, lurches forward where he lost his balance and knocks the bar stool over which knocks the next one, which knocks the next one etc. At which point my mate Vic R enters the pub, presumably to save a few souls from eternal damnation to see a bar stool flying through the air towards him. Vic R had to have a lie down before being escorted back to his car and The Owner was escorted from the pub and told to go home. Oh the embarrassment! They were also trying to blame me for mud on the floor, I would draw your attention first to my paws in exhibit one (above) and then to the state of The Owner's shoes. The defence rests m'Lud! I haven't seen The Owner yet this morning and I am not anticipating I will for quite a while!

Big Yellow Digger Driver's Dressing Down for The Tennis Court Fiasco

I knew it would happen! Yesterday The Owner was busy working and so I took myself for a patrol in the morning and felt I ought to include The Manor gardens in my route as I haven't seen what Big Yellow Digger Driver did to the tennis courts in the end. It is also about the right time to go and see if Adge the Badge has come out of hibernation yet.

The Owner reckons I sleep too much but I do at least wake up every day whether it is summer or winter. I might try hibernating sometime and see how I get on. Anyway, the tennis courts, I was just at the point of breaking cover through the herbaceous borders which were looking good I thought (Old Reg the Paper Boy has done a good job with them this year), when I stopped dead in my tracks. There was Manor Hoomun and Big Yellow Digger Driver stood by what remained of the tennis courts and there was a lot of pointing going on and hands on hips and stuff like that and Big Yellow Digger Driver kept pushing his hat further and further back on his head as the pointing got wilder and then Big Yellow Digger Driver got out his book and pencil and began scribbling as Manor Hoomun was making his point. I thought I would make myself scarce as I hadn't got a book and pencil to scribble in if the going got too rough, but too late, I had been spotted! "Tactics here Jack!" I thought. Always side with the more beneficial person I thought, so I risked the "not getting a crust from Big Yellow Digger Driver's sandwiches" and went and sat very firmly by the side of Manor Hoomun. It worked because Manor Hoomun said I had better come in and have breakfast so I did and he was always the more generous between Manor Hoomun and Lady Manor Hoomun when it came to breakfasts. I decided to abandon the patrol at that point as the belly was a little uncomfortable after two breakfasts. This morning Big Yellow Digger Driver has clearly been demoted! I knew he was on to a telling off by Manor Hoomun! I saw him taking a, frankly, ridiculously small little digger round to The Manor. I think I will keep well out of the way today and take a look at what he has done this evening when all is quiet again.

The Ducks

There are times when one is grateful that there are no cameras around and yesterday was one of them. The Owner decided to tell Slimy Salesman at the garage where they sell the very loud cars that go very fast that he was going to buy one of them. He was paying far too much attention to the one without a back seat for my liking but he went out in a big black one that was very high and had big wheels.

It still went very fast and was very loud but he told them he liked it so much that they told him he could have it for a day, so he would really like it. When we took it back there were loads of snotty nose marks all over the rear screen from me, left because he kept pulling away so fast and laughing out loud at my predicament in the back with my face pressed against the glass. In fact all of me was pressed against the glass as I recall!! He went and got Lady

Chocolate Lab Owner and Lady Chocolate Lab to show off to them. So now there are two of us in the back getting pressed against the glass. On one occasion I was already against the glass when he pulled away and Lady Chocolate Lab got pressed against me which I found a terrible affront but then realised it was actually quite pleasant! In this journey of torture we finished up at the pub near the river where I do my best to get all the rocks out from the bottom of it. I was busy trying to demonstrate my prowess at retrieving rocks from the bottom of rivers to Lady Chocolate Lab with a particularly stubborn house brick when I became aware of lots of laughter coming from the river bank and most of it did appear to be aimed at me! When I put my head above water to get a breath of air I saw what they were laughing about. Six ducks...... all in a circle..........round me............watching!!! Oh the shame of it!!!!!!!!!! I climbed back in the big black noisy car that goes very fast and shook myself off in there, with the laughter still ringing in my ears. Lady Chocolate Lab, being a K9 like myself, isn't known for laughter but I am sure even she was laughing when she got back in the car later. My only consolation in the whole affair being that I had made something of a mess of the inside of the car and I did notice The Owner throw the keys at Slimy Salesman as he virtually ran out of the door when he took it back this morning. I am expecting another row when he tells them he isn't going to buy it and they send him a bill from the car valet. I think I may be out when that arrives.

The Roses Buds are Breaking!

I have much on my mind this morning but it started yesterday really. As I predicted, a bill for the car valet turned up in the post yesterday morning which The Owner, also predictably, felt the urge to challenge. There then followed the first serious return to his old grumpy self that I have witnessed since his return from the hospital.

He opened the brown envelope and then went through a routine that I haven't seen for a while of holding his head in his hands and shouting to anyone close enough to hear, "How Much?!". Also predictably was the speed and ferocity with which he dialled the number of the garage which sells very fast and very noisy cars and demanded to speak with Slippery Salesman. There then followed an argument with many good points, forcefully put and ended with The Owner saying that he would never buy another car from them. I don't like to dispel any false impressions but that kind of implies that he had bought one before doesn't it? Then this morning, having had his breakfast he wanders outside and notices that the rose on the front of the cottage has started to open its buds. He spent the next hour hanging out of the bedroom window admiring "The wonders of nature". Then on the wander down the lane to the office we passed the pond and there....floating around.....looking far too at home....were two ducks! Now you will recall from the last post that I am having a pretty dim view of ducks of late, after the humiliation I suffered at the hands of a group of them in front of Lady Chocolate Lab, so I launched forth, into the pond and brought one of the little varmints back to The Owner. I'll give it quack quack quack! The Owner gave me a bit of a stare which seemed to imply he was less than pleased with me. Well the duck was alright when I let it go.......eventually!

Mice and Ducks

Yesterday was a traumatic day for me and I felt I needed to leave it until after dark before I patrolled anywhere! We left the cottage to walk to work and The Owner predictably starts sniffing at flowers and taking yucky pictures of blossom and other cissy stuff like that.

I had a quick look around the pond in case there were any ducks that required me to put them in their place but they had obviously learned their lesson the last time. Now, you will remember that my Bonio bucket has been empty and devoid of anything edible for a couple of days, well as we left the cottage The Owner gave me a carrot to carry, strange choice I thought but I will try anything once and I began to imagine what carrot would taste like and whether I should change my allegiance to carrots as the snack of choice. Well it was a bit of a dribble fuelled wander down the road carrying my mid morning snack and I now see why The Owner always puts his sandwich in a little plastic bag for the journey. We got to where the grandkids of Manor Hoomun keep their little pony, which frankly is little bigger than me and needs to grow a bit more before he can really call himself a horse at all in my opinion, when The Owner whips the carrot out of my grasp and gives it to the horse!!! I think you can safely expect reprisals for pinching my lunch! The Owner opens the office (which he has recently taken to referring to as his studio) door and I make a beeline for my Bonio bucket in case some have arrived over night. Well they might have done!!! But there, in the corner of the bucket, which was round so didn't have corners, was not one but two mice eating the crumbs from MY Bonio's!!!! Well I was so traumatised by the event I had to go and have a snooze in the sun by the door. In that half awake state that I like to spend most of my days, I was enjoying the warmth of the sun and dreaming of woofing and running and stuff when I became aware of ducks quacking. I thought it may have been part of my dream but I checked around in there and couldn't find a duck so opened one eye. Imagine my shock and terror! There on the door step, not a foot away, were two ducks looking at me. One of them even pooped on the door mat! When I tried that once (it was raining and I didn't want to get too wet) I got into a right old row. Well today he can carry his own damn carrot!!!!!

Bloody Dawn Bloody Chorus!

Well spring has finally arrived! How do I know this? Could it be the blossom? No, can't see that for The Owner's big head as he goes around sniffing at it. Could it be the cows out in the field for the first time? No, that's not it! Could it be the daffs in the woods at the top of the garden? No, managed to wee on them already!

Done guessing? Well I'll tell you! It was that damned blackbird shouting and hollering from the top of the hedge at the back, just outside the boot room door, from about half four this morning! Now I speak a bit of blackbird, being the educated, well bred sort of a K9 that I am. The Owner came down stairs (after I'd already had two hours of 'Oh what a beautiful morning' in blackbird), and put the kettle on. That's when it changed to "There's hoomuns, there's hoomuns! Ooooooooh there's hoomuns!" When I burst forth in desperation from the back door to have the first wee of the morning it changed to Aaaarrrghhh there's a dog, there's a dog, there's a dog, aaaarrrrrgggghhhhh! There's a dog there's a dog etc. as he disappeared over the old tennis courts (I have more to report on them later). Oh yes, be warned. The Owner has a new phone...... with a super duper camera on it. At the moment, all is safe as he can't work out how to use it. He has several pictures of his big toe and other parts of his anatomy too distressing to mention without sedation but he has no idea how he took them. It will only be a matter of time I suspect!

The Departure of Blackbird

This morning was a much more peaceful and ordered process as I awoke, a gentle buzz of birdlife in the distant background, and definitely without the assault on the senses which brought me back from the world of slumber yesterday. Let me explain, and I must point out that no blackbirds were hurt in the making of this story.

We got back yesterday afternoon from the office - sorry, studio - in daylight, which has been something I am not used to through the winter, but suddenly he is coming home an hour earlier at night. Being still daylight I felt a daylight patrol of the grounds was in order. Twas at that point I saw him, my morning nemesis! I had heard him shouting as we came through the gate, "Hoomuns are coming hoomuns are coming, dog, dog, dog, dog, dog, dog, dog, hoomuns are coming hoomuns are coming, dog, dog, dog, etc. But he had clearly now forgotten about me and was busy rooting through some dried leaves looking for heaven knows what when I came upon him behind the shed. Very intent upon his mission he had no idea of my presence as I crept closer and closer. When I was only the length of a box of Bonio's away from him I summoned my deepest and loudest woof which had a very profound effect on Blackbird and he dropped last night's worms and other stuff out of his bottom where he stood and then took off across the hedge and The Manor gardens with a loud "AAAAAAAAAAAAARRRRRGGGGGHHHHHHHHHHHH, it's a dog it's a dog it's a dog, dog dog dog dog", as he disappeared into the distance towards where Adge the Badge lives. If he tries to keep Adge the Badge awake with his early morning shenanigans I suspect he also may have an opinion on the matter too. I must confer with him later to see if he got woken up from his hibernation by Blackbird's infernal row.

On Mothering Sunday

It has been a strangely quiet day here today. The Owner came downstairs in a strangely melancholic mood and these are always a worry as you never quite know what his behaviour will turn to. He has moped around the house and lit candles everywhere, frankly I worry about the soot on the ceiling as you would imagine.

There are two special candles lit by the picture of his Mum who I never knew but clearly has a lot to answer for and seems to be in some way responsible so far today for his apparent melancholy. After two large mugs of tea and an equally large coffee he starts to fidget and this is the dangerous time coz you never know quite what scheme is beginning to hatch inside his mind. Suddenly he jumps up....... a plan has clearly formed! He goes out into the boot room and rummages around behind the fridge and drags out something covered in cobwebs and other dust. Something which clearly hasn't seen the light of day for quite a while. I think it is called an ironing board. His ironing and drying seems normally to comprise putting wet clothes in tumble dryer... taking dry clothes out of tumble dryer and throwing them into the basket in a heap. Then each morning the said heap is rummaged around until he finds the least creased shirt and putting it on with a jacket or jumper quickly over the top so no-one knows he hasn't ironed it. Several shirts which had clearly been the most creased for quite a while were liberated from behind the tumble dryer, brushed down and put in a heap for ironing. The iron was also liberated from under the big heap of shirts that were too creased to wear and all were put to good use. The heap of neatly folded shirts and towels and other stuff was growing steadily as he tried to convince, um, well himself mainly, that this wouldn't take a moment to do. Oh how we laughed, as he squirted water out of his steam iron all over me as I curled up on the carpet until, perhaps unsurprisingly, it ran out of water. So he goes grumbling off out into the kitchen to find a jug to replenish the water. Now picture this, the dining room carpet is covered with little heaps of freshly ironed stuff and there was nowhere for me to curl up for my mid morning snooze. So while he was out in the kitchen looking for a clean jug and making himself his second coffee of the morning (he is going to be so hyper later) I curled up on top of the two biggest heaps on the floor. Towels and sheets. I was a little lopsided but otherwise, after a bit of scratching around and rearranging, I was feeling quite comfortable on top. However on his return, he seemed a little less than enamoured with my choice of cushion for my snooze! I am now shut in the boot room since you ask!

Making The Morning Bread

Yesterday The Owner forgot to get a new loaf of bread out of the freezer. Now I did warn you he was in a funny frame of mind. So instead of going out and getting one in from the freezer in the shed like any normal and sane person would have done, he announces that he has all the ingredients and he will get up early and make himself a loaf of bread for his breakfast 'bread and marmalade'.

I just know this is going to end in tears! Half past four he comes crashing down the stairs this morning. Crashing, only because he wouldn't turn the light on because "it's spring and the nights are drawing out and we shouldn't need them on". I watched him, bemused, for a while as big bowls and pots and scales and stuff came out of the cupboard, before I headed for my comfy cushion by the fire. There was still a little warmth left in it and it would probably be safest in there. Why he was going to all that trouble escapes me as he has a perfectly good bread-maker on the worktop gathering dust. My curiosity got the better of me after an hour and I wandered out to see what he was doing. I was a little taken aback at first; well it was about the same shape as The Owner, except his normally greying hair was now white with flour. For that matter so was the floor, cupboards, stove, sink and even some up on the lights on the ceiling! I left quickly before it got me as well and returned to my cushion. I was awoken next by the smell of burning wafting through the cottage and noted a blue tinge to the air coming from the kitchen. So all was going well then! First batch failed he drags the bread maker out from under the layers of dust topped off with a layer of flour, which matched the rest of the kitchen. Quite why he doesn't go and just get a loaf out of the freezer I am not sure. It is now ten o-clock and the bread maker has long since finished and he is still asleep on the sofa! I was sure he had an important meeting first thing this morning; I wonder if I should wake him. Let me have another snooze first whilst I decide how I should do it.

It's Pigeons This Time

This morning, (early, since you ask) outside the boot room door I could hear that ruddy blackbird winding himself up to a crescendo. "Ooooooooooooh it's a dog! Oooooooooh it's a dog! Dog, dog, dog, dog, dog, cat, cat, cat, cat,cat,cat,cat. etc."

Why he changed to a cat I shall never know as there aren't any cats around here and if they were I feel they would have been doing the right thing and been in bed asleep. Which to be frank is where I wish I was at that time. I had got the first bit right, I was in bed and I had got the second bit right as well until he started his infernal row on the roof above me. Suddenly, he took off across The Manor gardens and all was quiet again for a moment, until two Hercules from Lyneham masquerading as pigeons flew across and landed on the roof of the boot room and started gossiping among themselves. "Do you wanna know who, who, who?", asked the first. "I'd love to know who, who, who.", replied the other one. "I'll tell you who, who, who!" said the first. "Who, who, who?", urged the second. Now, please don't misunderstand me, I love a bit of gossip as much as the next K9. But these two useless bits of raptor bait never got to the point and said who had done what. A quick woof disturbed them and they flapped off to go and annoy someone else with their pointless gossip. On reflection the woof was not the best way of getting my point across and achieving enough peace to return to my slumber. I was just drifting off again when I heard The Owner come grumbling down the stairs and then evict me from my bed to go up the garden whilst he puts the kettle on. "I was sound asleep when I dreamt I heard you bark Jack!" he said as he put my breakfast in my dish. There then followed much bread-making activity in the kitchen accompanied by singing and stuff but he is clearly getting much better at it as this time there was no scary sights with him covered in flour. However, much worse was to follow, it's very fast noisy car season again! To my understanding they still finished up back where they started! I think they must all have been using one of those useless Satnav things that The Owner threw out of the car window in a fit of pique last year after driving round and round Swindon town centre and not getting anywhere other than back where he started from!

Mowing the Lawns

Last night had its moments of great personal triumph for me and also moments of some confusion. Last night The Owner's friend, who for now I must call Bonio Man, (he has another name that The Owner is always calling him but I am too polite to mention and too innocent to understand) he came and gave me one of the Bonio's out of his own special box he keeps specially for me in The Owner's studio.

Then he took The Owner off to get some petrol for his mower. I tried my little 'Gimme another Bonio', dance when they got back but he didn't so he isn't my favourite now. But I'm sure that will change again when next he visits and responds to my little dance! I should explain that I find that The Owner's mower is something akin to his Dyson and terrifies me! On this occasion I thought I would steel myself and be very brave and I sat on the front door mat just outside the front porch and watched him cut all the lawns. I was so pleased with myself, at my bravery, that I launched forth when The Owner shut the mower down to go and see The Owner, that I forgot he had opened a bottle of wine and poured a glass and left them both on the table by the front door. Ooops! That's ok, he has another glass indoors...... and bottle. So my triumph was to beat my fear of the mower. My confusion involves my nemesis recently; Blackbird. Mowing finished and glass cleared up he opens another bottle and pours himself a glass and sits on the lawn. Behind the cherry orchard I can hear Blackbird giving it big noise with his "dog, dog, dog, cat, cat, catcatcatcatcat". I still don't know why as there isn't a cat for miles! Then comes the source of my confusion, Blackbird comes down and has a good rummage around in the grass box from The Owner's mower right by his feet, within launching distance of me. Now why do that when he was shouting only moments earlier about there being a dog nearby. Still it made a nice end to the day as I curled up beside The Owner with my chin on his lap as he drank his wine and watched Blackbird look for his tea. If he'd asked I would have let him have a bit of my dried food, although on second thoughts, no need to waste it! I think we may have a rook living in the trees that is either blind or stupid. One of them was clearly trying to show the stupid one something as it kept going "There, there!" and the other one would respond "Where, where?" They kept this going for about half an hour, I think I would have given up trying to show it by that time!

Water Delivery Driver

Yesterday I made a new friend! Water Delivery Driver turned up on the wrong day only it wasn't Water Delivery Driver. Confused? So was I! It was his van and I always have a grumble when he turns up. Not because I am being aggressive or anything but it makes him nervous and that amuses me. Mainly coz there are few in this world over whom I have any real authority.

So I psyched myself up for a big grumble at just the right point, and by that I mean when he has two big bottles of water, one in each hand and he is struggling to get in to the office door. This is the point at which it unbalances him most I have found and therefore gets the best effect. Well as he launched himself out of the door of the van and I was drawing a lung full of breath for a really big grumble, I realised it was not him! The Owner said his name was Relief (I think) and he looked at me and said "You ain't gonna mean that grumble are you?" and smiled. So I didn't, which was quite a good move coz he gave me a whole days supply of Bonio's in one go, which left The Owner quite speechless at the time and I really like Bonio's! Have I mentioned that before? Then this morning I was caught a little off guard. Relief's Van arrived again which was a little strange I thought so I may have been on for another Bonio or two again. Then Water Delivery Driver got out of the van. I am confused by this and not to mention caught out in the wrong place and without sufficient breath in my lungs for the customary grumble which was a bit of a shame but I promise to make up for it next time.

The Owner's Second Breakfast

Am I allowed to make predictions? Well I think I can make just the one at this point and with a certain sense of inevitability. I think The Owner will be having a tender tummy before too long and soon he will be running up the stairs holding his belly with a certain sense of urgency.

He was up early this morning, far too early. He has been busy making beds and flitting around energetically with the duster (not a pretty sight as the sun comes over the horizon) and then chasing me around the room with that ruddy Dyson. Oh how we laughed! With altogether far too much energy expended that early in the morning he predictably made himself a cup of tea and collapsed into his favourite armchair and fell asleep. Asleep, that was, until his hand went limp and he spilled his tea all over his lap! Then he starts fidgeting, well as you can imagine I thought this was due in some part to his rather tea stained shirt and trousers. But no, he wanders off into the kitchen with that rather strange way of walking reserved for when a hoomun has wet shirt and trousers and starts clattering around in the bread bin. Empty! Well I knew it was! I thought this would have started more flour filled hours of fun as he made some more, but no! A quick visit to the freezer in the shed and he returns with a frozen loaf of bread and a solid pack of bacon. He tried valiantly to separate the frozen rashers and eventually threw the broken bits, still solid, into the pan and then turns his attention to trying to thaw sufficient of the loaf to cut two slices off the end. Bacon just about thawed and bread buttered he balanced the plate with the bread on top of the chip pan. Well even I could see that the plate was barely the same size as the chip pan! We now have a plate and two slices of bread floating around in the bottom of the chip pan and the plate appears not to want to come back out of the hole it so easily slid through. Unwilling to go through the whole bread thawing routine again he retrieves his pruning saw from the shed and cuts two more slices of bread and tells himself that it will thaw from the heat in the bacon. Presumably the same bacon which has been off the heat for a good ten minutes now and has fat starting to congeal around the edges. He proudly carried the fruit of his labours into the lounge to watch BBC Breakfast with the bread glistening like the grass on a frosty morning and the bread covered in a layer of congealed fat. Like I said, I can safely predict he will soon be running upstairs to the toilet with a pained expression on his face.

Small Boy Visits

I'm sorry for the lack of further information on The Owner's frenetic activity late last week but as the events unfolded you really could have knocked me down with an empty Bonio box. It was about the right time when I would be expecting The Owner to have started running up the stairs holding his belly when I heard a minibus pull up outside the cottage.

Ever protective of my territory I went rushing out ready to have an opinion, or several if required, when out of this minibus got Strange Man who I did kind of recognise. He wandered round to the other front door and lifted out Strange Woman! Now I do recognise her, she always gives me cream crackers with Marmite on! Can't stand the Marmite, but you never turn down anything to eat do you? Inside the minibus there was another shape which sort of unfolded sniffed loudly and grunted in the way that teenagers do when more than a few yards away from the fridge. I think.... yes it is.......it is Small Boy!! That was why The Owner had been making beds. Strange Man and Strange Woman left and she didn't even give me a Cream Cracker, with or without the Marmite! She has just been moved from my favourite list to my non favourite list! So, we have Small Boy for a few days........ now what little misdemeanours do I need to offload? As it turned out I felt it wouldn't be right, he didn't need any help. Probably best to gloss over the tree that no longer has any branches or leaves but it did prove just how sharp his axe is! So that's alright then. Today he has just left and gone back home after Strange Woman came and picked him up and I have to say I was a little sad because I haven't seen him for a long while and it may be a while again. The Owner is strangely quiet this evening as well, I tried my little run around the carpet but I didn't really have my heart in it and it didn't make him smile either. The house is too quiet but I guess we'll get used to it again. Think I'll go and find my comfy cushion.......

The Small Boy and The Lawn Mower

Given my newly acquired bravery in the face of adversity such as The Lawnmower I attempt to get a better understanding of the process. Small Boy seemed to start it up and then randomly wheel it around the grass. The Owner of course refers to it as "The Side Lawn" but as you can see, with that many weeds in it I think just "Patch of Grass" is a far apt description. After about half an hour of randomly pushing the lawn mower about Small Boy seemed pleased with his attempts but The Owner seemed far less impressed and started going on about "Mist Patches". I'm not sure what or who Mist Patches is but I will report further on that when I get a better understanding of the matter. Now, how do I get off this pedestal and in doors for a Bonio without getting chased by Small Boy with Lawn Mower?

The Lesser of Two Evils

Well I made my dash for freedom and did indeed get chased by Small Boy with Lawn Mower which is quite a terrifying experience which I am not anxious to repeat. Even though The Owner was doing things like weeding and trimming to the lavender (Yuk & Phew!) bushes, I felt his protection was required. So I lay down at his feet among the bushes. It worked as Small Boy wandered off with his axe, looking particularly menacing, in the general direction of the woods at the top of the garden.

Defrosting a Chicken

This morning The Owner's household is not a happy one! It first started yesterday afternoon when we came back from the office. Sorry, studio. He shuffles off to the big freezer in the shed (and from the noises that one makes believe me I am glad that he doesn't try and bring it in and find space in my boot room for it) and liberated two frozen chickens.

Must mean we have guests coming today I thought. To make use of the remaining heat from the afternoon and evening sun he put the two frozen birds on plates and left them on the patio table just outside the boot room door. So far this is looking ok, but then a quick phone call diverted his attentions and he grabbed his fleece and ran out of the door leaving me behind! I guess an evening of solitary uninterrupted snoozing was going to have been my lot, but I could live with it. After a short while he returned and judging from the scents about his person I deduce he has been over to see Phlee Dog Owner. I started my very best 'pleased to see you back' bounce and was building to a momentous crescendo, one of which

I was quite justifiably proud, when he grabbed something off the table and ran out again and got back into Phlee Dog Owner's car. Without me, seeing as you ask! Well, long after dark he crashed through the front door giggling, so it has involved some quantity of red wine again then, and seemed genuinely disappointed that I didn't bounce about the place like a demented badger pleased to see him. There then followed much frying of bacon and stuff like that which splattered all up the walls and over the stove and floor and I think he is going to be in severe trouble when Cleaner Lady comes in tomorrow. This morning he remembered the chickens and rushed outside to discover two empty plates and a number of bits of plastic wrapping and a few bones, which seemed to cause a little anguish and turmoil in his mind. I guess it'll be KFC for ten again tonight then! Do you know he has got it down to twenty minutes for that little run now? So it was at this point that my breakfast decided to make a return visit together with what he seemed suspicious of being some bits of chicken. I can't imagine for the life of me how that got in there. Honest! The Owner grumbled considerably and disappeared under the stairs, returning with dustpans and towels and other such clearing up stuff. I thought, no need to waste good food or dirty the dustpan, just leave that to me! Have it cleared up in a jiffy! The Owner was having none of it though and set about clearing it up; I suspect he just wants it for himself! I think I'll take myself off up to the woods and find a nice sunny spot out of the wind and wait until he has finished with all that foaming carpet shampoo stuff and has had a chance to forget about his suspicion of my involvement in the demise of his two chickens.

Noisy Car Racing in Swindon?

I am finding this entire noisy car racing soooooo confusing. The Owner tells no-one in particular that this was the best one ever today, not sure why coz they still only got back to the same place AGAIN! Maybe it's a bit like getting stuck on the one way system in Swindon?

The Owner did that once in Swindon and we went past the same place four times to my certain knowledge! Until the shouting from the front seat got so bad I opted to go and sit in the boot out of the way in case some of that angst was about to come my way. Maybe I just don't recognise it and they are really in Swindon? I must check again next time and see if I can recognise anything. Anyway, the source of most of my confusion was a chance comment The Owner was shouting loudly during the race. When two of the noisy cars were trying to push each other off the road (actually the more I think about it the more this does sound like the Swindon one way system, I must watch more closely next time), The Owner began shouting very loudly "Come on Lewis! Come on my son!"?????????????????? I thought Small Boy was his son! I think I may retire to the calf sheds for a quick snooze in the sun whilst I contemplate this a little.

My Birthday!

So many birthday wishes (for a K9) this morning! I'm quite overcome! The Owner was up early this morning and I thought that it may be the start to another bad day, as do so many when he gets up early like that.

If only he'd turn the light on, he wouldn't stub his toe on things lying around the dining room or kitchen. Things which always seem to have something to do with me as it happens. When he opened the boot room door to let me out, it was with an unusually cheery "good Morning Birthday Boy!" As you could understand, it threw me little. Not the birthday boy bit, but the cheeriness! After breakfast he gave me a Bonio with a big ribbon tied around it which I devoured with great enthusiasm. Never did understand the idea of leaving a bit for later, I may get another one later if I look hungry or forlorn. I am beginning to feel at the moment that I perhaps ought to have not eaten the ribbon though. It was rather long and I am becoming a little concerned about how it may make its reappearance at the other end. If it's still in one long piece I may be there for some time! We're at the office, sorry, studio, already this morning and I have marked my birthday well, by having an opinion about the appearance of Electrician Yoof at the studio door. Although judging by the look on his face and the strange odour about his person afterwards I think my birthday may not be the only thing to have been marked this morning.

The Return of the Ribbon

I was in a certain amount of trouble at the weekend. Now I don't understand how a bit of old ribbon that I ate, which The Owner had tied around my birthday Bonio, went in as a big knot and came out in one very long length! The Owner found it most amusing as I struggled for ages with the problem.

Very insensitive of him I felt, particularly when he went and got his picnic chair to sit in the garden and watch. Quit with the wise cracks and lend a hand here, was what was really going through my mind. Whilst he sat there drinking his cup of tea and asking me if I would like him to go and get the Sunday paper for me to read I valiantly struggled to expel the whole length of ribbon. It was a small amount of satisfaction for me later when it got tangled up with the rotary mower and he had to untangle it from the blade underneath. I am guessing I won't be getting any more ribbon tied around my presents in the future.

Nothing Wrong with a Bit of Dead Deer.

He, The Owner, isn't talking to me today. He reckons I'm disgusting! After breakfast this morning I went off for a quick patrol through The Manor gardens and down to where Adge the Badge lives. I have to report that the tennis courts have been replaced with a big shed which The Owner told me was a summer house. That was when he was still talking to me of course.

You'd have thought with The Manor being that big they wouldn't have needed another house just for the summer! So out across the paddock I went through the wet grass when I stumbled across it. A deer which hoomuns would have said was a bit past its sell by date! True, it did pong a little bit, but that is the sign of a good bit of dead deer. So, eager to supplement my breakfast of dried dog food I opted to try this little delicacy. Just a little chomp I thought would help keep the hunger at bay until tea time. Feeling generally pleased with myself I headed for home and found The Owner stretched out on the sofa with a mug of tea in one hand and two slices of buttered toast in a plate in the other. So I sat down on the floor beside him and rested my head on his lap, when it happened. It was just a little burp, hardly worth mentioning I thought at the time. Over reacting or what!!!!! The Owner jumps up and knocks his tea and toast over and went rushing out holding his belly and hand over his mouth just like he does when he has been too long at the pub! And somehow that is my fault!?!?! Even if he were talking to me at all today I don't think I would be talking to him. So there!

Cat in the Pond

Sometimes you just notice things which you realise you should have known all along and yesterday was one of those days. I realised that cats don't float! I also realised that although when I, a K9, get wet through, it reveals my muscular figure as my wet coat clings to my rippling shoulders and thighs, a cat just looks kinda ridiculous.

Yesterday The Owner took me to see Owners Dad which happens altogether too infrequently. I say this not out of any necessary affection but because whenever I have gone there, Owners Dads Cat has offered me rich pickings from the remnants of barbecues or biscuits when he has overreacted to my appearance. So on this occasion, a barbecue not being one of the things on offer, I opted to lay in the conservatory nearest to a plate full of digestives which The Owner was devouring with great delight and frankly, to the exclusion of Owners Dad, despite his protests on the matter. Owners Dads Cat, who I shall refer to here as just Cat, left our little ensemble and went up the garden and lay in the sun under a funny little red tree beside the pond. In one of the neighbouring gardens Blackbird (and I don't think it is the same one as we have in the cottage garden as he spoke with a different accent) was venting forth on the presence of both a cat and a dog. "Dog, dog, dog, dog, dog, cat, cat, cat,cat,cat,catcatcatcat!" he shouted at the world as he took off from his perch on some apparent suicide mission over the top of the fence and swooped low over the pond and straight past Cat. Cat decided it would be good to vary his diet from the usual frogs and slow worms together with "on demand" dried food and include a little blackbird. So he lept forth from under the tree with claws drawn and missed Blackbird completely and it was at this point that Cat realised the flaw in his plan. He was three feet in the air, over the pond, and with no visible or practical means of support. I also have now realised that cats generally can make some very strange noises! Unlike myself when I get unexpectedly wet, I leap energetically from the pond to try and give the impression that I meant to do it, Cat just looks like The Owner trying to get out of the bath after using too much bath oil. I am sorry to admit that I am beginning to understand the pleasure in laughing at other animal's misfortune and can see why The Owner seems to enjoy it so much.

People Falling Over

Well I must apologise for not reporting on this yesterday but The Owner was hogging the computer all day writing about it all in his memoirs. I mean, who would want to read about a middle aged, slightly rotund bloke with a crusty old Barbour jacket and a dog? So, on Sunday it appeared to be a day of falling over. Not through the usual liberal consumption of drink but, well, let me explain.

Sunday morning was spent with a conspicuous lack of the promised activity i.e. vacuuming, mowing, changing of beds etc. until just after lunch when he jumps out of the chair and grabs my lead. Now the only place I wear my lead is in the pub (pub rules) so I got really excited and ran round and around until I nearly knocked him over, which did illicit a sort of growl from The Owner, so off we went to the pub. About half way up there I had been put on my lead because he reckoned I was sniffing too many posts and stuff. Then The Owner suddenly threw himself to the ground! I thought he must have wanted to play so I jumped on him and tried to stick my nose into many places that normally cause him to laugh but on this occasion he just grumbled as it turned out he had tripped over on a pothole. Since then he has been making plans to sue the council, the police, central government and Robert Mugabe. I'm not sure what he thinks Robert Mugabe had to do with it as I don't think he lives around here. After a few drinks, and eager to find a reason to get another drink after time has been called, he started to talk to Bar Maid. Eventually Bar Maid got fed up with talking to him as well and said she must be going and stood up to go. With that she threw herself to the floor as well. I couldn't see any potholes in the pub floor! The Owner jumps up and throws himself to the floor "To help her in her hour of need!" Well I thought they were all playing a game which looked kinda fun so I threw myself on top of the pair of them but it wasn't appreciated. Land Lord took me to one side whilst The Owner made her comfortable and held her hand a lot. Ambulance Man turned up and complained loudly about dog's hairs on his uniform so Kitchen Yoof was told to take me outside. I didn't think it was worth being banished! When a big ambulance turned up with flashing blue lights they also complained about dog hairs so I contented myself with weeing up their tyres. I've never been in an ambulance before but judging by the fuss they all made I don't think I am going to be invited to any time soon.

The Rook

Mornings for The Owner and me are a quite predictable transition from slumber to the outside world and work and other important stuff, apart from when I throw the odd curveball in; because I can.

Ordinarily it goes much along the line of The Owner coming grumbling down the stairs and putting the kettle and his toast on, letting me out, feeding me and then taking his tea and toast into the living room to watch the breakfast news whilst I go out for my early morning patrol. When I get back he is sat there either snoozing or watching something which has caught his attention and I settle down on the carpet for a snooze myself, until he is ready for his shower and then on to work. Today it had followed much the same routine until I heard a rook land on the chimney and his mild squawks came wafting down the chimney. I did no more than raise an eyebrow and then carry on snoozing when suddenly the stupid bird lost its balance and fell down the chimney! We then had The Owner rushing around the living room chasing a rook that was very intent on not being helped and had a lot to say on the matter. There was soot and feathers flying everywhere, as well as most of The Owner's ornaments, photos and books! Eventually The Owner managed to herd the rook out through the front door in a move that would have been worthy of One Man & His Dog, only without the whistles and the "Come by's!" After Rook's repatriation to the great outdoors The Owner returned and stood beside me, a little more awake than he was only moments before, and surveyed the carnage in the living room. It gave me a certain sense of pleasure to think that this was one big "Ooops!" moment that I was in no way responsible for, even in The Owners somewhat distorted version of reality!

My Routine

I have developed a little routine of late and I am beginning to see why The Owner seems to enjoy it so much. Most mornings his routine for himself is to make a mug of tea, put two slices of bread in the toaster, retire to the sofa and absent mindedly munch on his buttered toast and then shower before dressing and then shuffling off down the road to the office - sorry, studio.

Well, of late my own routine has not been dissimilar! On a recent patrol round the calf sheds I happened upon something organic and I confess I was at something of a loss as to exactly what to do with it for the best, roll in it, or eat it. So, the other morning on an early patrol, I decided to get my shoulder in it and then rush back to the cottage to see The Owner who was munching absent mindedly on his toast. He immediately went a funny colour and ran out leaving his toast on the carpet. Not one to leave an opportunity like that unused I cleaned it up for him. He called me outside and set about me with the hosepipe, so I went to the studio with a full belly and a clean coat. A not unpleasant experience I thought. So every morning since, after my breakfast, I have made a quick patrol up to the calf sheds for a quick roll, back to the cottage to show The Owner, he predictably goes a funny colour and runs out. Two slices of toast? Rude not to! Then he lurks outside with the hosepipe, so I have my "Shower". Not sure what to do when I have used up all the organic matter in the calf sheds. May have to widen my patrol and find a reserve supply.

Nettle Rash

Yesterday afternoon I was a little less than comfortable and this morning I have a little rash (in the gentleman's department seeing as you ask!). It was raining buckets yesterday morning here and I had the distinct feeling that The Owner was not going to be going out that door for the morning patrol very early.

Did I say distinct feeling? Should have read 'distinct wish'! You know where you are with rivers and ponds but when it is coming from the sky, water is an altogether unpleasant experience in my books. So, rain clouds empty, a lazy patrol was in order. We took off down towards the studio (See, he has even got me calling it that now) and I stopped at the end of The Manor garden wall to spray a little of my own water. The paddock just beyond the gardens wall is usually empty these days, so imagine my surprise when these brown calves, all ten of them, stuck there heads through the railings with a low bovine rumble right beside where I was weeing! Well I jumped (and who wouldn't) which is a dangerous thing to do in mid flow. Unfortunately in doing so I managed to dangle my gentleman's bits in the nettle patch! A most unpleasant experience and I admit I let out a little yelp, but despite my best efforts to wash it off, the stinging got worse. Even jumping in the pond brought little relief. I thought The Owner may have been suffering from the same problem at first as he was sat on the floor holding his belly with tears running down his cheek. But no! He was laughing at my misfortune to the point where he couldn't stand up! I am thinking his armpits need to be infested with the fleas of a thousand camels here! This morning the stinging has stopped and left me with more of a tingle and a rash which still has elicited little in the way of sympathy from The Owner. Weeing up posts etc. has been a delicate and careful affair this morning.

Never Right!

The Owner has an expression for moments when an apparent injustice has befallen him. In the dulcet tones of his West Country accent he would utter with great gravitas, "Never right!" and I think this is one of just those occasions. Earlier, I had been on patrol, a quick trip round the paddock to see if my mate Adge the Badge was about.

It was probably a little early for him so I returned to the cottage. As I came scampering through the door into the boot room there stood The Owner, by the washing machine. Now I know that it is a matter of some consternation when The Owner gets too close to the washing machine outside of his monthly cycle but this was a matter of GREAT consternation! He stood there with this look of concern, bordering on irritation, upon his face as he waved his old hat around on his index finger. How did he ever find that?!?!? After I had a little chew on it one day, when I needed a little comforting, I hid it behind his old jacket underneath my comfy cushion. Now you would be forgiven, as I thought should I, for believing that it would be safe from discovery hidden under there. So how did he find it? I went scurrying off to find my comfy cushion and escape from the accusing look which was coming my way........ but it was gone!!!!!!!!!!!!!!!!!!! I am finding the disappearance of my comfy cushion, the reappearance of his old hat (with added ventilation - K9 stylee) and the out of calendar sequence rumblings of that washing machine in the corner of the kitchen may perhaps all be in some way connected! As I said; "Never right!"

My World is not good

This has not been the most auspicious start to any of my days I have ever had. After the "theft" by The Owner of my comfy cushion last night and wilful destruction of the same by placing it in the washing machine with soap and smelly stuff and turning it on.

Then the subsequent discovery of not only his hat, which I had only slightly chewed, and his tatty old jacket, but several other little treats I had squirreled away under there for my personal pleasure. He has of course also discovered without any doubt that it was me who thieved his chicken, left in the sun one evening to thaw out by way of certain "evidence" hidden under my cushion, which he waved accusingly under my nose. I took myself off to the boot room after all that. This morning, I took myself off for the early patrol and returned to be reminded that there was only bare floor where my cushion would normally be. It seemed a fitting replacement would be one of his cushions off the settee. You know, the ones made of velvet. As soon as he saw me, I was getting a strange vibe from him. Even more so when he unceremoniously evicted me from the cushion by whipping it out from under me like a magician with a table cloth. So I sat, on bare carpet, disconsolately watching the telly, when there was this article on the news about my nemesis. Ducks! And they were laughing at me as they swam about their pond. I think I may go and find a hedge to sit under somewhere.....

My Cushion Returns

You will, I am sure, feel as relieved as I was that I eventually get my comfy cushion back from being ruined. Now you will be asking yourself as to exactly how or why it has taken him so long to return it to me after this ruinous process. He first stole it from me and then woke the washing machine up far too early in the month for what it has become accustomed to. It promptly had a hissy fit and pumped water all over the kitchen floor which he blamed me for as it was my hair that had blocked the filters. After his efforts at baling out the kitchen from soap and slightly hairy water and aided by two glasses of red wine he forgot about my cushion. I, however, was constantly reminded by the hardness of the floor! He was reminded when the smell of damp washing, left too long in the washing machine, came wafting through from the kitchen, so it had to be washed over again. This time he remembered to get it out of the machine but instead of just putting it in the tumble dryer so I could have it back again, he opted to dangle it over the fence to dry. It rained that night! Being made of foam it had absorbed most of the rain from the surrounding fields by morning and so had to go back in the machine again. Again placed on the fence to dry, it attracted the unwelcome attentions of Pigeon. Who landed on it and gave it the full benefit of his abilities in the "pooing on The Owner's car "department. Back in the washing machine again after an accusing stare was directed towards me (like I had anything to do with that!). This time it was put straight into the tumble dryer as I had thought it ought to have been right at the start. I don't like to mention that I was right all along, but I think I was! So this morning, after much ado about nothing, I was presented with my clean Comfy Cushion. Clean, that is, if you regard the smell of "spring blossom" as being clean. I am currently looking for a suitable something to roll in and then roll on the cushion to restore the equilibrium a little.

Parcel Shelves - What are they, What do they do? Discuss!

Perhaps I should first explain. When The Owner had a car, before he disappeared last year, I rode in the back. I like riding in the back, it's my favourite! He would normally open the tailgate and I would jump in, ok, there were one or two rapid changes of plan, when, half way through the jump, I would realise that the back of the car was already full of heaven knows what! In which case I would have to ride in the foot-well on the passenger side, at the front. But I like cars and that's the way I ride in them!

Now, back to the story in hand. I was sat in the garden watching a bee trying to land on my nose which as everyone knows is a particularly tiring activity, when a black car pulled up outside. I thought at first that The Owner had got a car again but no, it was Owners Sister! Black cars that go very fast are clearly a family thing, I have learned. She got out of the car followed by a little spaniel thing that had far too many opinions than was good for him in my mind...........and a horse! She said it was a dog, called Millie, but if I explain that I could almost run underneath her without breaking stride you'll understand my reasons for believing her to be a horse. It was then that my little faux pas occurred. The car door was left open and ever hopeful of a little trip out somewhere....... anywhere really, I hopped in! I thought I had better be a little nippy about it or else I may have been rumbled, so I jumped (in a very athletic manner I thought) from the front seat to the back seat and then without slowing, over the back seat to get into the boot.......... Now I have never come across a parcel shelf in a car before and I am guessing I may not come across that one again either, judging by the way that what was left of it, after The Owner helped me out of the car, was shovelled up and into the dustbin. Does anyone have a spare parcel shelf for a black car like the one The Owner used to drive? I may have a use for it!

The Owner's Sunday Paper

Today has been one marked by certain achievements on my part of which I feel justifiably proud. The Owner and I went to a barbecue last night although with two other dogs, who are my work day friends, so the scope for the odd dropped sausage or burger were a little limited.

This morning, very early, he was up again. Now this always worries me after his little disappearing act but after he had his cup of tea we wandered down the road to the office. On a Sunday! He opened up his computer and then shouted very loudly at the screen and then shut all the doors and we went home for breakfast. He was probably tired after last night! Now that seemed, on the face of it, a bad start to the day. But, it all looked much better when a car pulled up outside as I was sat under the hedge. It was the man delivering the phone directory! Oh you should have seen the look on his face when I fired up the big guns from behind him as he crept up to the front door trying not to make any noise. He looked like he had more legs than me as he tried to get back to the gate as I put my tail in the air and wandered off and left him to it. After The Owner fell asleep watching the noisy cars that go very fast back to where they came from on the telly, he got up and went outside and I then fell asleep myself. I was woken up by another car pulling up outside, such a busy day I thought as I chased off another man delivering leaflets. Two in one day!!! Now awake, I wandered off up the garden to find The Owner and stumbled upon him on the lawn, laid on a towel, glass of wine beside him and newspaper spread before him. Well I know how grumpy he gets if I lay on his towel so I ran up and tried to lay on his paper. Well he wasn't laying on it! So he threw me off it. So I jumped back on it. So he pushed me off it again. This time I stuck my nose in his ear as I jumped back on his paper. We arrived at a compromise and I was allowed to sit on the adverts page as long as I didn't leave any stains or smears. Once I had managed to roll on his paper and scrunch it up completely he seemed to lose interest and threw it in the bin with what I thought may have been a touch of a paddy. He must be suffering from last night's barbecue I think.

Burnt Toast and Fire Alarms

I'm in the boot room. He is not. He is just being a drama queen! I can hear him in there on the phone; the list he has researched on the internet so far extends to NHS Direct, St John Ambulance, the local doctor and the Samaritans.

He came grumbling down the stairs early again this morning and made himself some tea and put the toast on. Whilst I went off on my first patrol of the morning he went and sat down and started rummaging through the heap of papers from yesterday clearly looking for something particular. When I returned there were flames licking the underside of the grill and the dining room floor was covered in scattered newspaper. The Owner was sat on the sofa in the dining room, asleep. I thought, "Any moment now the smoke alarm will have its morning exercise and make it's normal row, as it does every morning when he does his toast", but until then I may as well get up on the sofa and snuggle up for a few moments. Now when Owner's Sister came up, her spaniel thing with too many opinions got up on the back of the sofa and laid along the back and I have seen other dogs do the same in pictures, so I thought I'd give it a go myself. Just as I got up there and was trying to work out how to lay down on it, the smoke alarm went off. It made me jump a little even though I was expecting it and my claws couldn't hold me fast and they slid down the side of the sofa. Well it's only a little scratch down his back!!!! No blood to speak of!!!!!! I think it may have been made worse by when he stood up, his head disappeared into the layer of toast smoke and he got a little disorientated. I was sent to the boot room which I think is the safest place. I can hear him in there now speaking to Air Sea Rescue. It's going to be a long day!

Lack of Mobile Signal in the Orchard

The Owner gave me a bit of a fright last night. The Owner gives me a bit of a fright most nights to be honest but this was one he hasn't managed before! After a hard days snoozing under the desk I was understandably tired and so went for a bit of a snooze on my comfy cushion.

When I woke up, it was getting towards dark so I went for a quick patrol, mainly to see where The Owner was and what he was up to. All his normal places had drawn a blank so I opted for a quick trip to see Phlee Dog Owner as The Owner sometimes has a habit of getting lost over there and coming back very late and smelling strangely of drink. If all else fails she is a dead push-over when it comes to liberating one of those doggy treat pigs ears from the box on the work top and I was getting a bit peckish. Wandering up through the cherry orchard on my way to the gap in the hedge, I rounded a tree and was scared out of my wits! In the half light this big clump of grass suddenly spoke to me!!! There he sits in the near dark, among the long grass, "Communing with nature" and scaring me half to death. Then the reason became clear! Nothing to do with any communion, natural or otherwise. More to do with there being no mobile signal in doors and his home phone being in bits and spread across the heater trying to dry out looking decidedly tea stained (and I had nothing to do with that! I'd just like to make that point) and apparently to go with the big matching stain across the carpet. I left him up there waving his head around as he tries to get enough signal to make a call. As I left I could hear him saying again, "Hello....Hello...... Can you hear me? No, the signal isn't very good here. Hello..... Hello..... Damn, lost the call!" No surprise there then!

On Fly Papers

Oh man, I am in a right pickle here! It all started innocently enough; we have a bit of a problem here at the moment with flies. Now believe me when I say they are a pain! They can even bite through my fur, and through The Owner's trousers which I think indicates either a very brave or very stupid fly. They have become such a nuisance desperate measures were called for.

The Owner rummaged around in one of his draws for at least an hour, (well it seemed like it at the time alright?) and produced, finally, a rolled up fly paper. Well I think he should have pinned it up first and then unrolled it, but would he listen to me? Oh no! It first got stuck to the hairs on his arm and in trying to remove it from there he got it stuck to his shirt. Pulling it off, that it got stuck to his right hand! Teasing it from his right hand his leg became stuck to it and then it all fell down again together with The Owner. Removing it from his hand by standing on it meant it was stuck to his foot and he walked around for a while like that lady at the pub with the loo roll the other day. Eventually he got it removed from every part of his anatomy that it had tried to attach itself to and re-attached to the ceiling above his desk. To start with the flies had clearly not been told how to use one properly as in the first three hours not a single fly had landed on it and just to rub salt into his wounds I saw six flies copulating on the desk. Now this morning I was busy at the keyboard myself entering up my blog and stuff when the damn thing came down again. All over me, as you ask! I now have glue all over the keyboard and it looks something like the carpet in the mornings after the slug that no one can find has been wandering around the office all night. There is a vast amount of fly glue all over me as well, my paws and claws are covered as well and to cap it all the fly paper was still empty but they are landing all over my back and sticking!!

The Rules of Fishing

Yesterday, after the fight with the flypaper I learned about fishing. I have never been fishing before but I have to confess I am still at a bit of a loss about the rules of fishing. The Owner, Pub Landlord and Recycling Lorry Driver went fishing at the lake which wasn't very far from here and I have to question myself as to why my patrols have never lead me to it before.

We all arrived at the lake and the three hoomuns got fishing rods out of the car which looked really interesting. The Owner managed to win the "tying lots of knots competition", which I thought would please him but he seemed a bit disappointed to have won. Maybe there are better competitions to come! They all attached a funny coloured stick to the end of the string and then tied a worm to the end of that. Then they threw it in the lake!!! All was quiet for a while and then they all sat down with a beer from The Owner's cool box and watched where they had each thrown their sticks. Well I couldn't quite work out what the floating stick was meant to do so I jumped in and swam out for a closer look. Well I really don't understand what I did wrong but they all started shouting at me! After about an hour of watching his floating stick and worm in the lake The Owner started fidgeting until in the end he got up and left his stick and worm in the lake and went to find someone to talk to. After he had gone I noticed something very strange, the stick which was floating in the water suddenly wasn't, it had sunk! Then it popped up again before sinking right out of sight! Then The Owner's fishing rod, which he had left on the bank, suddenly took off and started swimming across the lake before it too dived below the surface. I thought this must all be part of the game so I sat and watched as it kept popping up all across the lake whilst The Owner was talking to Pub Landlord. When at one point the rod popped up near where The Owner was standing he got very excited and started saying some very rude words! I thought that discretion was going to be the better part of valour on this occasion and went and sat in the car. I felt I probably wasn't going to get too much blame for his fishing rods going swimming if I was in there. When we got back to the pub they put me on a bit of old string which smelled far too strongly of fish for my liking and was not up to my usual standard of lead, I have breeding I do and that implies certain standards! I have to confess I was a bit surprised when they started telling the other hoomuns about events coz I don't remember there being a fish in there as big as they were saying. Although if there is, it has probably got a fishing rod trailing behind it.

Exercising with Small Boy

We have had Small Boy with us for the week so I have been a little preoccupied. Trying to understand Small Boy is even harder than trying to understand The Owner and I am quite worn out by the experience. I am also worn out by the exercise!! Me and The Owner have a very settled life normally.

The odd upset that I may have thrown into the mix (because I can, ok?) but generally life is very ordered. We get up and avoid the various calamitous goings on, if at all possible, that could signal the start of a bad day for The Owner and a quick patrol around the farm as we head for the studio. Then snooze until lunchtime when a quick shuffle up the road to the cottage before returning to the studio for more snoozing until it's time to go for an evening patrol and then home for tea. Alright, the evening patrol may involve a trip up the road via the pub but I can live with that. Small Boy arrives and we have walks three times a day with him as well as normal patrols with The Owner. Then yesterday he, Small Boy, has developed this new plan of putting my on a long lead and taking me off with him on long bike rides!!! The first one at ten yesterday morning was a bit of fun, but I had barely time to say "Bonio's three times a day would be nice please!" when we're off for the eleven o-clock and one at twelve and again at two... well you get the picture. I have hidden all my leads in the calf sheds this morning before Small Boy appears from his pit. I think strange woman is coming today to collect him so I can get some rest tomorrow. Do they do Ralgex for dogs?

Space Aliens!!!!

This weekend I have struggled a little. Small Boy went home with Strange Woman and the peace left behind in his wake was almost deafening. Our patrols were back to the regular mooch around the farm again, as opposed to the running at breakneck speed behind his bike for several miles, once an hour, on the hour.

Then on Sunday morning, just after the sun came up, The Owner is up and on the go with dish washers, washing machines and my nemesis The Dyson. Now this is normally the precursor to a visit from Owners Daughter but something about his demeanour said that was not going to be the case. Machines all fed and Dyson caged in the cupboard under the stairs again, a cup of tea for The Owner was in order, so we went and sat down and watched the very fast and VERY noisy bikes on the telly. They seem to me to be a bit like the very fast noisy cars we also watch on the telly as they go round and round the same roads and never seem to get anywhere. The Owner says it must be their Satnav although I am not sure what one of them is or if I should have one. After watching this for half an hour I went and sat out the front in the sun and then.... well....you could have knocked me down with an empty Bonio box! Two of those very fast and VERY noisy bikes pulled up outside. I was a bit wary to be honest and was a bit reluctant to go out and have an opinion on the matter. I had my suspicion that they may have been space aliens on the back of them!!! They had arms and legs, much like other hoomuns but they had shiny faces where their eyes should be! I was very glad The Owner was there for once! Then one of the space aliens took off its head!!!!! Oh saints preserve us I thought; this is going to be a messy day! But underneath its head was Owners Sister, had it eaten her? Then the other two space aliens took their heads off. One appeared to be Owner's Niece and the other, Mechanic. Perhaps they had all been eaten?! Well the space aliens took the rest of their skins off and all three looked deceptively normal and they gave me several Bonio's so they couldn't be all that bad. Later, they put their space alien skins and heads on again and got back on their very fast and VERY noisy bikes and went up the road. I stood there for some time after they had left to see if they were like the ones on the telly and came round again but I didn't see them. So the big question is, did I see space aliens? Or were they really Owner's Sister, Owner's Niece and Mechanic? And if they weren't space aliens where was Spaniel with far too many opinions and Horse? I think I need to go and have a lie down.

The Owner Plays Golf

Yesterday afternoon The Owner received a phone call which seemed to induce much excitement and good humour as he quickly locked up the studio and we shuffled off down the road towards the cottage. There then followed much rummaging at the back of his wardrobe until he re-emerged, triumphant, holding up a pair of very strange shoes. Bright colours, with tassels and spikes on the bottom!

They looked quite dangerous to me and I was not about to try and sniff them, mainly coz there was a lot of cobwebs in them and presumably several spiders, both of which have made my nose itch when sniffed at in the past. After a bit more rummaging he liberated a pair of the brightest patterned trousers I had ever seen! I need to watch this as I think more of his bizarre hoomun behaviour was going to follow. I was right, we went to play golf! Now I have never been to play golf before and judging by what followed The Owner hasn't either. I sat and watched carefully as all The Owners friends hit their little white balls down the strip of short grass. The Owner's first swing missed! Not the short grass; but the ball. It stayed resolutely on top of that little red spike he had pushed in the ground and balanced it on. Third attempt and he connected to the ball, which disappeared into the trees and the long grass. And as his friends disappeared out of sight hitting their little white balls as they went, The Owner was rummaging around in the grass looking for his. He also got shouted at for getting in the way of the group (who, by the way, were wearing the same strange colourful trousers as he was) that was following behind. I was curious, as I sat watching, as to exactly why he was searching for his ball over there when it was lying between my paws where it had landed. I tried to help! When he looked over in my direction I picked it up so he could see where it was. Well there was no need to say rude words like that!!!!!! I was only trying to help!!!! I don't understand hoomun ball games at all. My ball games are simple, you throw ball, I fetch it....you throw ball, I fetch it......you throw ball, I get fed up and wander off, you fetch ball. Simples! Then Grumpy Man with Hat came up and told The Owner he was causing an obstruction and asked him to leave the course. As we wandered back to the club house I was getting the distinct vibe that I was not popular over something. He may be sickening for something again I think. When we got home he threw his brightly coloured trousers in the washing machine along with one or two other items, put the soap and other stuff in all the right holes and poured himself a large glass of wine and went and found "somewhere to unwind". I couldn't help but feel, as I sat watching the machine trying to fill up, that all that water would have been better off inside it and it wasn't supposed to be flooding out from underneath and across the kitchen floor and on into the dining room. I'd go and attract his attention, but I don't want to get wet paws. When it gets to the living room door he'll probably notice.

My New Duvet

I appear to be in the do-do AGAIN! In fact of late I appear to have been permanently in the do-do, it's only the depth that has varied. Yesterday's do-do has had an unexpectedly beneficial outcome, something befitting the status of one who has breeding. Have I mentioned before that I was born and trained on Lord Bath's estate?

The night before last, quite late, he, The Owner, was asleep on the couch pretending to be watching the telly so I took myself off for a quick patrol of the garden. It was dark outside, really dark! On my patrol I happened upon something organic in the garden, although exactly what, I was unsure, as it was very dark. Never one to look a gift horse in the mouth I had a quick munch but the taste was not one I was familiar with so I was none the wiser as to its origin. Upon my return The Owner had stirred and was busy closing the house for the night so I retired to the boot room and snuggled up on my duvet. At some point during the night, and it caught me quite by surprise, my unexpected supper came back for an encore. Now I just knew that this was not going to go down well with The Owner so I tried desperately to hide it under my duvet but there was so much of it that it was sort of seeping out round the edges. When The Owner came down yesterday morning to let me out he didn't notice it at first, well, not until he trod on the edge of the duvet which leaked what was lurking underneath it and got all over his foot. I did check again in the light of day but I have to say that I am still not sure what it was. You may recall how the washing machine was on the blink, for which I was not responsible, which made cleaning my duvet one step beyond where The Owner was prepared to go for me so my duvet and half a tonne of soiled newspaper was deposited unceremoniously in the bin. I think Binman Hoomun may have a bit of a surprise this week when he has a quick nose through the contents of our bin to see if there is anything useful before it gets thrown in the back of the lorry. I think I may keep out of the way then. If they yuk and phew only half as much as The Owner did when he cleared it up I think I may not be very popular. Now I had some concerns, whilst watching this, about what I was going to lie on last night and was beginning to think that it may be the cold floor, but The Owner gave me a new duvet! Made of silk!!!!!! Now one is very posh!!!!!!!!!!!!!!!!!!!!!

The Odd Broken Dish or Two

I have come out of the way until the dust has settled a little out in the kitchen. I have noticed that The Owner has a tendency to just shove the clean dishes into the cupboard with no particular thought for any sense of order. It was ok when Owner's daughter was here sorting out the house for The Owner's return as she put everything in a proper place.

Now I was a little resentful of the intrusion at the time because I know how The Owner gets frustrated by tidiness and I was anxious that his return home should not do anything that would cause any anxiety. But I admit that the benefits grew on me a little and it did to a degree with The Owner as well. Now, apart from the odd intrusion of order when Owner's Daughter comes up for the day, the cupboards have lapsed into their former state of confusion as The Owner stuffs dishes and plates wherever he can see a bit of shelf or stack of other dishes and plates that look as though it may be able to accommodate another one on top. Personally, I always felt that all his glass roasting dishes balanced on top of his little breakfast dishes was an accident waiting to happen, but I'm a K9 (with breeding), what do I know? This morning he was up early again, which is always a recipe for a disaster later in the day (he tires easily), and the dishwasher was for a while the object of his attentions. Everything was unloaded and put into the disorganised chaos inside the cupboard. He was doing himself a bacon sandwich out there, so apart from the cooker now being awash with grease and oil which will invoke a severe case of frowning when Owner's Daughter next visit's, he opened the cupboard door for a plate........ and the dam broke. Plates, pirex, glass and tins all came out of the cupboard like a tsunami across the kitchen floor. I thought it interesting how those Pyrex dishes seemed to explode as they went. There has been much cursing going on out there which is why I have kept out of the way, just in case any came my way. But now he is sitting looking through the freebie papers for car boot sales, those that he hasn't been banned from, to see if he can replenish the cupboards with dishes and plates. The good news is that he has forgotten about his bacon sandwich which by now will be cold so I think that may be coming my way a bit later when he finds it again.

A Philosophy from Jack

One day you're a peacock,
The next you're a feather duster!
Choose your path wisely

The Mouse and Shakespeare

I have a new best friend called Mouse! He doesn't realise he is, but I can see he clearly has my best interests at heart. Last night The Owner had his tea early which means by late evening he will be getting bored. By the time the sun went down he is flicking from channel to channel on the telly, clearly bored.

So on goes the DVD player, innocent enough you may think? Let me explain; when I moved here from Lord Bath's estate (had I mentioned that I was born and trained on his estate?) I had never seen the inside of a hoomun home and had no idea of the concept of a telly. It took me some time to get my head around where the chimpanzees were inside his telly that week, but I eventually got my head around that. It took a little longer to understand the washing machine and I had to have an opinion on that once or twice. Anyway, TV understood, he, The Owner, finds it funny to introduce me to the concept of surround sound. Well, the surround sound speaker stands behind my comfy cushion and I was out of there pretty damn quick when the chimpanzee that hitherto had been inside the TV was suddenly having a lot to say from behind me! Last night, Mouse had chewed through the wire to my surround sound speaker and The Owner was clearly disappointed when he turned it on and it didn't have the usual effect of the sound wave blowing all the hair on my back against the grain

towards my nose. After much duct tape and swearing and the wire with a big lump in it like a worm with a knot in its tail, the customary "Wump" of the big speakers was heard as they were turned on. Last night it was Shakespeare and I now understand why Small Boy has such an aversion to all things Shakespearean. If he loves the woman why can't he just say so? Instead we have two paragraphs of waffle that I barely understood and all at ear-splitting volume! The Owner is of course in raptures over it.
So long as men can breathe or eyes can see,
So long lives this and this gives life to thee.
It doesn't mention the effect on my ears this morning does it?

The Dyson!!!!!!

I was set about earlier today by that ruddy Dyson. I swear it has a mind and can move by itself! The Owner and I came shuffling up the road at lunch time, now normally I would have been bouncing athletically from sniff to sniff whilst The Owner does the shuffling but today, well frankly, I couldn't be bothered so I gave the impression that I was walking dutifully to heel.

When we got back he potters around the kitchen and makes himself a sandwich and pours himself a cup of tea then grumbles off through the dining room to go and watch the news whilst he absent mindedly spills the contents of the sandwich down his shirt. Now I get quite excited at this point because whatever he spills I get to clear up. If he talks to anyone about it he tells them that he doesn't understand it as there is never anything on the floor and yet he has managed to get certain stains on his shirt. Well with my lightening reactions where a wayward crumb or two is concerned it doesn't take a brain surgeon to work it out does it! Anyway, I'm sorry I digress, he was wandering through the dining room with me bouncing excitably on his heels when we had to go past the Dyson, left out after clearing up the remains of last night's little accident with a plate of rice for which I hold no responsibility but apparently all of the blame. Just as we passed it I could have sworn it moved! More out of blind panic than any reasoned attempt to escape I shot forward to get away from it and straight into the back of The Owner's legs. Just as well he left the Dyson out as it happened, I thought, with all that mess now on the carpet.

DIY SOS

Last night The Owner had a bit of a traumatic evening although I have to say he brought it upon himself. It's a facet of hoomun behaviour that I find the hardest of all to fathom out. It is usually a woman thing as I am lead to believe but that doesn't stop The Owner becoming involved with this whole ritual.

I refer here to DIY SOS! Now I get the premise of the program; family of hoomuns buy a hoomun kennel that has more holes in it than a ferret's cage, they all live there in amongst building rubble and rolls of loft insulation for ages and then Father Hoomun gets all depressed and says he is a failure. Not sure why coz from where I stand their kennel looks about as good as my boot room so it must be alright. Then a whole army of Builder Hoomuns comes along and then makes it ten times worse by putting windows in holes in the wall and making it all look tidy and stuff. Then the hoomun family returns and start this whole thing of the eyes leaking that I don't understand. I thought hoomun eyes leak when they are unhappy or when they have hit their thumbs really hard with a hammer (which seems just plain stupid to me) but they are telling everyone how happy they are etc. Why do they do this eyes leaking thing and then say they are happy??? The bit I really don't understand is that The Owner joins in with eyes leaking and then tells me what a good program he has just watched! Hello! If it's going to upset him why watch it and if he is happy why have leaking eyes?? Hoomuns!!!!!!!!! I am going to find a good bit of badger poo to roll in I think.

My Friday - Good and Bad!

Oh where to start? Do we talk about Lady Chocolate Lab Owner or do we talk about Tesco Yoof? Well, to be fare I am not certain it was Lady Chocolate Lab Owner but on Friday he got up and did his normal stuff upstairs, whatever that entails I am uncertain as I hide when that happens ever since Owners Daughter invited me up there and then threw me into the bath.

Then we went for our normal patrol but instead of going to the office we came back here. Very strange I thought! He went upstairs and there was a lot more splashing going on and I was definitely not going to investigate for fear for my own personal safety and then he re-appeared, smelling funny. This was why I suspected he has been to see Lady Chocolate Lab Owner as he only smells like that when he was off to see her. I got a bit excited at this thought coz I thought I may have got to see my own love interest, Lady Chocolate Lab. He got a new pair of trousers out of a bag and put them on which looked kinda comical as his feet disappeared. There then followed much stabbing of fingers with needles and a lot of swearing. I did think that what he was doing would never last and I was right as when he did eventually get back his feet had disappeared again inside his trousers. Well after he put the needles and cotton wool soaked in blood and the Elastoplast box away, he stole my laptop and left!! I couldn't even voice an opinion on Facebook!!!! Home Alone I was!!! Today Tesco Yoof has been and delivered and he clearly thought he was a big strong hoomun as he insisted on carrying all The Owner's boxes up the path at the same time and opening the gate by himself. I feel it my duty to bring clever hoomuns down to earth a little and I practice daily with The Owner but a swift dart between his legs as he struggled past my wee tree brought his whole world tumbling down and all the boxes with him. A good start to the day I felt, I am of course in the boot room but it was worth it. I am of course still concerned about not getting to see Lady Chocolate Lab, if that was where he went on Friday.

4X4 Driver's Windscreen

Well........... I LIKE Sundays!!! Particularly Sundays like these. The Owner has done his housework which did reveal one or two misdemeanours' which I had hoped were forgotten some time ago and I was eventually allowed out of the boot room. After The Owner, (who has been going around singing, which is rather worrying) had done an hour down at the studio we, retired to the seat under the trees up the garden.

Now, I don't speak much squirrel particularly but I had worked out that Squirrel, who had been scattering his nuts, (metaphorically speaking) over the garden path was particularly vexed about The Owner blocking his path back to the nut bush and had a lot to say on the matter, fortunately, most of which The Owner didn't understand. So we retired to the cricket field with a collapsible chair and a bottle of beer which was extravagantly large in my opinion. Now, you have heard the saying "What goes around comes around!"? Well today was it! I was once castigated for retrieving the cricket ball which it would appear was not in the rules and today when some hoomun from another village smite the ball verily (it is Sunday after all) in a perfect arc straight into the bramble bush they called for me to get it out for them. Well there were prickles in there and I am a delicate soul!!! So I took myself back to the pavilion in the hope of a sandwich at half time. That was when 4X4 Driver came into the car park paddock. Everyone else parks there! But no, he has to go through to the cricket field and park! So this gentleman from the other village who it seems is very good at swiping the ball verily, took another almighty swipe at the ball, which looked kinda dangerous and indeed it was as it cleared the boundary fence that bites my nose when I have sniffed it, and went straight through the windscreen of 4X4 Driver's car. There was a lot of angst at this point so The Owner and I came home quite quickly. I do like Sundays!

More Leaking Eyes

Oh Saint Bonio preserve us! This hoomun behaviour trait is confusing me more than ever although I am getting some kind of a handle on it I think. He, The Owner, is in there now, with his eyes leaking again! The reason I think I am getting a handle on this strange hoomun behaviour is that I have been watching the TV and noticed something in common with both incidents.

Last time it was DIY SOS, and this time it is Village SOS. So, it is clearly something to do with SOS, I thought! Now a proverbial spanner has been thrown in the works of my thinking. At the moment he is watching a video called "The Colour Purple" which also appears to be having the same effect on his leaking eyes. I am thinking a frantic visit to the doctor demanding the attentions of Speshalist may ensue. Watch as I might I cannot see any reference to SOS in The Colour Purple but I will continue my observation and see if it comes later in the film. I will keep you informed! I think I had better go and find him a kitchen role or it could get messy!

The Speed Survey in the Village

I am thinking I may be in trouble here if the truth ever came out! It was an easy mistake I think, one hardly worth mentioning. But the ramifications could well be far reaching and one such ramification is building as we speak. I was on patrol the other morning up near the pub.

I couldn't go in as I was on my own and didn't have a lead (pub rules are that dogs must be on leads and under the control of a responsible adult............probably least said about the last bit, the better). 'Twas then that I came across the object of an hour or so of my amusement and attentions. Lying in the road, well, stretched across it actually, was a big rubber snake, two of them in fact. So I bit it! The snakes appeared to be coming from a grey box that someone had chained to the telegraph pole and when I bit the snake it clicked, as if in some kind of protest. So I bit it again! And it clicked again! So I tried the other one and that clicked as well! This was fun! So I pounced on it and bit it at the same time and it clicked quite a lot at this so I did it again..... and again. This was fun. At one point there was one car came past and it clicked at that as well. But that was just Lady Manor Hoomun on her way to do the flowers at the church. I had great fun with that until it died and fell apart and I lost interest. I am thinking that I may have inadvertently been responsible for destroying a speed survey of cars going through the village and in some way responsible for it recording an abnormally high volume of traffic and doing some impossible speeds through the village. Oh dear! But it was such fun at the time! It gets worse! Because of these results Police Hoomun has given the village a speed camera and they are looking for volunteers! I am feeling a little apprehensive about the way The

Owner is looking for his hi-viz jacket with a purposeful look in his eye. I will keep you informed.

The Owners Been in Police Custard!!

The Owner has one of his headaches that could erupt at any moment into a full blown hamstring injury. He has not had a good day, bless him! You may recall from my last missive he was trying to find his hi-viz jacket and was intent on volunteering for the village Speedwatch.

Having presented himself for duty his offer was spurned as it was generally felt the way he was salivating with excitement as he pointed the speed gun at Manor Cleaner Lady as she passed by on her bike was perhaps inappropriate. Undeterred, he returned to the cottage and after much rummaging at the back of a drawer produced a hair dryer. Armed with his new 'speed gun' and his hi-viz jacket he set up camp outside on the road pointing the hair dryer at passing motorists. It was all going well until he decided to make a citizen's arrest of one driver who turned out to be the Police Hoomun Inspector who's foot I wee'd on when he was asking inappropriate questions about The Owner when he went walkabout. After they released him from Police Custard, which sounded quite a messy thing to be in from what I could hear of it, The Owner decided to take me for a walk up on the hill. When I say walk, it really entailed me being on a lead running flat out beside The Owner, who is on Small Boy's bike. Up the big hill we went and that was when his day took a big turn for the worse. As we rounded the corner of the woods to come back down the hill, I thought I saw Lady Chocolate Lab down by the gate at the bottom and took off with a certain air of excitement about my general demeanour. I thought The Owner was joining in as no matter how hard I ran he kept up with me, whooping and shouting as he went! Well how was I to know that Small Boy had taken the brakes off his bike when he was here last? When we got to the bottom of the hill, well it wasn't Lady Chocolate Lab after all, which was just as well what with the mess he made of that gate. If my understanding of the things are correct, the five bar gate can now be considered a ten bar gate. Well I thought Farmer Hoomun may have been pleased at the increase in value of his gate but I must have missed something from the theory somewhere as Farmer Hoomun gave The Owner a bill and they always seem to upset The Owner. We may also have to visit Halfords before Small Boy visits next weekend as I don't think he is going to be too pleased with what The Owner has done to his bike! I am getting the strangest vibe from The Owner this evening; I think I may take myself to the boot room as a precaution.

Pigeon's Morning Visit

This morning I am not happy! This morning The Owner is not happy! This morning, perhaps for the first time ever we are unhappy about the same thing and from the same perspective!

Last night The Owner took me to the pub, perhaps predictably on a Friday evening but that is the kind of predictability I can cope with. Barmaid Hoomun was there yesterday evening although she is not the cause of OUR ire. Barmaid Hoomun I like, because she tends to give me little treats when The Owner isn't looking. But I am a K9 of some breeding, and not a little learning in hoomun terms, so although I can't speak hoomun, I can type it and I can certainly understand it, even some of The Owners more colourful language. So why does she have to talk to me in such an infantile way? "Does Jacky wacky want a Bickie Wickie?"?!?!?!?! Just give me the biscuit and cut the cackle! Some hoomun behaviour I will never understand!

Sorry, I digress already. When we came home last night the sun was just setting over The Manor and it does throw all kinds of golden light on the trees at the top of the hill opposite. This kind of scene tends to cause The Owner to wax lyrical and he grabs MY laptop and goes upstairs and sit in THAT window where the roses grow if I haven't managed to kill them first by weeing on them. Having been allowed up there once I can see that the view may have a certain appeal to a hoomun. So he sets himself up at the window, glass of wine to one side and MY laptop on the wide window sill. He was up there for some time and only came down when his wine glass was empty and required refilling. You'll notice the omission of the return of MY laptop, that'll be because he left it up there then! On the window sill, in front of an open window! This morning, Pigeon landed on the window sill and hopped up on to the nearest thing to a perch it could find, MY open laptop!!!!! The Owner opened one eye from his slumber and roared from his bed in a non appreciative manner, to which Pigeon responded by depositing last night's supper from his bottom all over MY laptop and flapping off out of the window. I am looking forward to my next encounter with Pigeon who is currently sat on the electric wires out of my reach saying "Coo" at the spectacle of The Owner and me working together to try and clean the keyboard. Anyone got any wet wipes? I may have a use for them.

Thoughts on Febreze

The Owner has discovered a new best friend and I have discovered another worstest friend. Something akin to The Dyson! I would like to point out that earlier he had already been terrorising me with that nemesis of mine as he laughs like some kind of maniacal despot (well, how I would imagine one would laugh having never actually met one) as he chases me around the living room carpet, destroying all my hidden bits of chewy stick I had brought in from the garden and thought I had hidden.

I thought my moment of torture was passed until he informed no-one in particular that Owners Daughter and Small Boy, who has been conspicuous by his absence this weekend, were running very late from their planned arrival due to Owners Daughter taking too long to put her face on before meeting her public this morning. This fills me with a sense of dread as he then has nothing to fill his time as previously planned. I believe you hoomuns have a saying about the devil finding work for idle hands or something like that? On this occasion the devil found a spray tin of Febreze to fill his idle hands with! All things, including me, my comfy cushion and my duvet (silk, obviously, as I have breeding, had I mentioned I was born and trained on Lord Bath's estate) were sprayed liberally with the stuff. He justifies it to me by saying Owners Daughter is coming but he is now prowling the house looking for something, anything else, to spray. He has now got another menacing look in his eye as he looks at me and I think I may yet be getting another liberal application of the devils spray. He is already calling me 'The Fragrant One', again! I think I may go and find some dead badger to roll in!

Small Boy and The Damson Tree

Small Boy arrived yesterday with Owners Daughter and I was so pleased to see them I did my silly run out around the tree in the middle of the lawn and back, twice. You may have noticed I have elevated the status of the bush to tree as it seems to have done quite well this year and is now blocking the path to the front door. It blocks it enough to make Postman's arrival at the letter box on a wet day a somewhat soggy affair.
Sorry, I digress already in my story. After much excitement and a crafty sneak of Owners Daughter's crust from her sandwich at lunch time, an afternoon of great activity looked promising! Small Boy was detailed to retrieve several of The Owners tools from all around the garden, behind hedges, up trees, wherever Small Boy had left them after using them on his last visit and from where The Owner had been completely unable to locate them which always seemed to be a matter of some frustration for The Owner. His frustration was helped little when Small Boy went up the garden and found them all so easily. The Owner then began compiling a list of many other tools which had gone missing over the years to see if he could find them with the same consummate ease. Small Boy was then sent up the damson tree to pick damsons, although I am not sure what they are as they are above head height, an area which tends to bother me little. Small Boy complained bitterly about his task and when The Owner informed him that small boys were always sent up the chimneys in years past, it did little to improve his demeanour. Small Boy, up a tree, picking Damsons, seems to involve throwing twenty or so to the floor and then putting one in the bag. When I say on the floor, I really mean they have to be first bounced off my back or The Owners head before hitting the floor. It would seem also that damsons stain quite a lot and I can see many purple blobs staining my back. Fortunately The Owner is unable to see the top of his own head and is therefore

oblivious to the effect it has had up there. I hope it stays that way or I fear his cheerful demeanour since Small Boy and Owners Daughter arrived may vanish. He has been out today and returned smelling of hospitals again. Unsure yet if I should be worried about that but I will keep you informed....

Men With Funny Shaped Balls

It is always a great source of excitement for me, when I play ball in the garden with The Owner. I pick it up and rush around the garden and The Owner gets very red in the face as he throws himself at the ball whilst I rush off with it in my mouth in a very athletic fashion. He then picks himself up and shouts a lot, not sure who at or what about but he does get very loud about it sometimes, before he chases me again and we do it all over again.

Sometimes I get a bit too carried away and I make the ball go hiss in my mouth and then it turns a funny shape and then The Owner throws it in the bin and goes and buys me a new one, albeit a little too begrudgingly sometimes. Today he is watching the telly, we have already watched the very noisy cars going very fast back to where they came from, (and incidentally, I have given up trying to understand the rules, as there always seems to be someone with a strange name, who, according to The Owner, doesn't do it right). Now we are busy watching loads of men running around a field chasing a ball which, frankly, ought to be thrown in the bin as it looks to me as though someone has bitten the ball and it has gone a very funny shape! And while we are at it why does he keep calling some of them Whales. I don't know too much about them as I have never met one, but I didn't think whales got out of the big village pond down near where Small Boy lives and when they do there is much wailing and gnashing of teeth by some hoomuns. Or should I have spelled that whaling? Whatever, there seems to me to be far too much testosterone in this room today, I think I may be developing one of my headaches! Last week The Owner went out for the day and came back smelling of hospitals again. I think I have heard him talking about making rangements. I don't think I have seen a rangement yet so I am not sure if I need to have an opinion about them. I will keep you informed!

More Pungent Flowers

I have been out in the garden, when it wasn't raining, and have been exploring the cherry orchard. Anything to avoid the noise coming from The Owner as he watches the Whales indoors! Walking round the corner, thinking that there are no more things to worry about as far as pungent flowers are concerned, when I stumbled across these! I may try and dig them up quick to avoid The Owner finding them! Just in case!

The Owner is Attacked

The Owner is up to something this morning and I am not sure what! Now I am not saying that The Owner doesn't do his housework regularly at all. He puts that ruddy Dyson round once a month whether it needs it or not, but not normally on a weekday during the morning! He is plotting something I am sure. He unplugged it from the socket where I plug my laptop in and unusually, he remembered to plug the laptop back in for me before it goes blip and disappears.

Then he grabs all the wire and the ruddy Dyson and drags the whole lot up the stairs, again nothing unusual except that it is during the day and mid-week, but what was particularly unusual was that he normally winds the wire up first before he carries it anywhere. I remember thinking at the time "That could be dangerous!", but I am only a K9 after all, what do I know? Within less than a minute he was back down the stairs and I can't help but think that head first was not in his plan and then I noticed the cause of his ire and predicament. He was being chased down the stairs by that ruddy Dyson and its wire had already caught his foot! He looked unusually pathetic laid at the foot of the stairs being molested by that ruddy Dyson. Well what have I been saying all along? It has got a mind of its own and it is a particularly malevolent one at that! He looked at me with a sort of pleading look in his eye but I was going nowhere near it or him whilst he was tangled up in it! He has made himself one of his very strong coffees and is sitting on the sofa looking for someone to tell about his plight. I am hoping his distress doesn't lead to him looking for his brandy bottle, he hasn't realised yet that it was in the recycling box that went out yesterday and still half full. He is not going to be happy and I think, as it is a nice day, I may take myself off up to the sunny spot behind the barbecue just in case he finds some way that this was all my fault.

Katia and The Blue Wheelie Bin

I had the fright of my life this week, well to be honest it was two frights together and I am suspecting I may have brought a little stress into the life of Manor Hoomun as well. The other night it was a little bit gusty here and the leaves from the trees were blowing everywhere. The Owner said it was Katia doing her best. I am not sure if she lives around here or not, but if she does, judging by the amount of rubbish she threw around the place that night, she isn't going to be very popular.

Sorry, I digress again. On this gusty evening The Owner was watching a DVD and snoring loudly, I am not understanding how he can do both but it is one he has seen many times before and can even recite the words to it when he isn't snoring, so I opted for a quick patrol of the neighbourhood. I was returning home through The Manor gardens and passing Manor Hoomuns car when Katia threw Manor Hoomuns new blue wheelie bin at me. Well I have been molested frequently by The Owner's ruddy Dyson, but never by an empty blue wheelie bin and to be honest it isn't going to go down as my favourite experience! Perhaps understandingly, I shot backwards in a state of fright and ran into Manor Hoomuns car which wailed loudly and had a lot to say on the matter. Lights came on everywhere and I feared I may have been sent to the boot room at The Manor so I ran as fast as I could for the gateway through the hedge to the cottage. From there I could witness Manor Hoomun and Lady Manor Hoomun searching the area for Truders. I am not sure who Truders is or why he was suspected as Katia was known to be behind it, but I am just glad that a finger wasn't pointed in my direction. Indoors, The Owner was still snoring; there is a certain comfort in knowing that some things never change.

The Wasp

I was only trying to have a little fun at The Owner's expense and it all sort of ganged up on me. It has been a little on the warm side here these last few days and as always on such occasions The Owner wanders home for an extended lunch and grabs a book, a towel and a beer and makes for the garden to cook himself. This is always the cue for much mirth and merriment as I try and get on the towel with him and he tries bravely to fend me off. He always wins on such occasions but it's fun trying. Yesterday he won, as usual and I had to lie on the grass which hardly befits one with breeding such as me, so every time he reached to turn the page I would stuff my nose under his hand which seemed to displease him, so mission was at least in part accomplished. I then opted to roll on my back onto his book and breathe in his face. Oh what fun! He didn't like that either. I was building up to the tail flick to knock the beer over when this strange looking creature crawled on my nose. Black spots on a red shell it had. Well I went a little boss eyed to see it on the nose but apart from a little tickle it wasn't too bad..... and then it bit me! Well I ran off, partly in surprise and partly in disgust, and found myself somewhere in the shade to lie until my nose had stopped hurting. After a while, The Owner went for another beer from the fridge so I sneaked back out and lay on his towel while he couldn't see me. Now that was fun because I knew it would get some less than favourable response from The Owner but not the one I was expecting! In the kitchen roof is a wasp nest and one of the .... sorry I nearly used a word then that I shouldn't...... No I cannot find a more suitable one! One of those sneaky bastards crept up and stung me! I am sure he was working at the behest of The Owner although I didn't see The Owner put it up to the job. This morning I have one ear normal and the other the size of a football and raging ear ache. I am not feeling very charitable today so watch out!

The Speshliss

The Owner is off to see Speshliss today! I am not sure who Speshliss is or what he does but he had better not upset The Owner as I think I have already done that as much as The Owner can cope with in one day! This morning we went off on morning patrol around the farm, across the paddock and round the cricket pitch taking particular care not to sniff at or wee up the fence that ticks and hurts; through the hunting gate and across the little sleeper bridge. Well The Owner crossed the bridge with rather a curmudgeonly grumble about slippery stuff and stinging nettles whilst I leapt across in a bright and energetic fashion, hardly breaking my stride. We crossed the field with the dead trees in, which are always good for a quick sniff at or even a wee up but taking particular care not to get too close to the fence that clicks and hurts in that field as well. Then around the back of the farm and back down past the silage pits and through the dairy yard and down to the studio. I have painted a picture of rural bliss on the morning patrol? Well I omitted the bit about the first rain in several weeks falling from the skies to "lay the dust", or so The Owner said. It had done just a little too much laying of dust really and the dairy yard was awash with mud as we crossed it. Back at the studio there is always cause for great excitement as The Owner always gives me a Bonio when we get back, had I mentioned that I like Bonio's? Well I am afraid I got a little too excited for the occasion and, well..... there were only the two muddy paw prints in the middle of his white shirt. Hardly worth mentioning here I thought. The Owner mentioned it quite a lot however! I just hope that Speshliss doesn't upset him as well or it may be a chilly evening in the cottage and that will be nothing to do with the weather either.

Broken Wires

The Owner returned yesterday from seeing Speshliss and smelling of hospitals again and with two muddy paw prints still on his chest. So after the little episode yesterday morning when he acquired said paw prints I felt that discretion was going to be the better part of valour and after evening patrol (twice, as he had left some shopping in the fridge at the studio and we had to go back for it) I opted for the safest option and went to the boot room for the evening. By this morning he was clearly feeling a bit better as I got some of his toast that he left on the plate and put on the floor. I wasn't intended to have it but I was not admonished too much for thieving it so that is as good as having been given permission. So to the studio we did go, and I bumped into my little terrier friend, "Chip". We greeted each other as K9's do and I ran excitedly to the studio hopeful of a Bonio. By the time of my arrival The Owner was already inside swearing at the computer so I came rushing in and under the table, ready to look cute in hope of a Bonio. Well I didn't see the phone wires! Or the broadband wire! Or his headset wire, and frankly he shouldn't have had them draped over my Vetbed! The Owner has had to wire up new leads and plugs and appears to be particularly vexed by the matter so I think I may go for another patrol. On my own this time!!!

Owners Daughter Has Done a Woopsie!!!

Well yesterday was a day of great significance and unexplained hoomun behaviour for me. The Owner told me that Owners Daughter had a bit of a woopsie in her car. Well when I have a woopsie it usually involves a shovel and a spell in the boot room whilst he clears it up. Hold that thought for a moment whilst I explain that her woopsie involved the front end of a tractor! Now I have seen the big buckets on the front of the tractors on the farm, indeed I have wee'd up some of them, so I know just how big they are. So how much did she do to need one as big as that to clear it up?!?!? Somehow in amongst it all it appeared to need a visit from Owners Daughter, Very Strange Woman, Diesel Dog Daughter and of course Diesel Dog. Perhaps it needed The Owners deft touch with a shovel or something. I left Diesel Dog to do his thing, which inevitable involved running up and down the path across the back of the garden like a demented badger, whilst the hoomuns went indoors and filled out Shoreance forms. Very Strange Woman needed a stamp for an envelope and The Owner had one left in his little book and gave it to Very Strange Woman to put on the envelope. It was at about this point that Diesel Dog's demented badger running involved a quick trip through the cottage and out the front door again. That was when the arguments seemed to start, as the only stamp The Owner had, was missing! I wandered outside partly to see where Diesel Dog had taken the stamp but mainly to get away from the argument about who last saw the stamp that was raging indoors. It is a strange sight to see a Diesel Dog running around the garden staring at the tip of his own nose where the glue on the stamp had firmly affixed the only stamp in Wiltshire and oblivious to everything else around him. I can't help but believe that he didn't really mean to run straight through The Owner's barbie at the top of the garden and that The Owner may have an opinion about that later as well as the somewhat less than favourable opinions that he was expressing indoors.

Fireman Friends

This morning I have made some new friends - Fireman! The Owner got up this morning when it was still dark. Why, was a matter of some mystery to me at first as today is a Sunday but then I realised when, with his second mug of tea, he settled down to watch the very fast and noisy cars drive all the way back to where they first came from. I worry as it is just too early for The Owner and he will be tired by the end of the day. After the race was finished and all the shouting at the screen had subsided he begins to fidget. This always means trouble of one form or another and this morning was no exception. Eventually his fidgeting had reached a kind of crescendo and he jumps up and goes out to the kitchen and puts the coffee on and several rashers of bacon under the grill. Grabbing the morning paper he flops back into the settee that I am allowed on to await the smell of bacon grilling gently. Well that smell came and went as I noticed the paper slip from his grasp and fall gently to the floor. I said it was going to be too early for him didn't I? Well I wasn't about to disturb him, I was comfortable where I was! After a while the smell of grilling bacon had been replaced by thick smoke billowing from under the grill, then a kind of pop as the flames started. I found that if I kept my head down low the smoke wasn't too bad and I could snooze on. Eventually The Owner aroused from his snoozing and became very disorientated when he stood up as the familiar surroundings of the dining room disappeared from his view when his head disappeared from my view in the smoke above me. I don't know how Fireman and his friends knew about it but as The Owner burst forth from the cottage front door on his hands and knees making far too much of a scene in my opinion, Fireman stood there with his hose pipe at the ready. His hosepipe was much bigger than The Owners and he didn't manage to squirt me with it, I like him! I like him all the more because he had a Bonio in his pocket for me, have I mentioned that I like Bonio's? In recognition of the Bonio, I only wee'd up one of the wheels of the fire engine. The Owner is now looking very sorry for himself as he cleans up the mess in the kitchen. I did say it was too early for him didn't I?

The Owner's Been Away

What a busy few days I have had! Full of strange twists and turns. Thursday morning, The Owner and I went off on patrol as normal, BUT, we came home again and The Owner seemed a little strange. Then Bracknell Lady Hoomun turned up, now I have met her several times before and she always gives me a Bonio or two so I like her. So I did my bestest little dance, but I didn't get a Bonio, so I thought I may have to revise my opinion of her. Then The Owner and Bracknell Lady Hoomun got in the car and drove off leaving me in doors at the cottage. I was beginning to fear they had left me as it had got dark and I was still on my own, but it wasn't quite so bad as I had tried all the chairs, cushions, beds and other bits that I am not normally allowed on. Then there was a rattle at the boot room door, in the dark. I was understandably concerned, not that we were about to be burgled, but that I was being disturbed and I still hadn't got around to trying a snooze on Small Boys bed! It wasn't a burglar hoomun after all, it was Phlee Dog Owner and he took me off to his home, after he fed me, so he went up in my estimation straight away! The Owner still didn't come back even though everyone was drinking wine and I even slept there last night. Their boot room floor was very warm; mine isn't! Still no sign of The Owner though. I did notice that Phlee Dog Owner wakes up after drinking wine with the same amount of grumbling as The Owner! Today, The Owner showed up with Bracknell Lady Hoomun and he smelled of hospitals again! I haven't finished yet! When The Owner and Bracknell Lady Hoomun arrived back, in the post box was a packet marked "Amazon" and it was addressed to me, more fan mail! Now I have seen how Amazon Lady pictures have a frankly less than necessary effect on The Owner, so I was quite hopeful that maybe Amazon ladies have lady chocolate Labs! So my anonymous fan from BH12 has struck again! More chewies! I shall be having a chomp on one or two of them later.

Nettles on the Nose

Today I was duped! Duped I was! By someone with no scruples! I have no idea what it means to have no scruples but The Owner always shouts that at the telly when he seems displeased with the Andrew Marr Show. Together with words like "Slimeball" and "Mandleson". I am not yet sure who duped me but I am suspecting it may have been Monkey Dog Thing as he has not yet exacted any kind of revenge for me encouraging him to wee on his lady hoomun owner's car seat some time ago and I am keeping my eyes open still. We are now past the final flush of summer and autumn is exerting its cold and windy grip around the farm. Our nettles, which I have given a particularly wide berth since I wee'd over one and it stung my little boy's bits, are mainly died down in the garden, so I don't tend to pay them any regard. Walking to the studio this morning with The Owner through the wind, which is fortunately clearing the smell of hospitals from his crusty old Barbour jacket, a waft of a sniff caught my attention from a small patch of weeds. As you would expect from a dog of my breeding and nature it required investigation so I sniffed it. Then I sniffed it again, a bit closer this time and it was then that I discovered how I had been duped. Someone (and I suspect it to be Monkey Dog Thing) had wee'd on some nettles (Presumably from a distance.) and I had just had a good sniff at it and I had now got a very sore nose. I am thinking Monkey Dog Thing may have got his revenge.

The Bovine Dinosaurs

This evening I am cold and wet, with the imprint of The Owner's yard broom still tingling on my shoulder. For those of you with not enough original thoughts in their minds, no I have not been rolling in anything even remotely badger! The Owner had had a difficult day, I could tell by the ferocity with which he threw his mouse pen back in its holster and his glasses across the desk. I knew we were in for an extended patrol as we always do when he throws his mouse pen like that and I was right, off we went across the fields and as we went he began to feel better. You can tell, because his grumbling got a little less verbose as we walked. The fingers of dark cloud extended lazily across the sky as the last vestiges of daylight disappeared and the world around us became cloaked in an eerie white glow. A host of celestial bodies cast their combined light across the cold slumbering world around us as we headed for the warmth of home and the promise of a long awaited belly filled with food. Well that's how it should have been except its damn cold in here as after only the first flush of frost, the oil has run out, because he forgot to order any oil throughout the summer again. As we crossed the cricket field, with the twinkle of light from the porch lantern a welcome and almost intoxicating sight in the darkness. I ran ahead in excitement at the prospect of my tea and through the gate into the paddock, next stop, the front door! In my excitement I had forgotten about the two barren cows in the paddock and they were lying in wait for me, either side of the gate, in the gathering darkness. Well, to say I pooped myself in terror as these two bovine dinosaurs emerged from the darkness either side of me with a loud "Moo!" would be a masterful stroke of understatement! In my panic I fell and rolled through fresh cow poo and I have to report it hasn't the same satisfaction as a good old dollop of badger poop! I am now cold, wet and in the boot room and The Owner is wandering around the cottage with three jumpers on and every once in a while he stops, looks at me, goes "Moo!" then laughs to himself as he carries on his wandering. I think he looks like a camel; he walks like one as well.

The Wasp Burning Stove

The Owner tells me off frequently for bringing things in from the garden, you know the sort of thing, little treasures for burying under my comfy cushion, manky piece of wood for chewing up later and various other little delights. I am thinking at the moment he is rather wishing he followed his own advice. You may recall how yesterday there was an absence of heating oil in the tank and therefore a corresponding lack of heat in the cottage. There was also a distinct lack of logs for the wood burner in the shed rendering a distinct chill throughout the cottage which he was clearly not prepared to endure for another evening. I have to say that his resolve was something I heartily approved of when he came home early and spent half an hour rooting around in the woods up by the barbie looking for sufficient fodder for the wood burner for the evening. He came struggling down over the lawn dropping more wood than he was carrying and disappeared back up to the woods for a second load. It was then that he thought he had struck gold when he happened upon a big bag of charcoal left over from a barbie in the summer and came rushing back to the cottage carrying his booty with the look of a small child who had just managed to nick his big brothers favourite toy. There was furious activity in the living room with paper being ripped and wood being broken up as he laid and then lit the fire. It was about then when I noticed an advancing army across the carpet. The bag of charcoal had become the home of preference for a colony of a thousand or two wasps that had hibernated for the winter. The warmth from the wood burner and the movement of being carried from the garden seemed to have upset them somehow and they were marching across the carpet to have it out with the first thing they saw moving....me! They seemed to have altogether far too much attitude for my liking so I went for a patrol and left The Owner to it. By the time I returned, he had most of the situation under control but he has been a little restless ever since. Anything that sounds remotely like a buzzing sound seems to put him particularly on edge. I bet he wished he hadn't brought them in. I bet even more he wishes he had ordered oil and firewood!

The Water Bucket

Life round here this morning has been a little difficult so far. The Owner has had to change his trousers already and my duvet from my bed in the boot room is hanging on the line to dry off a little. But the good bit is that we have a lovely clean kitchen floor and the boot room looks lovely and clean too. I suppose it all started last night really, the wood burner was warm and wasp free and outside it was raining and cold. To wee, or not to wee, that was the question. Not a difficult one as it turned out, if I tried to ignore it I felt I could probably last until morning and so opted for the warmth of the wood burner. By the time morning came around I was getting quite desperate, made worse as it happens by the rain overnight, with the water falling off the boot room roof into the gutter and then into the large bucket outside the back door. The bladder still hasn't recovered from the incident last year following the visit from the hounds and the sound of running water only serves to exacerbate the problem. When The Owner opened the door and let me out there was a certain sense of urgency as I ran up the garden to relieve the pressure a little. Whilst up there I could hear The Owner rummaging around in my food bin back in the boot room and so, pressure relieved, I made my way rapidly back to the cottage in anticipation of breakfast. Now this is where my morning started to unravel so early. It had been raining overnight and as I ran across the little courtyard (The Owner calls it the mews coz he wants to sound posh) I slipped a little on the wet concrete and slid straight into the big bucket full of gutter water right outside the boot room door knocking about five gallons of water over. The water hit the inside of the partly open back door which turned it neatly inside the boot room and all over The Owner. That which wasn't soaked up by my duvet or The Owners trousers , and the boot room not really being designed as a vessel for holding five gallons of water, turned its soaking attentions on the rest of the inside of the cottage. As I said, we have a nice clean kitchen floor now, a carpet that goes squelch every time you stand on it and a duvet hanging on the line dripping. Now I am no domestic goddess, but I feel sure that won't be dry for tonight. The Owner seems less than happy with me at the moment; I might make myself scarce for a while.

The Owner's Wet Trousers

Yesterday was not his best! The Owner I am talking about. It started out pretty much as it continued and I only fared a little better. As he closed the boot room door on me last night he was unusually comforting to me, ruffling my head as I walked past saying "Never mind old boy, perhaps we can have a better day tomorrow!" We had a certain amount of rain overnight the previous night which also continued through much of yesterday, so puddles were plentiful and deep as we left the cottage for the morning shuffle to work. He dragged the wheelie bin down to the gate and I sat just inside the gate until he had put it out in the lay-by and then he called me out. There were a couple of cars and a tractor coming from different directions, so he stood in the lay-by and waited and I sat beside him until the traffic had passed. It happened that the point where the car from out of the village and the tractor from the direction of the village was right outside the cottage and the road being not the widest road in the world, the tractor driver, without slowing, put one wheel through the edge of the lay-by. Right through the puddle as it happens! The Owner, after shouting a few words that I pretend not to understand, turned and shuffled back in doors to change into a clean and dry pair of trousers and a dry coat. I on the other hand, do not have that luxury; I only have the one coat, although at this time of the year I am doing my best to leave most of it over the carpet. So, him with dry clothes and me leaving a trail of water on the floor wherever I walked, we left for the studio for the second time that morning. There is still no water in the pond although being the lowest point for miles it does seem to have its fair share of puddles on the road nearby. As we approached the pond there was another van approaching at some speed, it was white so I felt The Owner would have had an opinion about the driver which was less than favourable. He stepped onto the grass bank to get out of the way and I did my thing and sat down beside him. White Van Hoomun drove through the puddle by the pond at great speed and I was right, The Owner did have an opinion that was less than favourable. So for the second time in less than an hour he is wet through and I am just wetter than I was previously. Being closer to the studio than the cottage and presumably because he had no more dry clothes at home, we continued our shuffle down to the studio. During the next hour or two, from the vantage point of my comfy cushion under his desk I could see The Owner's foot, with water steadily dripping onto the floor. Last night it was dark when we went home and although I can see very well in the dark, I suspect The Owner can't. A cars headlights appeared in the distance and he stepped sideways with the kind of steps that people make when they can't see where they are putting their feet and he stepped straight into a rather deep puddle at the edge of the road. There was much swearing and then silence for the rest of the day. I hope today is a little better for him.

Halloween and all Things Related

As I study hoomun behaviour, every once in a while I think I am getting the hang of it and then I get thrown another curve ball and I finish up in deeper poo, and not the kind I can get my shoulder down in either. Tonight was just such an occasion and I am now in the boot room but the back door is open so I have been able to get out and reap the spoils of my earlier misdemeanour. Top of my list of unfathomable hoomun behaviour is "Halloween". Now what's that all about then? All evening the hoomun kids from the little estate in the village have been banging on the door demanding treats from The Owner. I was understandably anxious that The Owner may have given them one of my Bonio's but he did give them a little hoomun treat which was a big mistake as it turned out. Word got around and half the neighbouring town's kids from around the county were beating a path to our front door. After the fifth group of kids banging on the front door The Owner was showing signs of losing his charitable bon homme so I thought I would help out a little and I lay in wait up the top of the garden. A car pulled up in the lay-by and I waited until they got up to the front door before I launched my charge. Silently racing through the cherry orchard, round by the satellite dish letting out my fiercest bark as I arrived in the porch....... well I didn't know he had ordered a Chinese take away to be delivered did I? Chinese Delivery Yoof stood rooted to the spot in terror and dropped the bag with the take-away all over the porch floor. The Owner didn't seem pleased to see his tea all over the floor as it happens. Chinese Delivery Yoof seemed unable to understand the mistake either and he seemed to imply that The Owner may be needing to get someone else to deliver his tea in future. So as I said, I am in the boot room but the back door is open. So if you'll excuse me, I am off to have another quick lick of the front porch floor. The Owner has cleared up but I think there may be just a bit more flavour to be extracted from the stone floor.

Terminal Five

Well, what a morning I have had already. I have been beyond Swindon and discovered that it is indeed a very strange and wondrous place! Early this morning, very early this morning, The Owner came grumbling down the stairs. It was so early that I had barely finished my dream of a bevy of lady chocolate labs carrying me shoulder high to a secret room that had the walls stacked high with Bonio boxes. I had not yet had time to get on to the one where I gamble carefree through the meadows and wake myself up when I hit my head on my food bin in the boot room through the urgency of my twitching. I wasn't about to complain as he then fed me. Then Phlee Dog Owner turned up in his car and off we went..... past Swindon! We arrived at a place that I think was called Terminal Five, which is a very strange name for a place, then Phlee Dog Owner jumped out, grabbed his bag and ran off through the crowds and left me and The Owner in the car park! I fancied a quick patrol of the big field but I couldn't find a way through the fence and it was far too high to jump over it. As it turned out it was probably for the better as there were what I thought may have been big buses although they were very high off the ground and they had funny flat arms coming out of their sides. I don't think they would get one of them down through the village picking up the kids for school in the morning! All these people were getting on them and then they drove off, albeit a bit noisily, and then this really big one went very fast and very loudly down this big road and then suddenly the front end was pointing at the sky and it was off the ground!!!!! All of its wheels!!! Off the ground!!!! I last saw it heading for the moon, I think! There was also a K9 called Sniffer Black Lab and he was totally out of control. He went round sniffing at all these hoomuns in a manner that most hoomuns seem to disapprove of. When I do that I usually get a sharp slap across the nose and a disapproving look from The Owner. Anyway, there was this lady hoomun with a big bag and Sniffer Black Lab went up to her and did paws and then she got tied up and taken away somewhere. When I do paws I usually expect a Bonio, I now realise that the other side of Swindon it must means something very different. I think I ought to remember that, it may come in very handy! We didn't see Phlee Dog Owner again but I think he may be very cross with The Owner when we see him again, The Owner took his car and he drove home again. I am a bit worried about those big buses still, I have been keeping a very wary eye upwards as the moon has now disappeared from the sky and the bus must be still up there somewhere looking for it. It is a very strange place the other side of Swindon and I am not keen to go again.

Checking The Sky

After yesterday witnessing such strange goings on the other side of Swindon, which the hoomuns around there seemed to accept as perfectly normal, it has been preying on my mind and to be honest I didn't sleep a wink last night thinking about it. I watched intently as the bus picked up the kids this morning to take them to school and it certainly didn't show any signs of lifting all its wheels off the ground and heading to the moon. Yet yesterday I watched a massive bus on big legs and wheels with funny things poking out the side, which frankly would have made it impossible to get round the corner in the village by the church, take on loads of hoomuns and then jump off the ground into the sky and head to the moon with altogether far too much noise for my liking! The Owner seemed to accept it as normal as well, but that doesn't mean much as anything he does seems to fall far short of being normal as far as I can see. I didn't see the big bus come back down to the ground so I have to assume that it is still up there somewhere and I have spent much of my time today watching, just in case it comes back down here somewhere. I may need to have an opinion if it tries to land in the village!

The Dyson is at it Again!

Yesterday it seemed obvious from the start that someone was coming to see us. The Dyson was dragged out of hibernation from under the stairs. That put The Owner in a bad mood, I thought, straight away, and so early in the day! Well, when he put all that stuff in that cupboard I remember quite distinctly forming the opinion it may be a little unsafe to push it all in and shut the door quick, but The Owner had clearly forgotten exactly what was behind the door as he opened the door with a flourish and promptly disappeared under a deluge of odds and sods that came tumbling out. I beat a hasty retreat to my comfy cushion in case I was blamed in some way for the fall-out which was quite fortunate as it happened because I found a crumb from a discarded Bonio underneath it. The Owner started pushing my nemesis around the carpets and it confirmed some of my suspicions about its intent. On the carpet and presumably out of The Owner's gaze, was a handkerchief which the Dyson devoured with great gusto and promptly blocked the pipe. There then followed much grumbling as he removed the blockage and cleared up some of the dust and my hair for the second time in as many minutes. Minutes later it turned its attentions to some length of speaker wire which wound itself around the brushes and prompted the use of words that I pretend not to understand. Now this all did not bode well for a peaceful day, however I may have been wrong as Owners Daughter turned up and had a box of Bonio's in her car boot and perhaps a little bizarrely, two bananas! I never did discover the significance of the bananas but I am very aware of the significance of a box of Bonio's. Of course the significance of a visit from Owners Daughter is that everything is turned off and not left on stand by and The Owner has been grumbling more than a little at having to get up and turn everything on again after he has settled down with the squidger which never seems as efficient at turning things on when the appliance it relates to is turned off by Owners Daughter.

Vic R Must Have Said Something

Yesterday was a bit of a strange day really. We set off, as if on patrol, about mid-morning as far as I can tell but we stayed on the roads up past the farm which left me a bit confused as normally any patrol that stays on the roads and goes past the farm is heading for the pub and as far as I can tell it was far too early for that. Even in The Owner's surreal world! Then we jumped over the hedge and across the fields. I hadn't been across here before so I had to have a few wee's up hedges and stuff, just in case The Owner got lost coming back. He was carrying something with a lot of red on it with him as we went; something I also hadn't seen before. We eventually re-emerged back on to the road up near where Vic R seems to come from and went up some steps and found a big stone thing which The Owner wouldn't let me wee up. He gave me a very hard stare and I reasoned that it was probably not worth the trouble I would be in if I tried. Sometimes you get those feelings when it gets into your mind to do something, have you ever noticed? The Owner sat there for a while swinging the red round thing by his side, seemingly lost in thought until Vic R appeared and a lot of other people also carrying red things. They all stood around the stone thing whilst Vic R spoke a lot and sung a bit and then he must have said something wrong coz there was a bit of an uneasy silence for a couple of minutes and one or two seemed a bit upset by the whole thing. I have noticed this kind of behaviour when one of the two ladies from the village has passed wind and everyone tries to pretend they haven't noticed. (Except the times when someone decides it would be better to blame me for the smell wafting around.) Even The Owner stopped his grumbling for a couple of minutes. Then everyone went up and put their red things on the steps of the stone thing and then talked a lot. Now I reckon they are all going to be in trouble later as when they all left none of them thought to pick up their red things which I believe were called poppies and left them on the stone thingy. Now I've seen the terrible state Church Warden gets himself in when the kids leave stuff in the churchyard that shouldn't be there and it really is not a sight for the faint hearted so when he comes and finds this little lot I feel sure he is going to have an opinion on the matter and it won't be a very positive one!

The Owner and the Slug

The Owner has had a less than perfect start to his day and so I am expecting mine to get worse! In recent weeks he has informed me that there has been a slug in the studio overnight. I was a little disbelieving at first as I had witnessed him going up the stairs to bed each night, I had heard him snoring away all night long and I had seen him come grumbling down the stairs again the following morning. So how could he have known? It turns out that the strange silvery marks on the carpet are not actually down to me at all, but are the "evidence" of the slug's nocturnal perambulations around the studio carpet. You would think with that much "evidence" (The Owner has been watching far too many crime dramas recently) as to where the slug had been it would be a straightforward process finding where it was. Even I couldn't find it! So each morning the carpet was further covered by the remains of a slimy trail and The Owner became more depressed that we couldn't find it. This morning he found it!! You'd have thought he would have been pleased, but oh no! There has been much huffing and puffing and yucking and I think it may be the calf sheds for me today for my own safety. We got to the studio as normal this morning and, as normal, he makes a mug of tea (I never get one unless Owners Daughter or Small Boy are here) and settles down to read his emails and other hoomun stuff. Placing his big mug on the desk beside him he absent mindedly took a sip periodically. It was during one of these sips that I witnessed one of those beautiful moments when two species really connect. Gastropod Mollusc and Hoomun, eye to eye! It seems that Slug, as we are now on first name terms, joined by a common bond of being on the rough end of The Owners morning temper, had apparently felt that he liked the sensation of the warmth of the mug through his belly and slithered up the side of The Owner's tea mug. Slugs eyes, by his very nature, are on stalks and so were The Owner's when he realised what he was looking at and was about to take a sip from. There has been a lot of yucking over the last half an hour and the tea mug has been thrown out and so has Slug. I'll be in the calf sheds if anyone wants me.

A Slug's Humour

Now I know very little of the behaviour of Slug or his family but I am beginning to suspect there may be a sense of humour there somewhere. Yesterday you may recall that The Owner shared a beautiful moment with Slug, as two species met, eye to eye. The Owner responded a little harshly and threw Slug (and the mug he had slithered up to warm his belly) outside in the cold. This morning when The Owner and I arrived at the studio he threw the door open wide and strode confidently inside expecting a slug free environment. He made his new mug of tea and went and sat down at his desk as usual to examine the contents of his inbox and probably swear a lot if usual behaviour is anything to go by. I was right, he did swear a lot, but not at the contents of e-mails on his screen. There, at a pretty precise angle of forty five degrees across his mouse mat, was a silver slug trail. He is now on a mission to find the culprit and the normal clutter on the desk has all been moved, examined, and then put back in place and all to no avail as yet. I have been kicked off my comfy cushion, twice, and it has been lifted shook out and put back again. I do appreciate the humour of leaving a slimy slug trail across the mouse mat but I am getting a little tired of being moved and then re-moved as The Owner searches for Slug again. I think I may wander home and see if the wood burner is any warmer.... and free of slugs!

He's Evicted MY Wood Burner

The Owner is up to something this morning and I have yet to understand what. I heard him come grumbling down the stairs this morning and put the kettle on, empty the tea pot and burp loudly, you don't really need a commentary on some of the other noises he made. The excitement on my side of the door is mounting as the next stage in the process will be to open the door to the boot room and then let me up the garden to relieve the pressure a little before BREAKFAST! Nothing unusual so far you will be thinking, and you would be right. Kettle boiled, tea made, he wanders off into the lounge, more burping and...... well you don't want to know the other noises he made as he wandered off either. As I am enjoying the breakfast chomp I can hear him in the lounge making noises at the wood burner. More excitement from me at the thought that the wood burner has been stoked up and will be roaring nicely when I have finished breakfast and go in to explore the living room and see what I may have missed on the lounge carpet last night that may be edible. There never is, but I live in hope. Nearly finished breakfast when I see The Owner come wandering past struggling under the weight of a big black metal box leaving a trail of dust on the carpet behind him which will probably command the attentions of that ruddy Dyson in a short while. I thought nothing of it, until I wandered into the living room..........and...........no!........... IT'S GONE!!!!!!!!!!!!!!!!!!!! That metal box he was carrying was the wood burner!!!!!!!!!!!!!!!! My friend!!!!!!!!!!!!! What is he doing????????????????? When we left for our morning patrol and the studio there was just an empty grate and a pile of ash where, until last night, was the object of much of my affection. Has he lost the plot again? I am beginning to think so!

Exit Wood burner - Bring On The Open Fire!

Well this answers the question about what The Owner was up to

yesterday I guess! We came home early from the studio yesterday and it was still daylight and The Owner made a mug of tea (with no slugs) and sat out the front of the cottage reading his paper. The Log Hoomun turned up with a load of logs. Now I was confused at this because there was nowhere to burn any logs anymore! Log Hoomun I have never really had an opinion about either way really. True, he has never brought me any Bonio's, but then neither has he ever upset me and he does always make a fuss of me. But today I did have an opinion. When Log Hoomun and The Owner had unloaded all the logs and put them all in the fuel shed he let me in the back of his van.... I like cars, they are my favourite! Log Hoomun and The Owner went to the shops and The Owner bought me a box of Bonio's, which incidentally The Owner has forgotten to bring to the studio this morning, so if Log Hoomun drove us to the shops for Bonio's there are two reasons why I should have a favourable opinion of him. When we got back The Owner went into the fuel shed and started throwing all the logs back out again! He also started using words that I pretend not to understand, I was shocked. When he had dug down through the heap sufficiently to get under the oil tank he dived under and emerged looking triumphant with the old log fire basket. So last night we were properly toasty and I had to re-learn old skills. The art of curling up in front of a real fire and going from sound asleep to wide awake and the other side of the room quicker than saying "Bonio's three times a day would be nice please!" every time the fire spits. Not completing that little task is just too painful to consider, and I have been there! I am looking forward to another evening in front of the fire. Happy days!

On Christmas Lights

We are approaching that time of year again when hoomun behaviour takes some very strange twists and turns which I generally find unfathomable, more so than the rest of the year. In the village, near the pub (and I'm sure that those two facts aren't necessarily connected), some folk turn their houses into a lighting system worthy of the landing lights at Lyneham. Including having some hoomun that spends over a month all lit up sat on the roof! The down side to all this light is that when on patrol one can't have a moment's peace and quiet to do - you know - doggie stuff, without being on display to the world. The Owner gets to shut himself away in the bathroom for a quiet moment reading the Sunday paper whilst he performs. I would like a few moments to myself to contemplate nature without having my activities all illuminated, but with those lights it ain't gonna happen.

So The Owner has been going around singing carols (and if I were Carol I think I'd have an opinion on the matter) and sounding generally far too full of good humour. Christmas is usually not The Owner's favourite time of the year, in fact The Owner normally uses another word in front of Christmas, one which I pretend not to understand and then Owners Daughter frowns at him very loudly and calls him Ebenezer. But all this jolliness was quite unnerving for a K9 as it would have to break at some point and this morning was it. The bread was still in the freezer and was singularly uncooperative when he tried to cut some for his toast so he managed to find just enough to cut two thin slices from the old stale loaf and put in the toaster. I think the toaster is treading on very dangerous ground at the moment, as it has developed a habit of burning his toast and this morning it did it spectacularly well, together with his fingers, the wall cupboard and his Pyrex jug and he has spent the day with his fingers bandaged and doing his best to extract every last ounce of sympathy from anyone fool enough to listen to him. I think tomorrow we are off to B&Q to get some new wall cupboards for the kitchen. I don't mind that at all as there is a burger van hoomun in the car park who I have managed to get the odd sausage or two from in the past, using the superior willpower of a K9 on matters relating to food. However I suspect the build and installation of these wall units could be a somewhat hazardous affair and may involve more bandages on fingers. I will report on proceedings over the weekend.

Windy Bridges

I was watching the weather forecast this morning, with The Owner, when I heard something which caused me to whirl around and look at him, looking for some kind of reassurance about what Weatherman Hoomun had just said. He said that it was going to be windy! So windy, in fact, that hoomuns should expect to get blown off bridges! Well I was about to go out on patrol when I heard this and I was understandable perturbed by what I had heard. At the far end of the cricket field there is a little bridge across the stream, now I can leap energetically across without having to use the bridge, but The Owner has to walk gently across and I really don't want to be around if he gets blown off the bridge! In fact, even if we go down behind The Manor, there is still a little bridge made of railway sleepers that he will have to cross. I think I may take his walking boots and hide them somewhere; I will be in dead trouble when he finds them, but the trouble may be even worse if he gets blown off the bridge! Hopefully we will just go to B&Q instead. Oh no! I have just remembered that there is a bridge to go over the little river just the other side of town.......... and another one in Chippenham!!!!!!!!!!! I may have to hide his keys as well!

The Owner's Soggy Trouser Leg

Now, I have a confession. The day was a lot more successful than I had feared. I nicked The Owner's boots to prevent him from getting blown off the bridge the other side of the cricket pitch, and then his keys to prevent him from getting blown off the bridge in Chippenham. The success was, that I managed to then get the missing items back, and then found, by The Owner, without arousing any suspicion that I may have been behind it. Now, for my confession, coz that wasn't it; I have a weakness, and The Owner has gone upstairs to change his trousers! The two things are connected. He ordered a take away and sat here and ate it. My weakness is not for sweet and sour chicken, can't stand the stuff! My weakness is not for rice, or noodles; can't see the point and the rice always gets in places I'd rather not divulge here. But he sat there with a bag of prawn crackers and I have a weakness for a prawn cracker (or two) and I, well, dribbled. Just a little! Not a lot you understand! And it just happened to be when I had my mouth above his trouser leg. He has made far too much of it in my opinion and has gone upstairs in a strop to change his trousers. Now, the good thing about being in trouble, in my opinion the best way of managing the trouble, is that you get it all over and done with in one go. You can't get into trouble when you are already in it so, well, he left his prawn crackers unguarded. Let's just say they are now not quite the prawn crackers that they were, "ex"-prawn crackers in fact and I have taken myself off to the boot room as a precaution. More of a certainty really.

Loose Wires on the Sound Deck

Last night The Owner said we were going to go "Out". I wasn't too sure where "Out" was at first but it turned out to be the village hall. Not sure why it has two names. Anyway, tonight The Village Hall will be known as "Out" and when we got there and went inside (I'm not really supposed to be in there) there were all these tables and chairs set out for hoomuns to sit at and some people with lots of makeup on kept popping out from behind a curtain and behaving in a very dramatic fashion. The Owner sat at the "Sound

Desk" and the "Lighting Desk". I'm not sure what one of those are either but it had lots of buttons on top and wires coming out the back and The Owner clearly thought it made him very important to have his own seat and two desks and his own light when everyone else had to sit in the dark with candles. I was told to sit under the "Sound Desk" on his bag so that I wouldn't be noticed by The Director (who sounded very important) and risk getting asked to leave. I soon worked out that when The Owner twiddled with one of his buttons and switches the lights at the front went on and off and made lots of different sounds quite loudly. I thought at first he may have been in trouble but The Director seemed generally pleased with his efforts, so it must have been alright. Things were going swimmingly as The Owner was slurping loudly at his wine glass and during the second half; he even kicked off his shoes under the table. Now in the studio that usually means he will rub my belly with his toes whilst he works, so I rolled over on to my back. One of the wires fell off the back of the desk as I did so, but I paid no attention to it and I thought no one would notice in the darkness. They were building to a very dramatic crescendo on the stage where the curtains are and they were clearly expecting something to happen at that point as they all stood around with their hands on their hips looking at The Owner who was frantically twiddling at knobs and switches as they began to harrumph a lot. The Owner, for his part was protesting loudly that he was trying to turn it on but they were having none of it. He was frantically twiddling, and they were loudly harrumphing, when the audience started sniggering, then laughing loudly and I suspected The Owner was getting quite flustered by all the attention, so I stayed under the desk. Eventually, The Director came down with an air of great authority and picked up the wire off the floor beside me, plugged it back in and suddenly all the stage was lit up again. Well I didn't know!!!! I thought Owner's Daughter could frown loudly but The Director has got the art mastered to a far greater degree from what I could see of it, although I couldn't see much as I had crept further back behind the table and out of the way. Well I wasn't supposed to be there, so I didn't want to get The Owner into any trouble, The Owner appeared to be in enough of it as it was.

Neffyou Comes to Visit

Last night we went "Out" again. I went and sat under the sound desk again but it wasn't The Owner's feet that appeared. When I poked my nose out, when the coast was clear, I noticed he had been left in charge of folding up raffle tickets. Presumably as some kind of admonishment for not turning the lights on when required on the previous night. Today we have had Neffyou come and visit with his mates. The Owner refers to him as Neffme as he says it makes it sound more personal and then laughs very loudly at his own joke. The first time he mentioned it last night it was mildly amusing and some fool laughed, someone who clearly had no idea about not encouraging The Owner in such matters. Thereafter, eager to seek more praise and popularity he was telling everyone and laughing very loudly himself. He was originally left in charge of selling raffle tickets but after he had scared two kids, one old lady hoomun and dropped the money box all over the floor, he was demoted to just folding tickets. Today he is busy with Neffyou down at the farm filming Neffyou's mates rolling around in the dust and straw on the floor. Their Mum's are going to be really cross with them when they get back. They seemed to want me to roll around on the floor with them, well that was not about to happen!!!! I remember what I had done in that straw when on patrol during last week!!

The Owner on an Icy Morning

This morning the expression "He who laughs last laughs longest", seemed to come to mind. When we left for morning patrol I observed the first proper frost of the winter, but temporarily forgot about the effects of frost upon the water. There had been quite a lot of water lying about overnight, the result of a couple of heavy showers during the evening, which the frost had turned to ice. My exit through the gate, with great excitement, was a somewhat ungainly affair and I ended up on my back with legs and tails going in all the wrong directions whilst The Owner laughed very loudly and pointed a lot. We continued the patrol, with me trying very hard to resist the urge to sulk over the insensitive way The Owner had behaved at my predicament and in fact was continuing to behave that way! As we got to the pond (still without water) The

Owner did a kind of little hop to get over the bank by the ditch and he too stepped on ice and fell on his back and waved his legs in the air a lot. I suffered in silence whilst The Owner made much of the whole affair and has been limping and wincing with every movement, eager for someone to notice his plight and ask how he is or something. Fortunately, no-one has obliged, so he may lose interest before long. I did manage to have a quick chomp on something a bit tasty that was lying under the hedge earlier. Come coffee time, I went up to The Owner for a little affection and mainly just to let him know I was there and not to forget my Bonio (I always have a Bonio when he has his coffee) when suddenly he went a funny colour and sent me under the desk out of his way!! It was only a little burp! Hardly worth all that fuss, I thought! He has been ignoring me for the rest of the day. I think he smells like a camel!

A Tale of Two Fires

What a busy time we have had, The Owner and me! Well actually it is The Owner who has been the busy one and I have been gainfully employed in keeping out of the way as it happens. Two things, and both, strangely, to do with fire! You may remember how Toaster got a little bit over the top in trying to upset The Owner's day at the start by burning his toast, along with much of the kitchen hanging cupboards. Well, I knew it had overstepped the mark and I was right, it was unceremoniously dropped in the wheelie bin. I wee'd on the bin later to signify my wish to be seen as siding with The Owner in his decision, just in case I overstep the mark myself one day and hope that he will remember and not throw me in there as well! So a visit to B&Q was in order for new units (and a sausage from Burger Van Hoomun when The Owner wasn't watching) after a quick stop by Curry's for a new toaster! When we returned home there was much unpacking of boxes and it was all going well until he went to get his electric drill/screwdriver. Battery flat! Boxes cleared away and wine bottle produced to while away the hour waiting for the charger to do its thing. I couldn't help but wonder whether the wine was a mistake, as we now have wall units that even I can see are not level. So much so that all the cups move to one side of the cupboard and the door keeps falling open! Now, the next fire. You may recall the eviction of my wood burner and the reinstatement of the open fire, together with all the hazards associated with it, like sparks and hot embers....oh yes, and smoke! The Owner has been back to B&Q and bought some bricks and some mud to stick them together with, and a big piece of metal (and another sausage from Burger Van Hoomun, but don't tell The Owner!). After much screwing (screwdriver charged up this time and no wine!) The Owner had fixed this big piece of metal across the top of the fireplace and then mixed up some of that mud stuff in the fireplace to stick all the bricks together. I feel Lady Cleaner Hoomun may have an opinion on mixing mud indoors when she comes later in the week but we'll see. The Owner arranged all the bricks and was very upset that some of them smell of wee! Now you see why I have kept out of the way? Well it was a heap of bricks in the garden and they are usually fair game for weeing up! After much banging and mixing The Owner stood up to survey the fruits of his labours and I must admit it did look quite nice and he ruffled the hair on my head and said "There we are Jack, that should stop the smoke!". So that was what this was all about! It didn't! Now I have mud, which The Owner calls Seement, stuck in my hairs on top of my head as well and I am worried in case I am seen out and about until I can get it out of my hair!

Kangaroo Chews

The Owner is being a little uncharitable towards me today and keeps calling me Skippy!

Yesterday a big parcel arrived from Oztralia. Now I have noticed just north of here is a place call New Zealand and The Owner tells me that Oztrailia is near New Zealand so I ought to try and keep an eye open to see the signs when next we go that way. In this parcel was some K9 chews with Kangaroo on the packet. Well I have looked them up on the laptop at home and they are indeed some strange looking critters! I mean, what happened to the rest of their front legs?!! So while The Owner was out of the way, and the packet of Kangaroo chews were unguarded, I nibbled the corner of the packet and "Borrowed" one. Well they were mine!!!! Sherlock

Holmes (AKA, The Owner) of course noticed straight away. How does he do that whenever I have been doing stuff he thinks I shouldn't do? Kangaroo chew inside me and telling off out of the way I opted to go and have a lie down on my comfy cushion, just for a few minutes. Well I fell asleep didn't I? Well there I was, in my dream, running through the paddock chasing Lady Chocolate Lab, when The Owner wakes me up with his laughing whilst pointing a finger at me telling me to stop twitching. Ever since he has been calling me Skippy!

I think he walk like a camel, smells a bit like one too!

Chrissmuss Morning in Swindon

Well yesterday answered several questions in my quest to understand the hoomun condition but posed several other conundrums for which I have absolutely no explanation!

Yesterday, The Owner came down the stairs as usual, except it was without the customary grumbling, he was singing! Singing about a Silent Night, which with his nocturnal grumblings and snoring is something unheard of in these parts. When I was let out of the boot room it came as something of a shock as he was wearing a piece of tinsel! Little else as it happened, as he fumbled around in the tumble dryer for his robe which he had forgotten to take out last night. Well if that was a bad way to start the day it got better, saying far too many "Yo ho ho's" to be plausible he presented me with the remains of my kangaroo chews that were posted to me from Oztraylia and also a packet of chews from my anonymous admirer known only as BH7 (Could be Blood Hound although I don't think they are numbered). I was immediately in trouble as The Owner left both packets unguarded whilst he made himself tea. Well they were mine!!!!!!!!!!!! I have been particularly careful not to twitch in my sleep ever since so as not to give The Owner any ammunition about Skippy again! We were collected soon by Volvo Hoomun and taken to his house, which appeared to be near Swindon! I like visiting houses, even in Swindon, so I wee'd up the door post to let others know I am about and went in, where I met Lady Volvo Owner, Volvo Daughter and Mother. They fed

The Owner and made him wear a paper hat which made him look quite silly but he didn't seem to mind. I have made a note that there wasn't even a sausage for me, reprisals may follow! I was then allowed upstairs!!! They didn't have beds for me to lie on with duvets and stuff upstairs but they had armchairs! Even I know that armchairs go downstairs! As I believe I may have mentioned before, anything seems to go when you are in Swindon! Compton Bassett seems a very safe place to be, I think. You know where you stand when you are in Compton Bassett.

Bath Time Again!

That's it! I am officially over Christmas! I am over hoomuns! I am over The Owner!

The Owner, as already reported, was up in a strange frame of mind this morning. I soon learned why when he stole my comfy cushion and put it in the washing machine. The day got worse, he disappeared upstairs to "Make myself beautiful!" as he puts it. I chose a small square of carpet to curl up on in the absence of my comfy cushion whilst he was out of the way. Then suddenly I hear him calling me from upstairs. Well after my experience at Volvo Hoomuns house yesterday where I discovered that there are sometimes armchairs and stuff upstairs I was eager to check it out so went off upstairs in answer to his call. That was when I discovered his betrayal! He put me in the bath!!!! He seems to think he can justify it by telling me I smell sweeter, I think I smell like a camel now. When he reached out of the bathroom door to get my towel he left a little crack in the door unguarded and I escaped. I take a little solace from being able to get dirty water sprayed up the landing walls, the stairwell walls, the dining room, the kitchen and it's probably best that I don't mention the living room here as its appearance seems to bring on an attack of the vapours from The Owner.

Visiting Friends

Yesterday I had a very good day! So much I did, so many people I saw, so many places I hadn't seen for far too long.

It started the previous evening when The Owner arrived back at the cottage in Phlee Dog Owner's car, but then left it out the front of the cottage and came in and went to bed. Early the following morning he was up again and he put me in the back of Phlee Dog Owner's car (I love cars, they are my favourite and I was so excited I had to wee up the gate post) and off we went, a long way, and then we picked up Diesel Dog Daughter! He drove a little bit further and then I was left in the car on my own, that was ok too as I like cars, had I mentioned that? When he returned he had not only Diesel Dog Daughter with him but Small Boy as well! Although he did smell of hospitals! We left Small Boy in the car park, I think he must have had an ooops and was being punished and in the absence of a boot room I guess the car park was next best thing. The Owner must have forgiven him as we soon went back for him and he had a bag with him this time so we all went to Owners Dad's next.

I managed to thieve some of Cat's food before The Owner chased me off so that was good. Then Horse turned up! Horse brought Owner's Sister and Mechanic too! Yet more excitement was to follow when Diesel Dog Daughter gave me a present which I was, frankly, less than enamoured with! Nail clippers for the K9! A bath one day, claws trimmed the next! This was not turning out so well! It turned out far worse for Horse when Owners

Sister picked up my K9 nail clippers and turned towards Horse with a, frankly, far too gleeful look in her eye for my liking!

I offer the picture as a sort of before and after image. This was me after my nails had been trimmed and before Owners Sister pounced upon Horse. You will notice my neatly manicured claws and the somewhat unkempt condition of Horse's claws. All in all, a thoroughly rewarding day; marred only by the brief incident with the nails! Oh yes, and the slightly regrettable incident with Owners Dad's sherry glass when Cat realised I was there.

The Dyson Has Started Its Demise (I Hope!)

The Owner dragged my nemesis out from its weekly hibernation and plugged it in. I don't hang around long enough to have any opinion on the way he uses it or anything further like that, I find somewhere to get out of the way of this demonic invention! Anywhere or anything will do for this purpose; I once tried to get behind the cooker out of the way. Now I know you are thinking to yourself that there isn't room behind the cooker, but you never know until you try, do you? Today I was a little more brave than normal and was peering round the corner of the bench in the hallway and bravely watched his activity. It was then I witnessed the first nail in the Dyson's coffin as with a loud pop the Dyson, The Owner and everything in the dining room disappeared in a large cloud of fine white dust. Now I couldn't help but wonder if that was meant to happen? I was soon answered by the amount of rude words that The Owner was using! After much banging and dismantling The Owner triumphantly produced a filter that he clearly was unaware was in it and pronounced to no one in particular that this was the root of the problem and put the ruddy Dyson back together again. He seemed to be of the opinion that he could finish terrorising me without the filter and was clearly pleased with his efforts as several little treats I had hidden about the dining room disappeared with a loud rattle up the pipe. I watched with some interest as it appeared to me to be a very clever way of doing things. All the bigger lumps were sucked up and collected in the clear box thing whilst all the fine dust was blown out of the vents and deposited on the table and the settee, indeed anywhere above ground level. I thought that was very good as I didn't have to walk in it and it was all out of the way above the kind of level where I can be normally blamed for anything. The Owner soon turned around and started using lots of rude words again so I guessed he hadn't intended that to happen. He is now trying to find a way of warming his hands; does anyone have a useful suggestion of thawing out my water bowl?

Russian Water

Today I will be keeping mostly out of the way! We had a bit of a thaw overnight and this morning, much of the snow has turned to slush or disappeared; which made morning patrol an uncomfortable affair. But at least my water bowl seems to stay mainly liquid which is a bonus for me! So, morning patrol and all associated grumbling about the weather, the cold, the damp and the fact that they didn't have his normal Sunday paper this morning over and done with, he made himself a coffee and selected a particularly nice looking Bonio from my tin to give to me (I hope) and we went and sat down. Have I mentioned that I am particularly fond of the odd Bonio or two? Mid-way through a heavenly Bonio chomp I heard an unusual noise, like rushing water, coming from the loft. Well it wasn't me as I have never been allowed up there, as dogs don't do step ladders. Well, this one doesn't anyway! Moments later, water wasn't the only thing to be rushing as The Owner ran outside and reappeared soon after carrying his step ladder. I thought "He is about to trap his fingers again and leak round his eyes." I was right! He did trap his fingers in the step ladder and run around with eyes leaking whilst holding his fingers! Sometimes I even surprise myself! Moments later after a quick trip into the loft The Owner reappeared, clearly having not found the source of the problem, (although I could clearly hear a lot of water rushing up there) he was running around the house, banging and shouting a lot. I couldn't help but wonder if all that water rushing out from under the boiler may perhaps have had anything to do with it, although I am no plumber. Clearly I was right as when he removed the covers the water sprayed the distance of at least twenty Bonio boxes laid end to end, after it had first soaked The Owner. I did once lay twenty Bonio boxes end to end and nobody seemed in the slightest bit surprised, but that has nothing to do with this story. The Owner rushed around with spanners and an air of authority, getting very wet until all the water from the tank, if it wasn't over the floor, was over The Owner! He is now sitting in a sodden heap in the middle of the lounge carpet with his cold mug of coffee and making MY square of carpet in front of the fire very wet indeed! I mean, where am I going to lie to toast myself???? Usually when such disasters befall The Owner it somehow transpires to be my fault and his mood looks very black indeed so I am not going to attract much attention to myself for a while.

Squirrel's Nuts

I think The Owner may be having a strong word with Squirrel when he next emerges from his hibernation which, judging by the temperatures out there already this evening ought not to be for some while. So maybe The Owner might have forgotten about today's little discovery by then. I have noticed during the late summer and autumn how Squirrel fervently hides little heaps of nuts all over the garden in case he wakes during the winter and fancies a quick chomp. Indeed last summer three chestnut trees appeared in the middle of the lawn as a result of just such an activity. They were doing well I thought and nearly high enough to have a wee up when Small Boy cut The Owner's lawns for him. Today, being another chilly morning in The Owner's world he went upstairs for an extra jumper before venturing outside. Grabbing last year's favourite fleece to put on, a large quantity of hazel nuts, chestnuts and acorns tumbled across the floor, presumably deposited there by Squirrel during the summer and autumn. I am thinking that maybe The Owner might not be so keen to show off by leaving his bedroom window open in all weathers now.

Frozen Ponds and Other Cold Stuff

Well, morning patrol is over and I am gainfully employed finding a comfy square of carpet to lie upon near the fire (when The Owner can be bothered to light it), together with imaginative ways of avoiding the ruddy Dyson. Which, incidentally, is still throwing all the dust it sucks up out through the vents and depositing it on the furniture, but The Owner clearly feels it makes a difference. I can still hear The Owner's laughter ringing in my ears at the look of confusion and befuddlement upon my face when I got to the pond a little earlier. I was feeling a bit frisky this morning as we strode purposefully out of the cottage and down the icy path where The Owner couldn't be bothered to clear the snow and just packed it down as he walked on it. I had a quick wee up my tree for good measure and launched forth from the gate and came face to face with Postman who was clearly as surprised to see me as I was him, judging by the way we both slithered a little and then fell in a big heap on the frozen puddle. He recovered himself and gave me a particularly hard stare which I felt was a little uncalled for and thrust some brown envelopes in The Owner's hand, which I suspect will mean more of his head in hands "How Much? mantra later. The Owner, with his collar up and hands stuffed firmly in his pockets, shuffled off down the road whilst I ran like a demented badger surveying my territory. There is an interloper at the moment called Jack Collie Dog who occasionally wee's on some of my posts but I am faster than him and I can wee higher, so no damage there then. We soon came to the pond and the cause of my ire this morning. As I said, I was feeling a bit frisky, so I thought I would launch forth into the water and make a big splash. Well I didn't know it was going to be frozen!!!!!!! I was sailing through the air, paws out-stretched, waiting for the splash when I made contact with ice and left a series of score marks from my claws in the ice as I pirouetted across the surface and came to a halt under the tree. Where, after a strange cracking sound the ice gave way and deposited me very unceremoniously into the water. The Owner laughed loudly at my predicament and pointed a lot as I clambered out of the ice and up the bank by the tree. I'm afraid all friskiness had departed my spirit at this point and I skulked home and left The Owner to finish the patrol alone. I think he walks like a camel anyway, and if he'd stop laughing long enough for me to get close I feel sure he would smell like one as well!

The Clean Kitchen Floor

The Owner has a new best friend, and whenever he gets a new best friend I manage to find myself in trouble. After his particular insensitivity yesterday to my predicament with the icy pond and then his subsequent taunting me with that ruddy Dyson, I was feeling a little less than charitable towards him. Then this morning, from the depths of his shopping bags that he didn't get around to putting away yesterday, he produced a pack of floor wipes. I had slept on my lack of charity towards The Owner overnight, aided more than a little by The Owner allowing me to sleep inside and not in that cold and draughty boot room and so was feeling a lot more forgiving. After coffee this morning he takes his new best friend and attacks the kitchen floor, although I couldn't help but feel he may have been better off starting at the far end and working his way to the door rather than the other way around. After much hard labour he sat in the only corner left uncleaned looking generally pleased with himself. Now I had noticed that when Lady Chocolate Lab Owner used to visit and The Owner had worked hard or achieved something worthy of merit she would give him a hug and then slobber all over his face as hoomuns tend to do. She, being not a fixture here any longer after he got a little unsteady on his feet one night at the pub on a business meeting and knocked the stool over and upset Vic R, I thought I ought to at least go and reward him with a fuss. Well I had absolutely no idea there was mud on my paws! And anyway, it was only a little bit of mud. Not worth the fuss I thought! I may not have spent last night in the boot room but it appears I am going to make up for it today and I am feeling less than charitable towards him again now. I have managed to find his jacket that he wears to meetings and dragged it out and on to the floor. I'll give him muddy paws!!!!

The Pet Shop

Today we have been to Town. Now I am in the boot room and The Owner is meowing at me which I think is very childish and immature! It is that time when my food bin requires refilling and because he created a fuss at my favourite shop of all time, about the labelling of the prices on the shelves not agreeing with the prices on the till, we are unable to buy my food from there ever again. Together with the garden centre and several other shops locally. So we went to Town to find another food shop and I have to say I reeeeeally liked this one. He put me on a lead when we got out of the car which usually means we are going to the pub and I was a little concerned that this far from home might be a problem if he had too much to drink and we had to walk home. But I needn't have worried! After a short walk through Town, where there were lots of lamp posts to wee up and stuff, we arrived at Pet Shop and went in. It smelled really good in there but The Owner was particularly interested in the shelf above my head height where there was lots of things for dogs, including dog whistles (we have three already) and it was then that I noticed that along the floor at my head height were lots of bins with interesting things in. One bin with pigs ears in (thank you very much, just the one then), then we moved along a little (loose Bonio's, one for now and keep one for later thank you). Then we moved a bit further and there were loose Shapes biscuits (just a couple then). Next move, chewy sticks (ok then, if I am quick). The next bin had something I had never seen before and proved to be my undoing. In it was this grey stuff, quite fine and powdery I thought, so I had a quick chomp of a sample. It was then I started to cough and it attracted the attention of Pet Shop Hoomun. It would seem that K9's aren't meant eat cat litter apparently! Well how was I to know!?!?! The Owner had to pay for the rest of my lunchtime snack which Pet Shop Yoof had been noting on his pad, which brought on an attack of the vapours, together with my bag of food. With the extra expense, he dispensed with the other things he had picked up to buy, including another dog whistle, but he had to resist the temptation to refer the whole process to Watchdog on the BBC as there aren't any other Pet Shops around here that he isn't banned from. So now, every time he passes the boot room door, he is meowing at me. Hoomuns can be so childish sometimes. Well, The Owner can be!

Some thoughts on a Blue Tooth

Well today I thought The Owner had finally lost it! There are a few, less charitable than myself and probably without the breeding either, who have alluded to The Owner having lost it ages ago. If indeed he ever had it in the first place. I have always chosen to hold on to the hope that whatever "it" is, there may be a small shadow of "it" still residing in there somewhere; particularly when in hope of a Bonio. Have I mentioned that I am really quite fond of the odd Bonio? He has been shopping again and I could tell from the manic giggling and chortling from the front of the car on the way back that he had bought himself something that had piqued his interest and fired his imagination. A dangerous combination I have come to realise! We arrived back at the cottage and there was much ripping of cardboard followed by a great deal of words that I pretend not to understand. The cross words were caused by the standard of packaging and the packagers ability to hide the little tab to pull on, by which it all seems to come undone. I found just such a tab one day on The Owner's jumper and it all came undone very easily after a quick tug on that. He was in frightful bait after that too! After first using his thumbnail, then his teaspoon, followed by his pen knife he eventually finished up by retrieving his hammer from the shed and beating it into submission as he does on every other occasion when packaging gets the better of him. It was at this point I noticed the rather odd behaviour start, all the previous behaviour being normal for him. I thought at first he was talking to someone, but there was no-one there. I thought then that perhaps he was talking to me but as I have not got any bricks for him to order let alone deliver them for him by Friday I guessed that he was not talking to me either. His new toy and best friend is a new Bluetooth Jawbone headset, I know, because he has been ringing everyone up whilst standing beside the washing machine when it is spinning and saying to them can you hear that? Then laughing uncontrollably as he explains that the washing machine (nearly as demonic as the ruddy Dyson) is right beside him and working flat out. He has even been knocking on the front door to get me to bark loudly and snarl a bit whilst on his "Bluetooth Jawbone". After the tenth time of doing that (maybe more, I lost count) I have stolen it from the coffee table when he wasn't looking and buried it in the garden! That should have put paid to the problem for a while although he is now rushing around upending all the furniture and other stuff looking for it, which is nearly as distracting as when he was using it! Next I predict he will be arguing with the insurance call centre and swearing about Merekats again. Today shows all the promise of a day without any peace at all. I think I may go and snuggle up with the calves in the straw bales. True, they do make quite a bit of noise, but it may be quieter than here!

The Train to Bath

Yesterday was a day of ups and downs. It started well, went through moments of terror and then finished on a high of chewy treats. The Owner took me to the station yesterday and I have never been to one of them before so I was particularly excited. I was a little confused at first as The Owner put me on a lead, I normally only wear a lead in the pub (pub rules) and it was quite early in the day for that. But then we jumped in a car and went to The Station. I use capital letters to add an air of gravitas. There were many posts all over the platform for me to wee up and I did my best! I didn't want to appear greedy and wee on them all but there was a group of small shiny posts all together so I thought I would just do them and call it a day. Well I've never seen a Zimmer frame before and I felt Old Lady Hoomun made far too much of my mistake to be honest! Fortunately the train arrived with a great deal to say on the matter and that was really quite exciting. Actually it was quite terrifying and a little bit of wee dribbled out which was a bit embarrassing. Station Master was a bit rude as well, he said to The Owner, "Keep that dog away from the gap"!!!!! THAT DOG????? Does he not realise I was born on Lord Bath's estate? I have breeding! And I can assure you that I have no intention of falling down there, so I hopped in a particularly nimble fashion on to the train, just to prove a point. Well it was quite nice on the train, lots of hoomuns and they were all very friendly, apart from The Owner who just grumbled a lot but that was normal. Then, from nowhere, it happened!! "Bing bong bing! All those for Bath get off here!" Bath?!?!?!? Is that where we were going? All this way just to have a Bath!! Have I been duped???? Well I wasn't going to get off there, so I tried to hide under the seat. The Owner dragged me out from under there and lifted me onto the platform. I was not going to make this easy for him so he had to drag me across the platform and I left a long line of claw marks behind me. All the way to the stairs! I don't do baths!!! Well I think the bing bong bing hoomun was only teasing as we didn't have a bath; instead we went to a hotel for lunch and met Lady Chocolate Lab and Lady Chocolate Lab Owner so I thought it was a good day out on reflection. When we got back to the cottage last night The Owner got his post and did his usual mantra of head in hands and saying "How much?" but there was a big parcel there and I could see my name on it. My friend called BH7 had sent me some more chewy sticks!!! I like my friend from BH7! I just wish I knew who it was!

The Bus and the Bus Stop

Today I have had an adventure, and for those of you, who are observing that my adventures of late have taken me into very different territory, you would be right and I am not so comfortable with it! Today I have been exploring and trying (desperately) to understand hoomuns in different places and circumstances. Today I was taken (on a lead and no pub rules applied here) down to the Bus Stop! I have never been on a bus before so I was perhaps understandably a little concerned when we got there. It seemed a little understated I thought, the Bus Stop. No doors, no curtains at the windows, in fact it was all windows, but I sat there, amongst some very strange deposits that even I could not have mustered, all over the floor. I was certainly not going to sniff that lot, I have breeding I do!! Then the bus turned up. Now I am seeing the connection here, Bus Stop and Bus, which stopped, but when it did the door opened and then it lowered itself! Well I was not about to get on that!! So The Owner had to carry me on, how embarrassing? We got to Chippenham on the Bus but he (Driver Hoomun) did seem to stop more than The Owner when going to The Pub on a Friday night when trying to show off his latest car! We walked to an office (and not The Owners) from another Bus Stop, (there seems to be more than one) but when we got there the doors were shut, but as we walked up to it the door opened, on its own! The Owner walked in but I was not about to follow, moving doors, and no one opening them?? I was carried in, how embarrassing was that?? I felt vindicated and insulted at the same time; The Owner was told he couldn't bring me in, "That Dog was not allowed in"! Hello? I have breeding I do! As we walked out I wee'd on the door post as a mark of disdain, although looking at the door pillar there were quite a few stains already there as well as the disdain that I was depositing. I am guessing that he won't be getting that job either! When we got to the Bus Stop in Chippenham for our return trip I was a little more prepared for the strange things that happen with Buses, however I was not prepared for what happened next. The Owner tried to whisk me up the stairs!! I was not about to go up there!!!!! I was carried up the stairs, how embarrassing was that? After our return trip on the Bus, home was a welcome sight and a comforting Bonio was called for, well, ok two were called for! Now where is my comfy cushion?

The Badger Poo Virgin!

Oh man was I in trouble last night! I know you hoomuns have a saying about a problem being better when shared, well I now can see the merit in the argument. Yesterday afternoon I was pleasantly surprised to see Lady Chocolate Lab and Lady Chocolate Lab Owner turn up at the cottage. As, presumably, was The Owner given that he was still wandering around in his boxer shorts and little else. That situation under control and his legs covered by some trousers, which he had only put in the tumble dryer five minutes before. He looked a comical sight as he wandered around for the next few minutes with steam coming from his legs and bum. We all four of us went for a walk across the hill. I was particularly pleased about this as I knew that up the top of the hill there is a badger sett and I have noticed there is evidence of badgers having been about over night when on patrol in the mornings. Now you're ahead of me here aren't you? Badgers out of hibernation means...........badger poo!!! So, whilst The Owner and Lady Chocolate Lab Owner wandered along the edge of the field at the top of the hill holding hands and other disgusting hoomun stuff I took Lady Chocolate Lab up to introduce her to a particularly gooey dollop of badger poo. Now it would seem that she is something of a badger poo virgin, but it must be a genetic thing with K9's as she took to it like a...... well, like a lab to badger poo really! We got really down and dirty in it, until I heard The Owner whistling for me to come back. The two of us ran flat out down the hill towards our Owners. Lady Chocolate Lab put her arms out to great her K9 as we bounded faster and faster towards them. I remember thinking at the time she isn't going to be happy any time now. The Owner, not wishing to appear at all grumpy did likewise, so I obliged and we all four of us tumbled over and over and down the hill, a combination of twelve legs, four arms and two tails. It was about half way through the tumbling that I became aware of a change in the tone of the shrieks, from those of delight to those of disgust. Another hoomun who has no appreciation of the finer points of badger poo! It was a long and silent walk back to the cottage and we were both subjected to a dose of the yard broom and hosepipe when we got back. Followed by a spell in the boot room! I am thinking that the boot room is not so bad when shared! I can't help but feel that I am somehow being held responsible by all three.....

Rat and The Heap of Dirt

We had a lazy start to the day today, The Owner and me, and to be honest, as he has been working from home today I have spent much of it curled up on MY settee with my chin rested on his leg. No, he has genuinely been working! There was a bit of an upset earlier in the day when we went on patrol, and I am blaming certain factions on Facebook for this, who have encouraged me to believe that maybe fox poo might be more acceptable to The Owner's delicate nostrils and sensibilities than my poo of choice, badger, for rolling in. I have to report, having found a small dollop over by the cricket pitch this morning, that it is not! The Owner took particular exception to my rolling activities involving the said fox poo, so I won't be trying that again anytime soon. Well, maybe. Come lunchtime, The Owner was sitting on MY settee, munching absent mindedly on a stale crust and I was sat beside him, dribbling a lot, when I noticed something move by the Ruddy Dyson cupboard. Perhaps I should explain at this point that there have been a lot of scratching's going on when the house has been quiet in recent weeks which The Owner put down to "Just the odd mouse, and it is a cottage so what can we expect?". Well, I am guessing that when he noticed it himself that wasn't quite what he had in mind! As I watched, there was more and more dirt being pushed out under the door and I did notice a rather large pair of whiskers at one point. Well when The Owner finally noticed it, the heap of dirt and rocks which I felt even Small Boy would have been proud of, was edging across towards the carpet. He jumped up with such a start that his mug of tea was sent flying although not so much as a crumb of his sandwich came my way and he nervously opened the cupboard door and instructed me to go in! Well I wasn't going in there!!!!! That is a job for Terrier!!!! Not a noble K9 with breeding such as I! I kept guard from the settee which was well off the floor as he nervously moved boxes and bags armed with a broom handle and his twelve bore. Presumably he was unaware of the rat the size of a small badger that was sat on the shelf watching him and I was not about to tell him in case I was sent in to retrieve it or something. Eventually he looked up and we had another of those beautiful moments when two species look into each other's eyes before Rat dived down the hole he had been so busy digging under the floors. The Owner has filled the hole with cement and piled some very large boxes over it. I just wonder whether that was the right thing to do really. I reckon in a few days time there could be a particularly ripe smell wafting around here for which I, for once, am not responsible.

The Sore Bottom

Yesterday we went on patrol and today, as the result of an ever so little incident, I am still feeling a little.... uncomfortable! The Owner had been working from home again yesterday, when I say working it was more of a very long snooze as far as I could see, interspersed by small periods of great activity. It was approaching tea time and he suddenly put his shoes on and grabbed his crusty old Barbour jacket and told me to get my butt off my comfy cushion. Never one to turn down an opportunity to do anything, I leapt energetically from my cushion and down to the gate. A quick shuffle down the road and we arrived at the farm, now this could have gone three ways and I was unsure which to anticipate. We could have been going for a patrol through the farm and up on the hill (good, there will be more badger poo up there by now!). We could have been going to the studio and that would have been another hour or so before tea. Third option.... yes it is Saturday.... we are going to the pub!! I like pubs, they are my favourite! It was about then that my discomfort began. I like to behave myself when wandering up the road with The Owner, I don't do leads, except at the pub (pub rules) so when a car comes along I go to The Owner and sit by his foot. It's what I do. We hadn't been on our way long when a car approached so I go and sit with The Owner, another car from the other direction as well, so The Owner stepped up on the grass bank, so did I and sat down beside him. There are only certain parts of me which are not protected by a layer of fur. We are enjoying the first flush of spring here and certain plants are just poking their noses through, determined to wreak havoc in my world. Where I sat, a stinging nettle was just emerging with a particularly vengeful frame of mind and the only bit round the back there which is unprotected was its point of contact. Stinging nettles on the bum is a sensation which I am not happy with and am in no hurry to repeat! I got absolutely no sympathy at all from The Owner! It seems that sitting in a pub with a K9 which was constantly licking his bum was not many peoples idea of a good Saturday evening out and so The Owner was soon asked to take me home. Serves him right! I think he smells like a camel anyway!

The Family Came Visiting

I had visitors today, Owner's Daughter, Diesel Dog Daughter and Small Boy! I like being with my family

Another Chinese Takeaway

The Owner has been a little grumpy of late, I mean grumpier than usual. I thought it best not to tempt fate too much by getting hairs and slobber all over the keyboard so I scribbled notes on my pad in the boot room and hid it behind my food bin. I can report on my adventures and findings on the hoomun condition in times to come.

He went off yesterday and came back smelling of hospitals again. Last night he announced that as it was Good Friday it called for a takeaway. Well I was as confused as you are, as far as I am able to tell today is Friday and I have found nothing about it to warrant it being called good. However, last night he ordered a Friday takeaway to be delivered. The attentive amongst you will recall the last delivery of Chinese takeaway when I caused a little problem when I appeared behind Chinese Delivery Yoof and he seemed a little overawed by my appearance. This time they arrived en mass with a car full of four Chinese Delivery Yoofs in a very posh delivery car. Well I was very anxious to make some kind of amends for the last occasion and so when the driver yoof jumped out to talk with The Owner he left his door open and the gate not closed properly. I took my moment and jumped in the car to say hello to the others, I reasoned I could say hello to Chinese Delivery Yoof when he returned from talking to The Owner. They seemed generally pleased to see me and squealed and giggled a lot which made me jump around a lot more, but when Chinese Delivery Yoof got back he must have had one of those bad heads that The Owner gets on a Saturday morning as he kept holding his head and said "My Dad'll kill me!.... His car!" over and over again. Not sure what he meant by that?! The Owner must have had a bad head too as he scowled a lot and then held his head in his hands as well. I was getting the distinct vibe that I was being held responsible for something.

The Lack of Gas For The Cooker

Yesterday morning there was a lot of grumbling going on and I tried as much as possible to keep out of the way. Experience has taught me that when The Owner grumbles a lot it usually ends up as my fault, so if I am keeping a low profile I don't draw attention to myself. It seemed the cause of his ire was that the gas had run out and his breakfast was only half cooked. He went and found his camping stove and that was in the same condition apparently, so I suspect that Owners Daughter will be getting the best end of one of his opinions when he sees her as I feel sure she borrowed it to go camping. I don't like camping as my comfy cushion gets damp! Just thought I'd mention that. After having an argument with Gas

Delivery Man on the phone, which predictably started with "How much?!?!?" it was arranged that Gas Delivery Yoof would drop a new bottle of gas off later that day. I have never met Gas Delivery Yoof before so was unsure what to expect. Later in the afternoon, after a day of The Owner going out to the kitchen every half hour and seeing if the stove would light up and then sighing a lot, a lorry pulled up in our layby and had a lot to say for itself, which made me a little nervous to be honest. Gas Delivery Yoof got out and fertled around in the back and produced a big bright orange shiny new gas bottle. Now we have two such bottles at the back of the cottage and in the absence of anything more appropriate I usually wee up them. It tends to make them rust a lot but I always feel a statement has been made when I wee up them. Gas Delivery Yoof put the new one down just inside the gate as he had forgotten his spanner so I took the opportunity. Start as you mean to go on I always say! He didn't notice anyway although he did start wiping his neck a lot and had a strange expression on his face as he carried the bottle round the back. He swapped the bottles over and then carried the empty one back to his lorry and put it down whilst he discussed important things with The Owner. You will be pleased to know that I managed to get one last wee on the old bottle before it was loaded up on to the lorry. It seemed a bit extreme the way Gas Delivery Yoof changed his jumper and jacket as soon as he got in the cab of his lorry. He sent one or two accusing looks in my direction too, but some people are just like that I have realised.

Observations on Rook Poo and Nest Building

Today The Owner's face was very black and I have to say that his mood seemed likewise so I have kept out of the way. It has been raining heavily all day so the sunny spot behind the barbie was out of the question, so I have spent the day curled up in the straw in the calf sheds. Our cottage is very old; The Owner says it is hundreds of years old so it is probably as old as him. In the shed is an old copper what they used to use for washing. The Owner refers to it as Zanussi V1.0 and then laughs very loudly at his own joke. I have been telling Rook for days that the chimney pot above the copper is not a good place for building a nest but would he listen to me? Mind you with the row his Lady Rook keeps making if he doesn't build it right he is probably deaf by now. Anyway, this morning Rook threw a particularly large twig down the chimney and forgot to let go. When The Owner went to get some logs he heard him in the chimney. What started out as just opening the firebox door for Rook to find his way out has finished up with bits of stone and copper everywhere and one Rook very reluctant to show his face. With the first row of stone and bricks already removed it was at this point that Rook chose to make his bid for freedom. I can't help but think if he had thought first about his escape route first The Owner may not have got covered in quite so much soot and rook poo and my life may have been a little easier today. This evening it is still raining, The Owner has wiped most of the soot from his face on a bath towel (I suspect that Lady Cleaner Hoomun will have an opinion about that tomorrow) and Rook is on top of the chimney again being berated by Lady Rook for using the wrong size sticks to build her the nest of her dreams. Equilibrium has been restored, which is more than can be said for the copper!

My Letter from the RSPCA

Well, so far this week I have had two letters from Postman. The first was early this week and I think it came from Blood Hound 7. Some nice treats for me I thought although The Owner was a little too keen to hide them from me, but my nose did not let me down. "Hah!", I thought, as I rummaged through his secret stash of wine bottles, "No problem!". I was, however, unsure whether I should be having an opinion on being sent "Wonky Chomps" through the post. Should I be drawing any conclusions here? Well, after being sent out into three inches of drought yesterday morning and being reassured that my skin was waterproof I did feel a little better when I found my way upstairs and snoozed on The Owner's bed until I dried off a little. Three inches of drought is quite a lot when spread over The Owners bed! This morning I had another letter addressed to me from the RSPCA. Whenever there are loads of letters after a name The Owner always makes them out to be very important so I was hopeful. Well I am so over the RSPCA!!!!!! Lots of letters to make up a name and not a tasty chomp in there for me!!!!! I am off to bed I think!

Home Alone

On Saturday I was left home alone! The very sound of it brings a shudder to my bones. I knew something was up as The Owner had been in the bath for far too long to be normal for a Saturday and some of the smelly things that he was spraying about up there were too hideous to mention. It wasn't long before Bracknell Lady Hoomun arrived, as if by way of explanation. Now, I like Bracknell Lady Hoomun as she usually brings me a tasty chomp or two as a bribe of some kind, so I did my best excited bounce and my very best excited run round the tree by the path that I wee on, but not a chomp nor treat did she give me! I was beginning to revise my opinion about her quickly! Even more so when The Owner threw a Bonio on my comfy cushion and when I went and got it they both were out the door in less time than it takes to open a Bonio box!!! I took advantage of my enforced solitude and had a quick snooze on the settee that I am not normally allowed on, then his armchair, then Small Boys bed..... in fact I tried everything that I am not normally allowed on. The only place I was unable to have a snooze on was The Owners bed as he had shut the bedroom door before he went. Although I was frankly not disappointed, as ever since I had a snooze on his bed last week, whilst I dried off after being shut out in the rain, there has been a strange smell of damp emanating from his room which I am frankly none too keen on. It was dark when they returned. My initial bouncing was a little difficult at first when the door opened, not because I had the grumps with him for leaving me, but because there was considerable pressure in my bladder which needed to be relieved first. Made all the worse by The Owner having left a tap dribbling in the bathroom! Bracknell Lady Hoomun was immediately forgiven for not bringing me a tasty chomp earlier in the day by arriving with a pocket full of Markies. The Owner however arrived with a kebab in his hand and so Sunday morning will be filled with either hideous breath that would de-scale the kettle at a thousand yards, which even I would not want to sniff, or an endless run upstairs to the lavatory holding his belly..... or both! Not sure why he does it really, far better to stick to something which is thoroughly wholesome.... like badger poo!

Survey Hoomun's Lunch Box

Well today has been a thoroughly rewarding day, all things considered, and I am feeling quite full. Although I have been on the receiving end of one or two nasty stares which I felt may have been a little harsh. On morning patrol we were heading for the farm and the warmth and, more importantly, the DRY studio. When we got almost there we happened upon two hoomuns who I believe were called Survey Hoomun, not sure why they both had the same name, perhaps they were related although I can imagine that may have been confusing at dinner times. So they were there with this tripod thing, and I have learned from my experience with the Zimmer frame on the station that it was not acceptable to wee up things with legs, but there was this red box, unguarded. So I wee'd on the box instead. Only a little wee it was, hardly worth all the fuss really! Survey Hoomun gave me a particularly hard stare and threw her sandwiches on the field, well how was I supposed to know the box had her sandwiches in??!!? But I made a note of where they went and retrieved them later, after all I am a retriever! A bit less pickle may have been better I thought. Then Water Cooler Hoomun turned up and he normally gives me a Bonio from my bucket so I got quite excited by the thought. But instead he gave me an apple.....I wasn't impressed! However he left his van door open and I had noticed an open bag of crisps on the seat so it all worked out for the best in the end!!!

The Studio Ceiling Paint

Today has been a busy day already, so much so that I have come back to the cottage out of the way of the frenetic activity now taking place in the studio. I have just selected a particularly tasty Bonio for a quiet chomp and sought the comfort and quiet of my comfy cushion instead. I also have my eye on a Markie which I have noticed under the side of the cooker. Well, I have always said that the ruddy Dyson is an instrument of the devil himself haven't I? There is a kind of malevolent consciousness about it which terrifies me, and I think this morning has proved me right. Yet again!! My guess is The Owner has a meeting today in the studio, as early this morning he threw the ruddy Dyson onto his shoulder and marched off to the studio with a certain sense of purpose about him. He then proceeded to vacuum the carpet, then my vet-bed and duvet, then behind the book shelves and, clearly warming to his task he went in search of more fodder to feed the damn thing with. Nothing was safe! My world was in frenzy as I ran from desk to desk trying to find some refuge from this mechanical Lucifer! Then he turned his attentions to Spider, who, together with many of his ancestors, has spent the last hundred years or more building cobwebs without limitations. Was nothing safe I wondered? Apparently not! I have been noticing two large areas of ceiling paint peeling a little and that was where The Owner turned his attentions next, which I was quite pleased about as the usual ritual when nothing further can be sucked up off the floor is to chase me around a lot with the Dyson hose. It was then that it happened!!! The effects of the ruddy Dyson were a little too much for the adhesive properties of two hundred years of paint on the ceiling and with an extra special suck from the Dyson hose; about half of the area of the ceiling paint came down as one piece! I thought I was seeing a ghost or something as the dust began to settle, this sheet of white paint was draped over the desk and the light unit in the middle of the ceiling and this big lump was moving around underneath it like a hamster under a freshly laid carpet. The only thing which gave away what was causing it was that the lump was swearing quite a lot using words that I pretend not to understand, so it had to be The Owner. Postman arrived at that point and opened the door and shut it again very quick. I guess we'll be getting our mail tomorrow instead! I think today, my comfy cushion will be about as far as I venture, for my own safety as much as anything else.

Oh No, Dog Dancing!!

I was sat there this morning with The Owner, the start of a peaceful Saturday morning, I thought. Our Saturday mornings are seldom out of the ordinary and seldom ever rushed as he watches Breakfast News on the BBC. He is too much of a snob to watch anything else and to be honest I don't mind as I watch Mike Bushell the sports presenter do strange things in the name of unusual sports which usually confounds any theories I may have been forming about the hoomun condition during the previous week. This morning I sat there and saw him start his report and pulled up a corner of my comfy cushion that I hadn't dribbled on or covered in other unidentifiable stains to watch his hoomun sporting antics. I could not believe what I saw!! Dancing Dogs!!!!! After watching this, for the next ten minutes The Owner was fidgeting in a way that I understand only too well, a plan is forming in his mind! I will be making myself scarce for a while as these kinds of plans usually are at my expense. I went up the garden and found the spot behind the barbie, true there was little sun and the wind was a bit chilly but it was safer than remaining indoors with The Owner when he is plotting ways of getting himself into the spotlight again.

The Log Delivery

Yesterday, Bracknell Hoomun and Lady Bracknell Hoomun arrived and brought some logs for The Owner. When I say "some" logs, I mean a lorry load! It took them ages to unload them and carry them round the back and put them in the fuel shed. The fuel shed is now full beyond even The Owners head height right out to the door. I assisted with the process as you would expect, until Bracknell Hoomun nearly ran me over with his wheelbarrow and he seemed particularly vexed by having to load the barrow up again with what he dropped. I left The Owner alone as he seemed in a particularly bad mood as well, after he dropped one of his logs on his foot, just in case he found a way that it was my fault. I went instead and assisted Lady Bracknell Hoomun, mainly coz she had a pocketful of Markies and every time she got down off the lorry, I got one! This morning The Owner is wandering round the house looking for something. In the last few days we have had several deliveries of treats for me. My anonymous friend Blood Hound 7 sent me some treats through the post and then Andrew Plod Hoomun turned up looking for coffee and he brought me some treats, of which I was allowed only the one. Well this morning The Owner is looking for them to give me one for being a "Good Boy". Well, in hoomun terms, a "Good Boy" I am certainly not. But I have to report that treats do somehow taste better when you just find them when you are not supposed to. I think the peace and air of fraternity in the cottage may be shattered when he discovers the empty packet in the boot room. I hope he finds it soon so we can get that bit over and done with for the day coz I just know I will be in trouble when he does. It's raining hard outside so I can't escape to the farm so it may be a long day.

Wise Words From Jack Labrador

More wise sayings from Jack Labrador - A Bonio in the hand is worth.......well......eating really!

More Wise Words From Jack Labrador

More wise sayings from Jack Labrador - Badger poo is a poo by any other name.

The Birthday Tea

Today is Friday and, perhaps predictably, we have been to the pub, "To celebrate your Birthday Jack!" he said. Am I missing something here? My Birthday, he gets the drink? The good news is that I managed to get him back home and past the pond without incident. Now, yesterday, we went to the studio. The Owner said to me, "Jack my boy, t's your birthday!" Well after past Birthdays I was immediately suspicious, I still remember the hangover! But, he offered me a dish of tea which I thought sounded a good idea. When Small Boy makes me tea I find it quite pleasant as an experience so I got quite excited and bounced around a lot. Well, three pints of tea was perhaps a little bit too much but you don't look a gift horse in the mouth do you? It was about an hour before the bladder became a little too uncomfortable, so The Owner let me out in to the paddock. Well I wee'd and I wee'd and I wee'd! The Owner was a little uncharitable, I felt, when he asked me if I wanted the Sunday papers to read whilst I was busy. When we got back to the cottage, Postman had delivered lots of chews and doggy chomps. Well, I had to sample a few didn't I? Not sure what was in one of them but it made me feel a bit funny and I finished up running from room to room. I couldn't help it!!!! The tally was; 2 pint glasses (full), a box of champagne flutes (now a box of bits), his favourite tea mug (no handle), his dinner plate (full), oh yes, and the table lamp (now without a lampshade). I am thinking that Birthdays may be overrated! I am going for a lie down!

Thoughts on Gold Foil Stuck to Noses

I have been more than a little charitable to The Owner during his recent "Medical Problems". I am not drawing any conclusions from his experiences and his palpitations occurring shortly after the arrival of his new medical dictionary! There is also a section I have noticed at the back on K9 ailments, which he is reading at the moment, amidst periodic glances in my direction over the top of his glasses (more of which later I am sure), accompanied by the occasional episode of K9 manhandling as he prods and pokes his way to disproving a further life affecting K9 affliction. Look, I am healthy!!! OK?!?!?!? I will of course draw no inference from the fact that the K9 section is at the back! However, after this morning, my formerly charitable feeling of "bon homme" has evaporated. Last night, he was drinking beer from bottles with funny corks in which he delights in firing around the room whilst trying to see how many times he can bounce them off walls, ceilings and other furniture and still hit me on the rump. They also come with gold foil covers over the top. This morning after breakfast and early patrol I had a quick sniff around the living room carpet looking for any traces of Bonio chomps from last night, or other edible detritus left behind, when a piece of this gold foil got stuck to my wet nose. It could be thought of in the same terms as hoomuns wearing mittens and then getting a hair in their mouths. Paws and claws are just not good at getting rid of bits of gold foil stuck to damp noses! The Owner, predictably, has found the whole matter very amusing and keeps laughing loudly at me every time he sees me and, as the foil in question is sticking up at the front of my nose, and in permanent view from where I can see it, keeps asking whether I prefer a cross hair or traditional blade sight. I responded by finding some badger poo for one shoulder and something indescribable in the calf sheds for the other. I was then banished to the boot room until the hose had been dug out of the shed and the yard broom rescued from wherever Small Boy had left it. I was then washed down in rather too rough a manner for someone of my breeding. He has now stolen my comfy cushion and my duvet and both are in the washing machine. The poo I found has been a particularly good vintage and has resisted normal attempts at removal. I am choosing to draw no conclusion at the moment from the fact that he is calling me in an altogether too friendly fashion from the bathroom, after much sloshing of water in the bath. I will report later on the glasses situation.

The Visit to The Opticians

I have discovered today what an optician is and I think tomorrow we need to discover a different one! Last week sometime, the electricity went off, and so when we wandered home after patrol, the cottage was dark and silent. All he had to do was to go and press the switch, but no, he starts to reminisce about his childhood and the three day week. I have yet to work out what a three day week is as ours around here are all seven days. Must be something that happens the other side of Swindon! He decided that an evening "By the light of the fire and a few candles" would be a good way to spend the time. Now something I have noticed about hoomuns is that their eyesight is not as good in the dark as us K9's. He went round to the wood shed and after fumbling around a little and swearing a bit, he re-emerged with an armful of logs. Inside the cottage his eyesight had improved none and I could see he was about to tread on his reading glasses in the middle of the floor. I was right!! He did tread on his glasses in the middle of the floor! Sometimes I even surprise myself! This necessitated us making a trip today into town to the opticians. He can be so embarrassing sometimes, when he feels a certain sense of injustice. No one else thinks his injustices are unjust, only in his little world. After selecting a pair off the rack that weren't bent and twisted like his old ones he went to pay for them as Mummy Hoomun was sorting out some for her small boy (not to be confused with my Small Boy) and Optician Hoomun said they were free. The Owners were not free! They were the cause of much holding head in hands and shouting "How much?!?!?" There then followed much shouting and arguing about how much he has paid in taxes and stuff and as a large crowd was gathering at the shop doorway to see what the noise was about I crept outside and awaited the end of the argument when he was asked to leave again. Rolling in badger poo is such a simple way of life, don't you think?

My Ride in The Pizza Delivery Van

Well, what an adventure I've just had! When we left the studio this evening we got to the road and there was much pondering as The Owner debated with himself over whether we turned and went to the pub or turned for home. It took a while, but eventually he decided and we came home. The Owner started to fidget until he fumbled through the letter box and out dropped an advert from the pizza shop offering two for the price of one. The naive among you would now be thinking that maybe the free one may be destined for me? Wrong! But that wasn't the adventure. Pizza Yoof arrived and came bounding up the pathway with far too much enthusiasm and bonne homme for all in a half mile radius. He stood at the front door, talking to The Owner and bounding around the front porch like a demented badger. He had left his car door open! And the front gate! Never one to turn down a trip out in a car I hopped in and then over on to the back seat and settled down to wait. Eventually he bounded back up the path and jumped in the car and shut the door. Excellent, I thought. We are off for a ride. Pizza Yoof turned the radio on very loud and started singing loudly and jumping around in his seat. I have to report his singing was going to win him absolutely no prizes on “The Voice”. My little trip was going well, I thought and then he rummaged in his bag and produced a biscuit which he had a quick chomp on as we drove along. I was getting concerned that a bit of that biscuit was not coming my way so I sat up and tapped him on his shoulder with my paw and woofed a bit. Well I think he overreacted and behaved in a very dramatic manner! Fortunately the pub sign was not showing much damage, unlike Pizza Yoofs car bumper! I was brought back to the cottage and couldn't help notice our formerly bouncy Pizza Yoof was a little more subdued, in fact, sort of, like, well... normal. He is out there now with The Owner and a length of wire and a bit of string and a broken bumper. I reasoned that I am going to be sent to the boot room when The Owner comes back in so I may just save him the trouble and take myself off there now. And he still didn't share his biscuit with me!!!!

The Hole That I Didn't See in The Pond

Well, the observant among you may have noticed that we have had a little rain over the last few days. Today the weather showed little signs of change. I know this makes me sound a little like the hoomuns I have seen around the village spending hours discussing the wevva.... and beer. On patrol (in the rain) with The Owner at lunch time I encountered some very strange hoomun behaviour which I am at something of a loss to explain. The pond was quite full and had spread right across the road. Nothing unusual in that, given the wevva, you are thinking. The unusual bit was Road Workman on his little digger, in the middle of it, digging a very large hole under the water. I found out later that he was digging a hole for new sewer pipes which will probably give The Owner some comfort that his taxes are being well spent. Now how did I know he had dug a hole under the water? Well, as you ask, The Owner stopped to chat and try and impress Road Workman with his knowledge on digging holes and to show off his new wellington boots as he stood in the water. I had a quick sniff around his digger and wee'd on his tracks. Then I walked across the front of it and was somewhat surprised to get a mouth full of water and found myself unable to see anything through about four feet of murky water in the hole that Road Workman was apparently digging. The Owner showed his usual sympathy at my predicaments and laughed loudly as I spluttered my way to the surface again. The water was very muddy, and so was I when I clambered out. The Owner was far too busy to worry about drying me off a little with a rub down with a towel when we got back and soon disappeared back to the studio leaving me at home. He left me looking for some way of drying myself off a little. Well I am predicting there may be words said when he goes to bed later, I found just the spot to dry off a little and keep warm. I don't think The Owner will be happy with it though. The boot room is dry enough! :)

The Aftermath of The Owner's Damp Bed

I was sooooooo right yesterday, when I predicted there would be ructions when The Owner went to bed last night. I had fallen foul, or rather in the hole that Road Worker Hoomun had dug in the road, which by then had become a victim of the pond which had spread to include all the road, the ditch and some of the field. Because he was sat in the middle of what was formerly known as the road, I felt that I could have been easily excused for not realising there was actually a hole under there. That was until I fell in it of course! I had no sympathy at all from The Owner who laughed at my downfall in a particularly raucous fashion all the way home as I dribbled water behind me. As he hadn't towelled me off and had left me at home alone I found my way to his bed as somewhere warm and dry to lay for a while until I dried a little. My prediction was that he may have an opinion or two when he went to bed himself and found it to be a little damper than he had been expecting. The evening had gone well and he ruffled my ears absent mindedly as he watched the TV and slurped loudly at his wine. It almost seemed a shame that it was going to end so loudly later, but hey ho, I am just a K9 after all. What could I do? Well, as predicted, soon after he went up the stairs there was much wailing and gnashing of teeth coming from his bedroom. Well what could I do? You're right - hide! So I have found that there is enough room - just - for me to squeeze down the side of the tumble dryer and hide behind the fridge. As long as I don't mind sharing it with several odd socks, two pairs of boxers, a towel..... and a sink plunger! No idea what the sink plunger was doing there either! I think he must have slept last night in Small Boys bed as he isn't here during the week. When he came down the stairs this morning I heard him put the kettle on as normal and empty the tea pot as normal, but the door to the boot room didn't open for some time. This was a little worrying as the bladder was getting fairly stretched and not helped by the cramped spot I had spent the night. When the door was finally opened he stood there, in his boxer shorts, arms folded in a very uncompromising manner and a scowl on his face, which was frankly enough to have even silenced those two old ladies in the village that smell of lavender (yuk and phew!) who never stop talking. I have a feeling today could be a very long day; I was even put on a lead for the walk to the studio this morning!

My Collision with The Owner

Today I was beginning to feel I may have been forgiven for the damp duvet incident. The day had gone well, The Owner had his coffee and sat on the step in the sunshine and gave me two Bonio's. It's not often I get two Bonio's! Then, a little earlier than normal he grabs his phone and his keys and says "C'mon Jack, let's go and have some lunch shall we?" and we wandered home. I should explain that last night The Owner had mowed the lawns, even the ones around the back and the paths up into the woods by the barbie. It must mean that someone important is coming to see him or he would never have bothered with the back of the cottage and the paths in the woods. So, unusually, it is possible to completely circumnavigate the cottage without getting stung in one's important little places. Now big words like that do tend to impress me with my own brilliance! Whilst The Owner went inside I stayed outside and had a poo, which always leaves me with an irresistible urge to run very fast. So I thought I would run all the way round the cottage very fast. It was great fun! I was nearing the end of the third circuit when it all went horribly wrong. As I rounded the corner of the porch on the front door The Owner was wandering out with a plate and a sandwich in one hand and a mug of tea in the other looking for a nice spot to sit and have his lunch. Well I hadn't allowed for this! I also felt he was making just a little too much of the whole affair with the way he threw his sandwich and drink in the air as I ran into him. There was a certain amount of venom went into the way he cut some more bread for a replacement sandwich, but the good news was I noticed where the sandwich went and when the dust has settled a little I will go and find it. I think until then I may keep out of the way a little.

More Wise Words from Jack Labrador

More wise words from Jack Labrador - A bird in the hand is worth two in the bush just means you weren't barking loud enough to scare the little varmints away in the first place!

Yet More Wise Words from Jack Labrador

More words of wisdom from Jack Labrador - A horse may run quickly but it cannot escape its tail. Turn the tables and chase the tail instead - it always works for me. I never catch it though!

The Owners Acceptance Speech

The Owner is feeling very pleased with himself today. The gullible among you have been buying his first book! He is already trying to write his acceptance speech for the National Book Awards. I have the laptop so he is currently sucking thoughtfully on his pencil and then scribbling furiously before screwing up the paper and throwing it at the waste bin. You notice I didn't say in the bin; that was because it has already disappeared under the weight of two packs of paper. It could be another long day.

Diesel Dog Has Landed

Well, what a few days I have had! Sundays, as I may have mentioned before follow a set pattern. The Owner gets up, makes a cup of tea and feeds me, then takes said cup of tea through to the living room and puts the telly on and shouts at The Andrew Marr show a lot. He says things like Slimeball Mandleson and other words that I pretend not to understand. Then he makes a second mug of tea and picks his paper off the front porch and then sits in the dining room and rants a lot at the paper. Grateful that his rant isn't at me I snuggle up with him on that sofa (because I am allowed) and awaits the next disturbance which will be at coffee time when he has a coffee and a glass of sherry. After the coffee and sherry disturbance to my snuggling and snoozing I settled back down again, only to be disturbed soon after when a van pulled up in the lay by so I felt obliged to charge about the garden a little and act all brave. Well I was more than a little surprised to see Tesco Delivery Yoof there so I rushed around in an entirely different manner hopeful of a Bonio. It was then that the day took a little random turn. Enjoying my snuggle, I had a quick stretch and turned over, when out of the corner of my eye I felt sure I saw something rush past. Opening both eyes I was unable to see anything that may have been responsible so I settled down again, after a moment or two I was even more sure I had seen it again but when I looked the room was quiet and still, much as it always is. I was just having another stretch and climbing off the sofa when Diesel Dog ran through the dining room and the boot room and out the back door, apparently for the third time in as many minutes. I finished my stretch and was about to start looking where he had gone, when I was T boned in the side by a demented badger masquerading as Diesel Dog! I ran out the front door, mainly just to get out of his way until he had worked it out of his system, but the fool followed me! So I ran harder, so he ran harder. I ran harder still, so the demented badger known as Diesel Dog ran harder still. After the fourth trip round the garden, taking in the boot room, the kitchen, the dining room, the hallway and the porch before going outside the cottage again, I took a little sidestep as we entered the kitchen and stood behind The Owner's legs where he was making tea for Owners Daughter and Diesel Dog Daughter. Diesel Dog got quicker and quicker in his efforts to catch up with me, whilst I watched from the relative safety behind The Owners legs. Three more trips round unsuccessfully looking for me and he spotted me. I thought my peace was about to be shattered but he just kept on running. I was quite worn out just watching him!! I was lucky it was a warm and sunny day so I went and had a snooze behind the barbie in the woods, every time I opened an eye I could still see him running. It was all just too much effort and I still feel tired.

Walking on Water

This morning I have made an important discovery for animal science!!! Cats do walk on water, albeit a little shakily, probably in need of a bit more practice. I was on early morning patrol and am happy to report that the pond has had so much drought flow in to it that it is now full and overflowing.

We have had a problem recently with a fox using the front lawn as its own private lavatory for which I at first was getting the blame. Although as The Owner has always said, if I do one it usually requires blue and white road signs around it and to be treated as a roundabout. So he finally realised that these were far too delicate and small to have come from me and the admonishments I had received thus far were all in error. Did I get an apology? Nah! So, on patrol I was, near the pond; when I heard noises in the little copse around the back of the pond. I thought to myself, "Jack my boy, here is your moment to explain to Fox that he needs to adjust his pooing activities before The Owner catches up with him". So, with my stealthiest paws on and crawling on my belly, I crept through the copse from the cricket field towards the pond. As I got closer I realised that Cat, who is new around here, had the same idea. He was creeping up on Fox too. So I crept closer and Cat crept closer. Cat had obviously been blamed for pooing on his Owner's lawn too. He crept right up behind Fox, (who was either very brave in the face of adversity or he had seen neither of us,) and was about to pounce, and I was right behind Cat. Well the excitement just got too much for me and I let out a very loud bark. It had the desired effect on Fox, who legged it round the side of the pond and across the fields, but I am guessing that Cat was unaware of my presence until that point, as he ran straight across three lily pads and only realised he was on water when he was nearly at the other side...... and sank! Up to that point he was doing well I thought. Brave as ever, I jumped in and rescued him. Which seemed to be a little under-appreciated and I now have a little scab on the top of my nose which is a little distracting as I can see it if I squint a little. If I snooze I can shut my eyes and it won't be such a problem I think. I'll be on top of the straw bales in the calf sheds if anyone wants me.

Lynx

I was sitting there all quiet watching the telly with The Owner when I whirled round looking for some explanation or reassurance. The man on the telly started talking about this cat and described it as Lynx. To me, it looked not dissimilar to Cat that tried to walk on water earlier last week, and who incidentally has still not forgiven me and growls whenever I walk past on patrol. When The Owner wears Lynx he certainly doesn't look quite so furry. He seems to think it will make women fall at his feet in a heightened state of carnal desire. Of course, they don't and that may be due in part to the application of half a bottle producing a stench worthy of a large lavender bush and capable of descaling a kettle at a hundred yards, and also because of his constant laughing at his own jokes. I am failing to see the connection here unless Cat on the television is also wearing the same stinking stuff. I will try and find out more over the coming days.

Breakfasts Second Course

How do hoomuns just KNOW? The Owner does it all the time, I do something which I feel he wouldn't want me to do and I do it when he isn't around. Then when I wander in through the back door he is there, arms folded, foot tapping with that accusing look in his eye. Today was just one of those such days! It was raining when I went off for a mini patrol after breakfast, when I happened upon something organic and decaying nicely in the woods near the barbie. I had a little room left after breakfast so I thought a quick chomp wouldn't hurt. When I got back to the cottage The Owner was sat watching the telly with his cup of tea shouting at Robert Peston on the news. He holds him in similar contempt as That Slimeball Mandelson and so there was a lot of shouting going on so I was anxious not to cop any of that flack and knowing he wouldn't have been too impressed with my little snack I crept in on my belly and slid around the corner of the sofa to get to my comfy cushion. How did he know????? His first words were "What have you been up to?" in those accusing tones he reserves for such occasions. I tried to creep under the sideboard but there was more accusing looks to follow. Ok, so I did deposit my breakfast and my extras on the carpet at his feet, but all the accusations were a little harsh I felt. I just wish I knew what it was I had eaten as it was perhaps not quite ripe enough. Perhaps that was what the problem was; The Owner was saving it for himself! But I still would like to know how he just....... knows!!!

The Owner and The Ambliance

We have had major things going on here today! The Owner had been shouting at Robert Peston on the telly again this morning, which is always a bad start to any day and then he thrust his hands deep in his pockets and we stomped off to the studio. I walked a little behind him all the way down. Not out of any sense of duty you understand, more a sense of self preservation. When we got to the studio he opened some letters and then started shouting at them too. This was followed by the phone and then the computer. The day was not going well! Eventually, he, The Owner, made himself the customary eleven o clock coffee (which always means I get a Bonio, have I mentioned that I like Bonio's?) at half past ten. Now aren't you impressed that I can tell the time as well? He hadn't finished his coffee when he wandered off outside. I awaited his return for the other half of my Bonio but he didn't return, so I went outside to see what he was doing. I found him, lying like a heap of crumpled ironing outside on the floor, which I thought may have been a little unusual. And so, apparently, did Dairyman Hoomun and Lady Dairyman Hoomun, as they helped him back into the studio and flopped him into the chair. This big delivery van, with lots of blue lights and far too much to say for itself, then came into the farm and I am told they call it an ambliance which was ok as ambliances come with ambliance drivers and they may give me a Bonio. I was a little disappointed as they all paid The Owner far too much attention which will only make my life difficult when they have gone, and they didn't give me a Bonio. Next thing I knew, they'd whisked The Owner off into the ambliance. Well I was, by now, beside myself with concern! Not only had they not given me a Bonio but they had encouraged The Owner to go with them and he hadn't given me the other half of my Bonio yet. It really is just too much; I may have to pee on their wheels if I see them again. I think The Owner is going to be a little difficult this evening if he has had any attention during the day from Ambliance Hoomun and Lady Ambliance Hoomun.

The Helmet

Oh dear! I'm in trouble - at least I will be when everyone has worked out what happened. It was an uneventful day at the studio, periods of snoozing broken only by intervals of slumber throughout most of the day. Disturbed only occasionally by a brief period of delicious activity as I terrorised the new postman, such a pushover in the face of K9 superiority! Being summer(ish) The Owner keeps the studio door open and I snoozed in the doorway all day in the sun, until nearly at the end of the afternoon when I opened one eye and noticed Dairy Yoofs friend turn up on his bike, get off it and then push it into the little garage beside the studio. At exactly that moment I heard The Owner put his glasses down and pick up his phone and keys and that means only one thing - home and then - dinner!!! I rushed out the door eager to wee on the gate post before I leave my territory unguarded for the evening. I stopped in mid wee when I noticed something with lots of colour and kind of round sitting in the middle of the yard. I reasoned that if I was going home I needed to get this new addition to the yard wee'd on quickly, just until the morning when I would have more time to do the job properly. I was halfway through my wee when I heard Dairy Yoofs mate call out to someone, not sure who, "Can you pick my helmet up off the yard?" Ah! So that's what it was then! I thought it may be time for a little subterfuge so I quickly ran round the outside of the studio and reappeared from the other direction. Clever eh? Couldn't have been me could it? I think Dairy Yoofs mate was a little suspicious, if the look on his face as he put his helmet back on his head was anything to go by. I got the distinct vibe that my efforts were less than appreciated from the stern look he gave me as I dutifully walked to heel beside The Owner as we headed for home. I feel that maybe tomorrow would be a good time to make myself scarce and spend a little while in the calf sheds out of the way.

Cling Film Poo!

I had a very strange experience this morning which unsettled me to be honest! To put things into some kind of perspective I need to take you back a day or two. One afternoon The Owner had called in Plumber Hoomun as there was a vast escape of water in the cottage for which I was in no way responsible. It was in the bathroom which, because of its definition, i.e. bath, I have nothing to do with. So, Plumber Hoomun arrived brandishing two new taps for something in the bathroom. He had much discussion with The Owner about which tap should be installed but whilst that took place he had left his box of stuff by the gate... so I went to investigate. Nothing wrong with that I am thinking?!? What I found, in part, interested me greatly. His box contained lots of "Tools", none of which I had ever seen before. But what interested me particularly was his packet of sandwiches, perched on the top, wrapped in cling film. Nevertheless I decided I ought to pass comment on the quality of them and the filling. To be honest I did get a little carried away in my sampling and forgot myself a little and..... well...... ate them all. I thought I may have got away with it as Plumber Hoomun spent ages looking for them, inside his van but attention was diverted when my hoomun friend Acushla Hoomun arrived bearing Bonio's. In fact, in the excitement I had forgotten my input into the reason Plumber Hoomun spent half an hour searching his van for his dinner. So, today, breakfast consumed, it was time to go and have a quiet moment on the side lawn. Quiet moment enjoyed, and bowel evacuated, one always has to have a quick sniff and a check to make sure all is in order. You just have to do things like this! So I did. Whoa!!!!!!!!!!!! Who wrapped them all neatly in cling film???!!! It wasn't The Owner, he was inside! It took me a while to figure out the connection. I need a lie down!

The Bells

Such a weekend of embarrassment I have had. It all started on Friday with some fool telling The Owner that the whole country was being asked to ring a bell for three minutes just after breakfast. Having found an old bell in the bottom of a box somewhere, he dusted it off and chose to ignore the crack in it even though it sounded more like my food bring thrown into my metal food bowl, and began clanging furiously. The lady hoomun on the telly rather foolishly announced that many churches across the country are also ringing bells so he stuck his head out the boot room door and noticed no bells ringing at our church. Whilst composing a letter in his head to my mate Vic R about the lack of public spirit etc. he was out on the road waving his bell at driver hoomuns who he clearly felt were in need of his advice and direction. Which was most of them. Then police hoomun turned up! How embarrassing? Someone had reported a madman waving a bell in a particularly threatening manner at hoomuns as they passed the cottage. I went up the garden and off on patrol and left him to it. Well, I have a reputation to uphold! And I have breeding I do. I am not the one who gets brought home in a police car, or now, gets taken away in one. Then yesterday was a day of fun for me, The Owner had been told to get himself home from the police station and had arrived and was busy composing another letter to someone called MP. He must be really hip and happening, whoever he is, if he is only known by his initials. So I kept myself very entertained with the cyclist hoomuns who were coming past the cottage in large numbers. I would have a quick snooze in the sun up by the barbie and then when I heard them coming down the road I would run very fast (on silent) and then burst through the gap in the hedge making lots of noise and see if I could get a wobble out of them. I was having great fun when I heard some more coming down the road. So I started my charge....lady hoomuns this time... such fun as they always wobble more and louder (have you never seen a loud wobble?) I was nearly at the hedge and ready to burst forth with lots of noise, I am such a master at my art, when I heard lady cyclist hoomun say to her mate, "My friend lives in there!" Brakes!!! Brakes!!!! That would have been soooooooooooo embarrassing! It would have been a bit like The Owner saying hello to someone in town who he thinks he knows when it isn't them..... except that is funny.

More Wise Words from Jack Labrador

Obstinacy and vehemence in opinion are the surest proofs of stupidity. (Which reminds me, I haven't seen The Owner in a while.) ~ More wise words from Jack Labrador.

Even More Wise Words from Jack Labrador

"It is the mark of an educated mind to be able to entertain a thought without accepting it." Aristotle ~ But with no mind at all everything is entertaining! More wise words from Jack Labrador.

Lady Chocolate Lab – Caught Out Again

I am Soooooooooooo over Lady Chocolate Lab!

Yet More Wise Words from Jack Labrador

"That which doesn't kill us makes us stronger." - Friedrich Nietzsche - Now here is a man who understands badger poo!!!!! More wise words from Jack Labrador.

The Water Main

I felt a little uncertain about events of this morning at first. Morning patrol accomplished, it just left the journey to the studio before a Bonio to chomp on would appear out of my Bonio Bucket. Then The Owner would do his emails and stuff whilst having a slurp from his coffee mug. As we approached the farm everything appeared normal, and I have come to expect this sort of thing when disaster is about to befall, when from nowhere it came! There I was, weeing up against a clump of grass on the side of the road, when suddenly it started to wee back!!!! Then the drain in the gully started to have an opinion on the matter too, followed by the cracks in the driveway, a second drain, another clump of grass (which I hadn't wee'd on yet) and the area around the gatepost, (also not wee'd on yet)! With that much water around it is usually something to do with me I have noticed, or at least I get blamed for it, so I tried very hard to keep out of everyone's way just in case. I opted to go and sit in the field behind the fence to distance myself from the water and any attached blame. It was then that I noticed the water was off down the road past The Owner and heading straight for Farmer Hoomuns cottage. If water could have a vengeful look in its eye, this was just the occasion when it would have had it! I couldn't help but think that The Owner was getting worried as well at this point, in case he got the blame as well! The water then suddenly disappeared down another drain, which I have noted; if it can take that much water in one goes it is worth knowing about! You never know when that kind of information may come in handy! After much excitement on the farm with hoomuns of varying shapes and sizes talking to their phones and scratching their heads I heard The Owner pronounce his verdict with a great sense of authority on the matter. We have a water leak!! A big water leak!!!!!! I will keep you informed.

My Trip to Lundun

Yesterday morning The Owner was up early and polished his shoes (always a bad sign) and then dragged his suit out of the wardrobe. Not off a hanger, you understand, but from the bottom where he had thrown it after a disagreeable meeting a month ago. This of course liberated one or two of my little misdemeanours. Well he had left me on my own a couple of times and I wanted somewhere different to lie and the wardrobe door was open! So this was the first accusing stare I had received that day, there will be more. And it was only a few of my hairs after all!!! So, suit de-haired and put on, I was expecting the usual cursory Bonio to be thrown my way and then abandoned to my own amusement for the day. Instead he picked up my posh lead and told me to get in the car!!! We went to SWINDON!!!! I was a little nervous until we got to the station where I relaxed a little. I knew that we get trains from stations and they go to Bath, I have been there before. I had also learned not to wee on the old lady's Zimmer frame legs. They are apparently not for my benefit! However I was taken a little by surprise when the train came from the other direction, but a very grumpy chap who clearly had no understanding of my breeding told The Owner "Be careful with that dog and mind the gap with it." With IT!!! So I wee'd on his trouser leg and felt much better for it. The Owner said we were going to Lundun! When we got to Lundun there were so many people! I don't even see that many people at the village hall! We walked across the big station; I have never done my best walking to heal quite as well as that before. Not to demonstrate my considerable prowess at walking to heel, just that I wanted to keep The Owner close by me. Well I was a little out of my comfort zone, alright? Then we came across this huge badger hole and all these people went down it! What kind of a place was that???? As we got close to it I noticed that the stairs were all falling down the big hole, well I frankly wasn't surprised with that many people standing on it. Then The Owner went to jump on, well, I wasn't about to get on that!!! It moves!!! Oh the embarrassment! The Owner picked me up and carried me down it. Those badgers must have been very well organised as they have trains and everything down there. I must have a look again at the badger's sett on the hill when next I go for a quick roll. When we got off the train, and came back out of the badger's sett, we arrived in this park which The Owner said was a Kings park. I did look but didn't see a King. What is a King anyway? Should I have one? Anyway it was about that time of day, the time of day when certain functions need to be attended to, so I found a secluded spot behind a tree and tried to ignore the big offices full of hoomuns watching. Then The Owner.... what was he doing?????? He pulls a carrier bag out of his jacket pocket and PICKS IT UP!!!!!! I told you the world was very strange the other side of Swindon didn't I? And it has even affected The Owner. I pretended not to notice out of politeness but I have to report I am in no hurry to repeat that particular journey. You know where you stand with cows. As far away as possible usually, but at least you know.

Revenge is a Dish Best Served Cold!

Yesterday I met a lady. One who clearly recognises breeding! The Owner and I were walking back to the studio for the third time that morning, (why he doesn't write a list escapes me) when Lady

Hoomun With Horse happened upon us. The Owner always says that it is a woman with a funny growth between her legs.... and then laughs very loudly, so it must be one of his special jokes that no-one else understands. As Lady Hoomun With Horse got closer she uttered words I will cherish forever. "I do admire your dog", she said to The Owner. "He is so handsome and well behaved!" I was beside myself! I have made notes and will not be weeing on her car door or her handbag should I see her in the pub one day. The Owner was predictably dismissive and said I had my good days and then, scowling in my direction, added "Sometimes!!!" Talk about deflated!! Owners Daughter arrived last night and stayed in the spare room. After The Owner had brushed off all my hair and other bits and pieces from where I managed to get a sneaky forty-winks when The Owner was out one day, he then passed it all off as a freshly made bed, although I suspect she had other ideas. What is the saying about revenge being a dish best served cold?? Well the more observant among you may have remembered how Owner's Daughter forcibly deposited me in the bath one day? Well..... let me just say, Owner's Daughter is not, habitually, an early riser, I am. I have a cold wet nose, and the grass in the garden was very damp this morning. An early morning poo causes me to get very excited and run very fast in no particular direction. Except today I found a direction.... straight up the stairs. Let's just say she was up and out of the bed with a certain sense of urgency at this point, after the deft touch of a wet nose up the back of her leg. It was a good start to the day! Now, what to do next? Has Old Reg the Paper Boy delivered the paper yet I wonder.

Family Fun in the Garden!!

Yesterday, amid much excitement, Owner's Dad arrived together with Lady Auntie Hoomun and Accountant Hoomun. I thought Accountant Hoomun was a strange name for a hoomun but he did give me a Bonio so I will play along with strange hoomun behaviours. Lady Auntie Hoomun also gave me many Bonio's so I will forgive her for what followed. Whilst I was giving a Bonio my full attention all of them ran outside and closed the front door behind them. Feeling it was all a mistake I ran to the back door..... it was shut! I ran to The Owner's bedroom window... the door was closed! I was suspecting that this was perhaps not a mistake and they had deliberately abandoned me. Bereft, I consoled myself with a sneaky snooze on the velvet cushions. When they returned, my K9 snifter, which never lets me down, deduced they had been to a pub somewhere.... without me! More Bonio's followed so I was in half a mind to forgive them until Lady Auntie Hoomun kept insisting I joined them in the garden for "Family Fun and Frivolities!" My comfy cushion, or better still the velvet cushion on my settee with which I am building a good bond of late, seemed a far better option in my opinion! I checked the car to see whether Cat was there and got chased away so I suspect he may have been hiding in there and was scared to come out as the cows were in the paddock opposite.

Now, after my recent trip to Lundun on the train where I witnessed The Owner and other hoomuns picking up the evidence when us K9's had a poo, I have come to consider myself something of an expert on the matter. However, a question was posed to me yesterday which I have to say baffled me slightly. I understand how some K9's, labs in particular, work tirelessly to assist their blind owners, (I work tirelessly, on the other hand, to confuse The Owner. It's slightly different, yet equally successful) but the question was posed, who picks up their poo when they have one? It all sounds terribly messy if you ask me...

The Pile of Washing

We have had visitors we have! A car arrived in the lay-by in front of the cottage and out got a familiar shape, Polly Dog! I have met Polly Dog before when she came to see me with her Hoomun called NieceinBornmuff. Well NieceinBornmuff has apparently now changed her name, as The Owner now informs me that she is called NieceinBlandford. I am unsure why hoomuns change their names like that, I will investigate and report. Out of the car also got Musician Hoomun carrying a bundle of washing, I thought, as I wee'd on their car wheel. The Owner and the other two hoomuns carried the bundle of washing in doors and the tea ritual, which I have witnessed so many times when hoomuns come to visit, was started by putting the kettle on. I had assumed that the bundle of washing had been brought up because their washing machine was broken or something. The Owner had to take his washing to Owners Dad's once when his washing machine sprung a very large leak and cast water upon the kitchen floor in a very dramatic fashion. So I reasoned that maybe they also had a very wet kitchen floor and felt it my duty to point out that I was in no way responsible. Cups of tea made and great attention on my part being paid to who was going to be the easiest to get a Bonio from, when the strangest thing happened!! The pile of washing started to move... on its own!! Then made noises! Then a toy hoomun arm appeared... followed by a toy hoomun leg, and altogether far too much of an opinion on just about every matter you could think of!! Well I have never seen a hoomun as small as that before! Do they make lots like that or is this a one off? I watched this small hoomun with an air of caution for the next hour or so, you know where you are with The Owner but the Heap of Washing Hoomun was unpredictable at best. I was quite grateful for a lie down in the boot room that night; I had one of my headaches coming on!

The Owner's Velvet Cushions

Look! He wasn't using the cushions, so it seems perfectly reasonable to me that I can! Ok?

The End of a Good Day!

Yesterday was a good day! There was much frantic activity during the morning by The Owner; he had announced that he was going to have a day off which I had assumed would mean we would "do things". But instead he started painting. He painted the walls, he painted the doors, he painted himself, he painted the bath, he painted the sink; he also got some paint on the beams which I gather was his intended target. The oven was another of his targets and I now understand that the rungs inside the oven are meant to be bright and shiny! At some point in the afternoon, after he had stolen my duvet from the boot room and thrown it without due ceremony into the washing machine (he seemed to think it was getting smelly, I thought it was getting about right) Owners Daughter arrived. After successfully communicating mind to mind and getting her to retrieve a Bonio for me from the tin, The Owner went and got several armfuls of newspaper and went to throw it in the boot of Owners Daughters car. I am always hopeful of a trip in a car somewhere so I jumped in quick, fully expecting to be removed amid much bellowing but I was allowed to stay!! We went first to the recycling centre and then to the pub in the next village, where I met not one, but two lady chocolate labs and two swamp collies. And I got fed when we got home! It is a very comforting feeling at the end of a day when things have gone well; I even let The Owner sit on my settee.

The Trailer Monster

Yesterday was Friday! Has the K9 (with breeding) lost it I hear you ask, to make such a simple fact worthy of mention in a post? Well, in my understanding hoomun days are twenty four hours long, my Friday is currently standing at 33 hours and is showing no signs yet of drawing to a close. I don't know what has got into my hoomun!! For the purpose of clarity let us just call Friday the bit up until midnight last night and the rest we shall hereafter refer to as Saturday even though the two are normally distinguished by an extended period of slumber and snooze. After work on Friday we ambled up to the pub so The Owner can enjoy the odd pint (or four) but I really don't mind as it means I go too, and then I can hone my skills in extracting the odd morsel from any who come within my powers. Mainly lady hoomuns as they are easier since you ask. So far, yesterday was remarkable only in that it was starting to draw to a close. Until The Owner got a phone call.... as he was getting ready for bed! There then followed much frantic activity until his mate, who he refers to as The Ugly Sister, (no idea why as I thought being a sister made you a lady hoomun) came bounding through the door with far too much enthusiasm in my opinion. I am not normally allowed in his car but today I was actually encouraged to!! Now comes the worrying bit, we went off the other side of Swindon. A long way the other side of Swindon! I was on my guard for strange things happening! Friday became Saturday and after much discussion and a lot of swearing at Ugly Sister's Satnav, (which seemed to have an opinion on just about everything) and several hours driving, we arrived at our destination. At least that's what Satnav seemed to be suggesting. To me it seemed more like a bit of dual carriageway with no distinguishable features. The Owner found the right place for The Ugly Sister and has not let it rest since. It was very dark and The Owner got out and let me out for a wee. He put me straight back in the car as he said he had to "Couple up the trailer!" which sounded very important. At least in The Owner's mind it did! I am not sure if K9's do trailer coupling or not but The Owner seemed very pleased with his efforts as he got back in the car. We then travelled off into the dark of the night. With not much to see I settled down and enjoyed the journey, this proved to be my undoing. We came to a roundabout which clearly had a lot of street lights and I wanted to see whether there would have been any which required wee'ing up. As I opened one eye and looked up, there it was, directly above me, a MONSTER!! Just the other side of the back window.... the kind of monster you would expect to find the other side of Swindon and it was looking in as we drove along!! In my half-awake state, defence of my hoomuns was my only concern! Well actually it was more because it scared the poop out of me, but I feel sure there was at least some desire to protect my Hoomun. I leaped up and had a great deal to say on the matter...... well how was I to know it was the trailer and it was meant to be there??? Their laughter ringing in my ears for the rest of the way home, I began to plot my revenge! Expect reprisals!! I am looking forward to my bed tonight and if he tells one more delivery driver to "Watch the dog as he may be grumpy, he didn't get much sleep last night!" it won't be the delivery driver that needs to watch me!!!!!

Jack Two Baths

Last night I was becoming a little concerned about The Owner, he is such a worry! He kept saying to me "You're going to smell soooooo nice tomorrow!" I think I smell perfectly ok anyway, but how could he know about this morning by last night??I pondered on this all night, sat in the boot room. It didn't keep me awake as such, the fridge did that! I am sure it gets noisier!! Well, I got up this morning, still pondering, and chased The Owner for my breakfast. He was grinning at me in a particularly malicious fashion which unnerved me a little. I had a bath! Twice!!!!! I was whisked off my feet with no regard for my dignity and carried upstairs. As soon as he does that it is sure to end in tears and I do my best to ensure the tears are his and not mine but I was deposited without due ceremony in THE BATH!!! With lavender (yuk and phew) bubble bath!!!! I can feel nightmares coming on for tonight already! I think I may be in trouble later when he goes to bed, when I jumped out of the bath I ran across the landing and had a quick trip around his bedroom and across the bed. I ran down the stairs and out into the garden at which point I couldn't help notice that there was a dollop of badger poo in the woods at the top of the garden and, well, sort of,............................ well .... rolled in it! I couldn't help it! I did notice that my second bath of the morning, in the pond since you ask, was a little cooler than the first bath. Devoid of any badger poo on the shoulder The Owner made me walk to heel all the way to the Village Hall. There was lots of people there, nearly as many as I saw in Lundun last week and many of them seemed to be very friendly (unlike The Owner who had a very unfriendly scowl). I had the feeling I was some kind of celebrity! That was until I was shut in a cage in the back of Lectrician Hoomuns car. In a cage!!!!!!!!!!!! I have breeding I do!! Had I mentioned that I was born and trained on Lord Bath's estate? The good thing was that The Owner didn't realise that I was being fed lots of cake through the bars of the cage in which I had been incarcerated. I wonder what's for tea.

Am I Famous

Today is a day of celebration - I think! I was recognised this morning at the gate by cyclist hoomuns as they rode past. I was sat there sniffing nonchalantly at the breeze, trying to work out what to go and sniff at next when suddenly they were upon me, before I had time to work out a suitable opinion to have about cyclists wearing too much brightly coloured Lycra (although I think that is an opinion in itself) when one of them started trilling at the top of her voice "Look, there's Jack!". The other one went "Aawwwwwwwwwwwww!" I am unsure at the moment whether that was good or not. I will practice my response for another occasion. The Owner has been telling me this morning that I have an ISBN number which is the reason for my day of celebration. I have a question now, what is an ISBN number, do K9's have ISBN numbers and should I be having an opinion on the matter?

Attacked By The Squidger

Last night The Owner took to calling me Earle! He sat there watching the TV where we learned for the twenty fifth time how to build an Airbus A380. I pretend to be interested as it keeps him from feeling dejected I guess, that a K9 (with breeding) may have understood the intricacies of building an Airbus A380 on the first watching. On the coffee table in front of him is spread an array of remote controls which he calls Squidger's, one might even call it an arsenal of Squidger's. There is one for the TV, one for the set top box, one for the surround sound, one for the DVD player, one for the DVD recorder, one for the video cassette player (very old school,) and a spare. So having selected his channel on the building of an Airbus A380 and set the volume level he placed the squidger on the arm of his chair and settled back to watch. Again! I curled up on my comfy cushion, which, as it happens, is right below the arm of his chair. After a few moments the squidger landed on my head in a very unceremonious fashion. I assumed there was some reason for this being thrown at me so I sort of included it into the folds of my comfy cushion to ensure it couldn't be seen and therefore used again and settled back to enjoy a snooze with one eye and kept the other on the Airbus A380. We were just getting to the interesting part where they bolt the wings on when he changed channels, and then turned the volume up. I was a bit mystified by this! Then The Owner gets up, whilst the volume levels were going up and down quicker than the price of a box of Bonio's and starts pulling all the cushions out from his chair. Having not found what he was looking for, presumably the TV remote; he selects "The Spare" from his now dwindling arsenal of Squidger's. Tuning back in to watch the Airbus A380 he had missed the best bit and the thing was now airborne, as was the volume level on the TV! I was unsure what he was trying to do. Flicking channels and always back to watching the Airbus program and volume levels up and down as fast as you could say "Bonio's would be nice three times a day please!" After a while of this he got fed up and turned the TV off and announced he was going to bed. I got up from my comfy cushion and left his TV remote on the cushion for him to find for the morning. But it would seem that he was blaming me for the somewhat erratic control of his channels and volume. Ever since he has been laughing as he walks past me and saying "Are you sitting on the remote again Earle?" I think he may be sickening for something.

Blowing up a K9's Nose is Un-Cool!!

There are times when I really wish The Owner's armpits were infested with the fleas of a thousand camels! May I just explain that as a K9, having hoomuns blow on, or even worse, up our noses is the worst thing imaginable and will always be met by an unfavourable response. This morning, as autumn extends her chilly grip across this great land of ours (excluding the other side of Swindon obviously) in anticipation of the frosty mornings, The Owner was out in the garden tidying up and putting stuff away. His attentions were particularly caught and occupied by the hosepipe. The short section at the end was particularly shop-soiled and was removed, The Owner then removed any residual water left in the pipe by blowing down it. Well I wouldn't, it has been within weeing height all summer! Fast forward to this evening. The day, largely being at its end, I was starting to snooze gently on my comfy cushion. In the course of my slumber I was suddenly and rudely awoken by the most violent and explosive urge to inexplicably sneeze. Once the convulsions had subsided I opened my eyes to seek the cause of this situation and could see nothing to explain what just happened. The Owner was sat in his chair reading his Sunday paper, the fire was gently crackling in the grate. Assuming it to be "one of those things" I turned my attentions back to slumber, only to be hit by a further irresistible urge to sneeze to the point where I farted and a little bit of wee came out. Opening one eye I could still see nothing to cause this reaction and drifted back into slumber. After a chance opening of an eye I saw The Owner's paper shaking, and then I noticed the piece of hosepipe he had removed earlier in the day poking out from under the edge of his paper and advancing in the general direction of my nose to claim victory in its third attempt at inducing nasal failure. I know there isn't such a thing as nasal failure, but there is now, I just made it up and it works for me, OK?????? He walks like a camel anyway, sells like one as well.....

My Trip to Sainsbury's

I have had a bit of an adventure this evening! The Owner needed to go to Sainsbury's for some groceries. I was confident that this may include the odd Bonio or Markie so I allowed him to go, but wait up... he is taking me too! Sainsbury's are my favourite!! We went off with Ugly Sister in his big car but The Owner had "Basins" to deal with in town so The Owner opted to get out and walk round town. After presenting Bill with a brown envelope we wandered to Sainsbury's which The Owner referred to as Sainsbugs and then laughed loudly at his own joke. When we got to Sainsbugs (he has got me at it now) I sat outside and was put on trust. Which means I have to sit outside in the rain like a lemon and get wet! To others it means I am not tied up outside the shop and have to behave myself. I sat there getting wet, awaiting the return of The Owner and as it was raining there was little option of any treats from passers-by. I was understandably despondent and then I heard it. Inside they have a ping pong ping announcement thingy which asked for Mr Jack Greening to report and then they said "Jack, will you go to the checkouts?" I didn't need asking a second time, it was wet out there! I rushed in and Shop Manager Hoomun tried to greet me (I thought) with open arms. Well it was The Owner I was looking for so I was not about to let him catch me! I ran (athletically) down the row and more shop hoomuns joined the game and I have to report it was quite fun, but it was The Owner I was looking for so I didn't have time to play and I ran on. More shop hoomuns... no match for my athletic manner. Although I have to report they were becoming more cunning and quite persistent. Not a problem.... I would run around them! Ah... first problem... shiny floors and wet paws....not a problem, it won't take them long to rebuild that stand. Traction was becoming more of a problem as I ran into the olive oil stand and slid into the special offer half price wine stand which I imagine The Owner may have a deep affection for. I found The Owner, predictably, at the sherry shelf. Well I don't think it would take them more than a day or so to put it all back together which is better than some of The Owners little mistakes, they are still in bits after twelve months! I am thinking we may have to shop in Tesco's from now on. Shop Manager didn't seem very friendly!

ABOUT THE AUTHOR

Jack Labrador is written by Adrian Elmer, inspired by the actions, reactions and utter confusion displayed by his long suffering dog Jack. All stories have the semblance of some kind of truth in that every story has a small bit which has genuinely happened at some point or other, the rest is pure fantasy and conjecture as to how Jack would look at it.

Adrian has written many plays and pantomimes and recently published The Major's Diary on Kindle; it will be available soon as a paperback, both available through Amazon.